Spirited praise for CASEY DANIELS' Pepper Martin Mysteries

"Sassy, spicy Penelope, AKA Pepper, Martin, wearing her Mochino Cheap & Chic pink polka dot slingbacks, will march right into your imagination! . . . I, for one, can't wait to read more of Pepper's ghost busting adventures!"
Shirley Damsgaard, author of *Witch Way to Murder*

"Imagine Carrie of *Sex and the City* going *Six Feet Under.* . . . Hip, original, out-of-this world fun!"
Laura Bradley, author of *Sprayed Stiff*

"Spooky mystery, a spunky heroine, and sparkling wit! Give us more!"
Kerrelyn Sparks, author of *How to Marry a Millionaire Vampire*

"Wonderful, wonderful."
MaryJanice Davidson, *USA Today* bestselling author

"There aren't many better settings for solving a murder than a cemetery. And there aren't many better clients for a would-be investigator than one of that cemetery's dear, departed residents."
Linda O. Johnston, author of *Nothing to Fear But Ferrets*

"Write faster, Casey Daniels."
Emilie Richards, *USA Today* bestselling author

By Casey Daniels

THE CHICK AND THE DEAD
DON OF THE DEAD

CASEY
DANIELS

The
CHICK and the DEAD

AVON BOOKS
An Imprint of HarperCollinsPublishers

This is a work of fiction. Names, characters, places, and incidents are products of the author's imagination or are used fictitiously and are not to be construed as real. Any resemblance to actual events, locales, organizations, or persons, living or dead, is entirely coincidental.

AVON BOOKS
An Imprint of HarperCollins*Publishers*
10 East 53rd Street
New York, New York 10022-5299

Copyright © 2007 by Connie Laux
ISBN: 978-0-06-082147-0
ISBN-10: 0-06-082147-7
www.avonmystery.com

First Avon Books paperback printing: March 2007

Avon Trademark Reg. U.S. Pat. Off. and in Other Countries, Marca Registrada, Hecho en U.S.A.
HarperCollins® is a registered trademark of HarperCollins Publishers.

Printed in the U.S.A.

10 9 8 7 6 5 4 3 2 1

This book is for all the in-laws and all the out-laws:

Peg & Tim
Jim & Cindy
Michael & Chris
Karen & George
Nancy & Art
Bill & Joann
Bob & Bonnie
Mick & Jim

The
CHiCK and the DEAD

Chapter 1

It all started with Gus Scarpetti.

More specifically, it all started when I was leading a tour at the cemetery where I work and smacked my head on the marble step of the mausoleum where Gus Scarpetti's mortal remains were resting, but not in peace.

High heels. Uneven ground. Gravity.

Not a good combination.

If I didn't know it when I woke up in the emergency room with doctors peering at me and asking me if I knew my name and what day of the week it was, I sure did after that. Because after that . . .

Well, after that, I started seeing dead people.

Did I say *people*? Let me correct myself. After that, I started seeing *a dead person*. Singular. As in one gone-but-not-forgotten Mafia don—the aforementioned Gus Scarpetti.

Luckily, the whole ghostly experience didn't last more than a few weeks. I did some investigating and, thanks to me, Gus's unfinished business here on earth got finished. After thirty years of his restless spirit looking for someone who could help, his murder had been solved. By me. Gus had finally gone to the Great Beyond. Or the white light. Or wherever it was that ghosts went after they served out their time here.

And like any logical person, I figured that was—as they say—that.

Except apparently it wasn't.

Because just minutes after I said my final good-byes to Gus, I walked into my office at Garden View Cemetery and came face-to-face with a blond wearing a cardigan sweater and a poodle skirt. Saddle shoes or no saddle shoes, I knew we were not talking twenty-first century.

The awareness stung like a shot of Botox, and for a couple of long seconds, all I could do was stand there and listen to my blood rush in my ears and my heart slam against my ribs.

That, and stare.

At the woman perched on the edge of my desk, her legs crossed and one foot—and the saddle shoe on it—swinging. At her bobbed, wavy hair. And the pink chiffon scarf tied around her neck. At her pink cardigan, the one with the loopy D written in rhinestones over her heart.

She was a ghost. I knew it as sure as I knew my own name was Pepper Martin, and realizing it made me feel, well . . . I'll leave out the part about being pissed, exasperated, and leery, and just settle with saying I was not a happy camper.

I backed away, but my office isn't very big and there wasn't far to go. The doorknob poked my butt.

"No. No. No. No way can I see you." I held one hand out in front of me, emphasizing my point. "No way can you be here. You're not Gus."

She snapped her gum and blew a big, pink bubble. "Don't have a cow! Of course I'm not Gus. Do I look like Gus?" The woman sat up and pulled back her shoulders, the better to emphasize a bust-line that was nearly as ample as mine. "No way Gus has a chassis this classy," she said. "Gus is the one who sent me."

"But Gus is dead." Okay, it was an understate-ment, but I thought I should mention it, just in case she didn't know. I looked toward the far wall. If I had a window—which I didn't—I would have been able to see across Garden View—which I couldn't—toward the mausoleum that was as flamboyant as Gus was himself. "I solved Gus's murder. This is the rest-in-peace part. For him and for me. No more ghosts."

"You think?" She grinned. "I've got news for you. That's not how it works."

I didn't have to ask, I knew the *it* in question was my ability to see and talk to the dead. As far as I knew—at least until right then and there—that *dead* meant Gus and only Gus.

Which meant that with Gus gone, I was offi-cially out of the private-investigation-for-the-dearly-departed business.

Or at least I should have been.

Struggling to make some sense of it all, I ran a hand through my carrot-colored hair. "No way this is happening," I told the woman. "I hit my head on Gus's mausoleum. Not on yours. I don't even know who you are. I shouldn't be able to see you."

"But you can, right?" Her smile was perky. Have I mentioned that I hate perky? She hopped off my desk. "Thanks to that accident of yours, you have what's officially known as the Gift."

"Oh no!" I sidled along the wall until I was standing on the opposite side of the desk from where the woman stood. "Whatever this Gift thing is, I don't want it. Take it back. No Gift. Not for me. I just want my life back. My regular, old life."

"Really?" She fluffed her skirt and adjusted the knot on the gauzy scarf around her neck. "That's not what Gus says."

"In case you haven't noticed, Gus is a mobster. One of the bad guys. That means he's not exactly the most honest person in the world. Whatever world he happens to be in. And besides, when did you have time to talk to him?" I thought back to what had just happened out near Gus's mausoleum. One second he was there, the next . . . poof! "He just went to the big spaghetti dinner in the sky."

She shrugged like it was no big deal. "Time doesn't work the same here as it does there. Gus, he told me all about you. He said he was pretty sure you'd moan and groan about how much you hated working for him but that deep down, you're really grateful that he showed up. After all, before he did, I hear your life was dullsville."

"He told you that?" So, Gus was over on the Other Side talking behind my back. You think he'd give me a little more credit. After all, I was the only one capable of seeing him. I was the only one able to hear him and talk to him, too. Without me, Gus Scarpetti would still be hanging out over in his mausoleum watching the guys in his old crew bring him fresh roses every Thursday, the day he was gunned down outside his favorite restaurant.

Of course, before Gus showed up, I was pretty much sitting on the sidelines watching life pass me by, too.

A dead-end job here in dead city.

A fiancé who dumped me rather than risk hurting his social status when my dad traded his medical license and our more-than-comfortable upper-middle-class lifestyle for prison pinstripes.

A mountain of unpaid bills and a social life that gave dullsville a whole new meaning.

None of which made me feel any better about being bad-mouthed by the bigmouthed dead.

"What else did Gus tell you?" I asked the woman.

She grinned. Like she'd known all along that my curiosity would get the best of me. "He said that before you met him, you never had to prove yourself. And that now, you finally realize how smart you really are. He said before you met him, you thought your life was good for nothing but sitting by a swimming pool and getting a really good tan."

And that's a bad thing?

I didn't bother asking the question, mostly because I didn't really care what this throwback from the last century thought. Partly because after spending a few weeks with Gus dogging my every step, I was sensitive to the fact that ghosts might be sensitive to how they couldn't tan.

Then again, I suppose I might have kept my mouth shut because there was a kernel of truth in what Gus had said.

Before I met him, I had resigned myself to my

not-so-happy fate. Go-nowhere job. Go-nowhere life. Before I met Gus, I never would have dreamed that I was capable of solving any murder, much less one that gave a whole new meaning to *cold case*.

Of course, before I met Gus, I never had to deal with mobsters, dodge the FBI, or worry about hit men, either.

Ice settled in the pit of my stomach, and I dropped into the guest chair opposite my desk. I swallowed down my misgivings and eyed the woman carefully. I didn't want to hear the answer, but I had no choice. I had to ask the question. "You're telling me that I can't see just Gus, right? I can see—"

"Other ghosts. Sure." This ghost didn't seem nearly as disturbed by the news as I was. "It's cool, isn't it?"

"Yeah. Cool." My assessment of the situation was not nearly as enthusiastic as hers. "But what if I don't want to? See ghosts, I mean."

There was that shrug again. "I told you, honey. That's not the way it works. We don't get a choice about who lives, who dies, and when. If we did, do you think I'd want to be dead?"

She had me there.

"So you're—"

"Didi." She answered the question before I could ask it. "You'll pardon me if I don't shake hands. You know how that works, too, right?"

I did. After all, that was precisely why Gus had needed my help in the first place.

Being incorporeal, ghosts can't do anything for themselves. Not anything that has anything to do with our world. They can't touch things. They can't feel things. And the one time Gus had tried to latch on to my arm to pull me out of the path of an oncoming car . . . well, I found out the hard way, that didn't work, either. His hand went right through me, and the instant it did, I was left chilled to the bone for days.

No way was I going to risk that again. I waved away Didi's apology and asked another question I knew I should have left unspoken. "And you're here, why?"

"Because Gus said you could help me."

"Gus is crazy."

"Some people would say you are, too."

She didn't need to remind me. I'd spent the better part of the first weeks of my relationship with Gus wondering if I'd gone off the deep end. That was right before I spent the next few weeks being ambushed, followed, and shot at. Yeah, call me crazy. No way was I going to do that again.

"Look . . ." I rose to my feet, the better to look commanding and in control. "I don't know what exactly Gus told you, but whatever it was, he's got it all wrong. I'm not playing detective again. Been there, done that. It may have been exciting, but it was dangerous, too, and how dare Gus, anyway?" The thought hit out of the blue and sent my temper soaring. "The nerve of that man, thinking he can send people . . . or spirits . . . or whatever you are . . . over here and just assume that I have to help them. You can go back to wherever you came from and tell Gus that he's not the boss of me."

I sounded like I meant it, even though I did leave out one vital fact: Technically, Gus was my boss.

He'd paid me nine thousand dollars from a secret stash he kept in his mausoleum back when he was still alive.

Of course, on the flip side, I'd kept my part of our bargain. I'd solved his murder. I'd unraveled a mystery even the cops couldn't figure out. I'd earned my nine thousand bucks, damn it, and I deserved a break.

My mind made up, I breezed past Didi and headed for the door. It was close enough to quitting time to justify a hasty exit, and besides, I knew how ghosts could be, dead set—pun intended—on getting their own way. I stopped at the door to deliver my parting shot.

"It's not going to happen," I told Didi. "Not now. Not ever. So you'd better face the facts. I'm not going to risk getting killed again."

Remember that part about being commanding and in control? It should have worked. After all, I was a hairbreadth away from scraping six feet, and Didi couldn't have been more than five two. Still, she wasn't the least bit intimidated. I could tell because instead of giving up and apologizing for ruining what should have been my Gus-is-finally-gone celebration, she grabbed her purse and fished out a compact and a tube of lipstick. She added a little peachy color to her lips and smacked them together. "You're the only one who can help me," she said.

"Not my problem."

It wasn't, and just to prove it, I took another step toward the door, distancing myself from the whole thing. "I'm not the one who chose this goofy Gift thing. I'm not the one who decided to help Gus, either. I wouldn't have given him the time of day if he wasn't such a pain in the ass. But that was then and this is now and Gus is right, I'm way smarter now than I used to be. Smart enough to know that I'm not going to do it again. No way! No bad guys are going to take potshots at this girl again." I poked my thumb toward my chest. "In case you're not getting the message, that means that if you want someone to solve your murder—"

My office door opened, and I jumped out of the way at the same time I gulped down the rest of my words. Instantly I felt heat rise in my cheeks. My boss, Ella Silverman, stepped into the room, and I knew there was no way she could have missed the fact that I'd been in there talking to myself.

While I scrambled to come up with something that sounded even vaguely like a justification for my behavior, I watched Didi fade like a bad TV picture. She disappeared in a wisp of what looked like pink cigarette smoke.

Breathing a sigh of relief, and hoping it was the last I ever saw of Didi, I turned my attention back to Ella and wondered what I could possibly say to explain myself.

It was only then that I realized I didn't have to.

Explain myself, that is.

Something told me Ella hadn't even noticed that I'd been carrying on a conversation with thin air.

Ella's eyes were bright and her pupils were huge. Her cheeks were as red as the ankle-skimming skirt she was wearing along with a white peasant blouse embroidered with colorful flowers. If that wasn't enough . . .

Well, it didn't take a detective to see that Ella

couldn't stand still. She just about line-danced across my office, each step making her red and blue bead earrings twitch and sway as if they were alive.

"Ella?" Automatically I stepped toward her, wondering what was wrong at the same time I told myself that *wrong* didn't usually make people act like they'd just won the lottery. "Ella, are you all right?"

"Oh, Pepper!" Ella's eyes twinkled in the light of the buzzing fluorescents on the ceiling. "I hope you don't mind me coming in at this time of day. After all, you should be leaving for home right about now."

I checked the clock that hung on the wall opposite my desk. She was right. Sometime while I was busy dealing with Didi's annoying ectoplasm, the big hand had ticked its way past the twelve. It was officially after five and I was officially free to leave.

Which didn't explain why I stayed right where I was.

What did explain it was that I knew that aside from being my boss, Ella was a real trouper. She'd even shown up at Garden View with clean clothes for me the night I was a hit man's intended target. He'd missed me, but he didn't miss the thug standing just a couple of feet away from me.

I had no idea how much blood could spurt from a bullet wound.

Hence the need for a change of clothes.

Cleanliness aside, Ella was a nice woman. A nice, normal, middle-aged woman who took her job as community relations manager here at the cemetery as seriously as she took her responsibility to her three teenaged daughters. She was level-headed and professional, which didn't mean she didn't have a fun side, too. She could tell jokes with the best of them. Sometimes they were even funny. And I'd heard from other members of the staff who had worked here longer than me that she threw one hell of a Hanukkah-Christmas-Kwanzaa party.

But she usually didn't hyperventilate.

"Something's up." Didn't take a detective to see that, either, but since Ella didn't know I was a detective, I figured I didn't have anything to be ashamed of. "Ella, what's wrong with you? You look like you're about to shoot into the air like a rocket."

"Do I?" Ella laid a hand on her cheek. "I'm burning up!" She didn't sound upset by the realization. She didn't look worried, either, the way you'd expect someone to who'd just discovered that her temperature was up in the stratosphere somewhere. She paced to the far side of my office (it didn't take long) and came back again, grinning from ear to ear and fingering a button pinned to the front of her blouse. It was the first I'd seen the button, and I took a closer look. It was the size of a quarter, with a turquoise background and the letters SFTD written on it in bright yellow, showy script.

"Pepper, I have such exciting news!"

The announcement drew my attention away from the button and back to the woman wearing it. She shuffled in a little dance pattern across my office.

All this back-and-forthing was starting to make

me nervous. I waved her toward my guest chair. "You want to sit and tell me?"

"I couldn't. Sit, that is. It's just . . ." She clutched her hands at her midriff, right below a swath of embroidered flowers. "Well, I hardly know where to begin. I suppose at the beginning, right?" Ella giggled. It was something she didn't do often, and it was that more than anything that worried me.

"Do you need water?" I asked her. "A cup of tea? Maybe I should see if Jim is in his office and—"

"Jim's meeting with the cemetery trustees," she said. "And I don't think he'd appreciate this anyway. I mean, he knows about it, of course. Since he's the chief administrator here at Garden View, I had to clue him in. But he doesn't understand. Not the way I know you will. That's why I wanted to share my news with you. And while I'm at it . . ." Ella pulled in a deep breath and let it out again slowly. "Well, I have some good news," she said. She looked away. "And I'm afraid I have some bad news, too."

Bad news as in I just found out I had the Gift and could be eternally bugged by the eternally undead?

I thought not.

"Whatever it is, I suppose you should tell me," I said to Ella because I knew that no matter what she had to say, it couldn't be as bad as everything I'd heard from Didi. "Start with the bad news. Get it over with."

"But it won't make any sense. Not until you hear the good news."

"Then start with the good news."

"Which isn't really fair because then you'll think

I'm insensitive and you know I'm really not, Pepper. I think of you the way I think about my girls. I mean, you're a good worker and a fine young woman and I—"

"Ella!" I screeched. It was the only way I could get her attention. "Spit it out, will you! Not knowing is way worse than any news you could ever tell me."

"Yes. Of course. You're right." Ella pressed one hand to her heart. She forced herself to stand still, and I could tell the effort cost her dearly. All that nervous energy, and Ella looked like she was going to burst at the seams.

"The good news." She cleared her throat and raised her chin. When she spoke, her face was transcendent. Like she really had just won the lottery. Or gotten her lousy ex, Jeffrey, to finally pay all the back child support he owed. "The good news . . . are you ready for this? The good news is that Merilee Bowman is coming. To Cleveland!"

Chapter 2

I would have lied if I had the energy.

If I hadn't spent the day exposing a killer, saying goodbye to Gus, and getting up close and personal with another ghost—and the realization that this Gift thing just might plague me until I was a ghost myself—I might have managed some bit of bullshit that would have made Ella believe I shared in her excitement.

The way it was, the only thing I could do was chirp out a confused "Who?"

Ella's expression dissolved like my social contacts had once my plastic surgeon dad had been convicted of Medicare fraud. She blinked at me in stunned disbelief.

"What do you mean, who? Merilee Bowman." Ella pronounced the name very carefully, as if she was sure I simply hadn't heard her correctly. She touched a hand to the button pinned to her blouse. "*The* Merilee Bowman," she said. "You know. *So Far the Dawn*?"

I looked at the yellow, flowing script, and suddenly the button on Ella's blouse made sense. Even if all the pieces still didn't connect. "SFTD. *So Far the Dawn*. That's a movie, right?"

Big points for Ella. When she sighed with exasperation, at least she didn't do it too loudly. She couldn't stop herself from rolling her eyes, though. "Pepper, Pepper, Pepper." She shook her head. Clearly, I'd gone from fine young woman and model employee to world's biggest disappointment in no time flat. "I can't believe you young people these days. Yes, *So Far the Dawn* is a movie. But it was a book before that. Don't tell me you've never read it?"

The way she asked the question, I knew she was convinced there wasn't a soul on earth who hadn't read the book. Who was I to burst her literary bubble? "I saw the movie," I said instead, deflecting the whole question of book reading before I was forced to confess that the only thing I'd read in as long as I could remember were the sex quizzes in *Cosmo*.

"At least I think I saw the movie. Once. A long time ago. It had something to do with women in gowns and guys in uniforms and . . ." I knew this was important to Ella, so I thought really hard. "Horses?"

This time, she didn't even try to muffle her sigh. Her excitement smothered beneath what was apparently my suffocating cultural deprivation, she went over to my guest chair and plunked right down. "Maybe we should start at the very beginning," she said.

I wasn't convinced it was the best idea. Especially since it was after five o'clock. But since I'd already taken Ella's excitement and ground it under the soles of the adorable silk and lizard T-strap pumps I'd bought with some of the money I earned from Gus's investigation, I didn't want to do any more damage. Dutifully, I took a seat behind my desk.

"I'm right, right?" I asked her. "*So Far the Dawn* is a movie, isn't it?"

I could just about see Ella fight to retain her composure. She closed her eyes, drew in a breath, let it out slowly. "It's not just a movie," she said, giving me a look that told me she was about to set me straight, whether I wanted it or not. "It's *the* movie. *The* single most romantic and wonderful movie ever made. Based on *the* single most romantic and wonderful book ever written."

"And this Bowman woman?"

"Is the author of the book." There was only so long Ella's nervous energy could be contained. She hopped to her feet. "She's coming here, Pepper. To Cleveland. Because this is where she lived when she wrote the book. This is where the book is set. It's a classic, the story of a Union family's lives and loves during the Civil War. Now do you remember it?"

I did. Or at least I remembered what I'd remembered before: women in gowns, guys in uniforms. Horses.

"So what's the big deal?" I asked, because I figured she didn't want to hear me say that, try as I might, there wasn't another thing about the movie that I could recall. "So the author's coming to town. Authors come to town all the time."

"Merilee Bowman is not just an author. She's a

superstar, Pepper. A supernova in the literary world. No one's ever written a book like *So Far the Dawn*. Not before and not since. It's sold millions and millions of copies and it's been translated into every language in the world. There are *So Far the Dawn* conventions and study groups. There are reenacting weekends and groups that come to town to tour every location she mentions in the book. There are collectors who specialize in dolls modeled after Opal and Palmer, the heroine and hero of the story. And some who collect out-of-print editions of the book. And some who like—"

"Those creepy porcelain figurines of the characters." Another memory sparked and I thought of my aunt Carolyn, my mother's sister, and her affinity for what my mother kindly called "collectibles." "You don't do stuff like that, do you?"

Ella's shoulders shot back, and she arched an eyebrow at me. "Stuff like what? You mean collect? You bet I do! It's how I got involved in the fan club."

I didn't bother to point out that Ella wasn't the groupie type. Apparently there were depths to Ella that I had never even guessed existed. "That's what the button is all about, right?" I asked with another look at the lurid yellow letters pinned to Ella's chest. "That's a fan club thing."

"My idea." She beamed. "It's a way for us to identify each other. I started the button campaign right after I took office as president of ISFTDS."

The alphabet soup of letters floated through my brain.

Ella must have realized my attention span was drifting away with them. "The International So

Far the Dawn Society," she explained. "I've served
as local chapter representative, national secretary,
and now I'm president of the international group
for the next two years. I'm proud to say that I was
instrumental in arranging Merilee Bowman's visit.
I didn't want to announce it. Not to anyone. Not
until it was official. But I just got word and . . ."
She dropped back into my guest chair. "I'm so
happy, Pepper, I could just cry."

She looked like she was going to, too, and I was
so not in the mood. Not after the day I'd had. I
decided to humor her and tried for a smile that
looked at least a little bit genuine. "So this author
is coming to Cleveland. That's great."

"Not just to Cleveland." So much for humoring.
Tears splashed onto Ella's round-as-apple cheeks.
"To Garden View!"

Suddenly Ella's mood made a lot more sense.
"You're going to get to meet her?" This I did understand. I imagined myself one-on-one with the
genius who had combined silk and lizard into T-
strap pumps, and suddenly it all made sense. I
grinned and gave Ella the thumbs-up. "That's so
cool."

Ella was too overwhelmed to speak. She took a
moment to compose herself, and when she finally
did, she hiccupped over her words. "Merilee is
something of a recluse. She moved to California
right after the book was published so she could act
as a consultant when they were making the movie,
and she's stayed there ever since. These days, she
lives on a two-hundred-acre compound surrounded
by a wall and plenty of security. No one ever sees
her. The fact that she's agreed to come to Cleve-

land is a major breakthrough." Another round of tears put an end to Ella's explanation, and I was forced to fill in the blanks.

"She's got family buried here at Garden View?"

Ella nodded.

"And she's going to visit them while she's in town?"

Another nod. It was all she could bring herself to do.

"And she's coming to town because . . ." This was something I couldn't figure out for myself. I had to wait until Ella was calm enough to continue.

"The movie has been digitally remastered, of course," she said, sniffing. "Surely you must have read about it."

I didn't bother to point out that I'd been too busy trying to stay alive.

"The premiere is scheduled to coincide with the original publication of the book. That was back on July 12, 1959. Between now and July 12, the society has all sorts of things planned. Miss Bowman has agreed to a television interview. Her first since the original movie premiere. There's going to be a big gala, too. You know, with everyone in Civil War–era costumes. It's going to be fabulous."

I dunno. Hoop skirts and pantaloons? That wasn't sounding fabulous to me.

"Oh, and the museum, of course."

The P.S. from Ella jarred me out of my thoughts, which was just as well. I had this frightening vision of myself captive inside the confining clothing women wore back in the way-back-when. I skimmed a finger under one strap of my Victoria's Secret

IPEX demi to get rid of the thought and turned my attention back to Ella.

"Thank goodness the old Bowman home was never demolished like a lot of the other houses in the Ohio City neighborhood. And it's still in the family, too. Isn't that remarkable?" Ella sure sounded like she thought it was. "That just shows you what a sweet and caring person Merilee is. Even though she doesn't live here, she's maintained the family house all these years and now she's donated it, and it's being restored and turned into the *So Far the Dawn* museum. The gala will mark the grand opening."

"Well, you are going to be busy, aren't you?" It seemed a kinder question than *And I'm supposed to care about all this why?* I took another look at the clock and rose from my chair. "I should let you get to it."

Ella took my statement at face value. Like it was no big deal, she waved one hand. "Most of the groundwork is done, of course. Had to be before now. Merilee's appearance is the icing on the cake, so to speak." Her smile faded, and she sighed. "There was never a chance Elizabeth could make it, of course. But I was so hoping Kurt could be here."

I was tired. That had to be the reason why when I wracked my brain, I couldn't figure out who Ella was talking about. Kurt wasn't a boyfriend; Ella hardly ever dated, she said she was too busy with her job and her girls. And Elizabeth wasn't someone on the cemetery staff, either; tired or not, I'd at least remember that.

I gave up. "Elizabeth?" I asked. "Kurt?"

"Elizabeth Goddard? Kurt Benjamin?" Her eyebrows did a slow slide up her forehead, and Ella pinned me with a look. It still didn't register, and she surrendered with an exasperated groan. "Opal and Palmer in the movie! Everybody knows that. Elizabeth died back in the sixties, but even so, I can't believe you wouldn't know her if you saw a picture of her. She was a gorgeous blond. And what an actress! As for Kurt . . . come on, Pepper. No way you don't remember him. I don't think there's a female alive who could see that movie and not remember him. I swear . . ." She fanned her face. "Postmenopausal or not, that man makes my hormones shoot to the moon! He was so handsome and such a rogue. Remember that scene in the movie? The one where he's saying what he thinks is his final goodbye to Opal?"

Clearly this was something Ella enjoyed talking about. She was off and running.

"Opal's leaving for Baltimore, remember. She's going to marry Charleton Hanratty, the swine who's making millions—well, I suppose it wouldn't have been millions in those days, but you know what I mean—millions smuggling illegal arms to the Confederacy. And remember what he says?"

I didn't. My blank expression said it all.

"Palmer looks deep into Opal's eyes and says, 'There never will be another woman like you, Opal. There never will be another woman I love. But don't think that means I'm not going to try. With every woman I meet.'" Ella squealed with delight. "Doesn't that just make you tingly all over?"

It didn't. As a matter of fact, as lines went, it was pretty lame. Rather than point it out, I asked the logical question. "And this Palmer guy . . . I mean Kurt . . . he's not coming to the premiere because . . . ?"

"Because he passed away, of course. Just a couple of weeks ago." Disgusted by my knowledge (or lack thereof) of current events, Ella slapped one hand against her thigh. "And we had a commitment from him, too. I swear, meeting him, that would have been one of the true highlights of my life. Right up there with the births of my children. One look from those smoldering eyes of his . . ." She sighed again.

I wrinkled my nose. "Come on. The guy would have to be what, like ninety years old or something?" A shiver skittered up my spine. "How creepy is that."

"He was eighty-three when he died. Not all that old. And still as handsome as ever. Besides, he'll always be Palmer to me. Those flashing eyes. That dark, dark hair. That bushy mustache. Remember what Opal said the first time he kissed her? She wasn't in love with him yet, or at least she wouldn't admit she was. She said it felt like kissing a caterpillar." Ella laughed. "If he kissed me, I sure wouldn't be thinking about caterpillars."

I had tuned out at the first mention of kissing and caterpillars in the same sentence and figured this was as good a time as any to put an end to Ella's fan frenzy. I headed for the door.

"Well, I'm happy for you," I told her, and I was. "I hope it all goes really well. The gala and the premiere and all. I'm sure you have a lot to do and—"

"But, um, Pepper?"

The excitement had drained from Ella's voice,

and I remembered what she'd said when she first walked in.

The thing about the good news.

And something about bad news, too.

My stomach clutched, and I stopped and turned to see that she had risen from the chair.

"You're not going to tell me I have to wear a hoop skirt, are you?" I asked.

It was her turn to look at me the way I'd been looking at her since she started jabbering on about *So Far the Dawn*. She finally got the joke, but she didn't laugh. "Maybe you should sit down," she said.

The tightening in my stomach intensified. I decided to stay right where I was.

Ella cleared her throat. She tugged on her right earlobe, and the earring in it jiggled. "Well . . ." She looked at the ceiling tiles. And the scuffed wooden floor. She took off her SFTD button and straightened it, even though it wasn't crooked to begin with. Carefully she pinned it back into place. "Like I said, good news and bad news. The good news—"

"Yeah, Merilee. I know that part."

"And the bad news . . . well . . ." She shifted from foot to foot. "Merilee's coming. Here, Pepper. To Garden View. And when she does . . ."

I guess I was getting pretty good at this reading-between-the-lines thing. "I get it." I breathed a sigh of relief. "You said it yourself. Merilee is a recluse. And she's famous. That means when she comes to visit, the press is going to follow. You're thinking newspapers and TV reporters, right? And you're telling me I'll need to work longer hours."

"Not exactly." Ella sat back down. She stood

up. "You're right about the press and the reporters. In fact, Jim called me into his office earlier this afternoon. He says the grounds crew has already seen some photographers hanging around."

"Paparazzi?" The very word was exciting, and I combed my fingers through my hair. Not that I actually expected them to be lying in wait to catch a shot of me when I walked out of the office, but there was always a chance. And it sure would beat the other kinds of shots that had been aimed at me as of late. "That's terrific," I told Ella. "Great publicity for Garden View, right?"

"Publicity? Sure. If we're careful and we do everything just right. That's going to mean coordinating with Merilee's secretary and hiring extra security and coming up with a plan to funnel people in and out. Plus, of course, we need to worry about any funerals that are scheduled. That's more important than anything."

"So we're back to the whole extra hours of work thing, right?" I wasn't exactly looking forward to it, but hey, Ella's bad news could have been a whole bunch badder. And a little extra money wouldn't hurt, either. Sure, I had the nine thousand bucks from Gus. Or at least I used to have it. After catching up on my bills (there were plenty of them), a shopping trip to Saks (where the T-straps had come from), and an afternoon spent online tiptoeing through the White House Black Market, Victoria's Secret, and BCBG sites, credit card in hand, my bank account balance was dwindling fast. "You can count on me, chief," I told Ella. "I'll be here."

"Well, that's just it, Pepper. See, I'm sorry, but you won't be."

That got my attention.

I already had my hand on the doorknob, and I stopped and looked over my shoulder at Ella.

"I'm sorry," she said. "Really. It's not my decision. I'm not supposed to tell you that. As your immediate supervisor, I'm supposed to take responsibility. But I'm so sorry about it all and I couldn't live with myself if you thought that—"

"What?"

She gulped. "That I was the one who decided to lay you off."

"What?"

Ella hurried over to where I stood. "I'm sorry," she said for like the fifth time in thirty seconds. "I know this is a lousy way to break this to you. I know it's a lousy thing to do, but with paparazzi and TV cameras and reporters . . . we think they'll be swarming the place. And like I said, we have to concentrate on funerals and on the residents who are already buried here. Their loved ones need to have access, of course and with it all . . . well, Jim decided and I agreed, reluctantly, but I agreed . . . that there won't be time to conduct any tours. But don't worry!" Ella jumped in with the words of encouragement, such as they were. "There's no way we're going to eliminate your job. You have my word of honor on that. As soon as the excitement dies down, you'll be right back here where you belong."

Most of the summer off? Honestly, I'd never been squeamish about working on my tan. But there was the whole paycheck thing to think about, and thinking about it . . .

I guess my expression must have said it all because the next thing I knew, Ella was giving me that motherly look.

"I know exactly what you're thinking," she said. "What are you going to do to fill all those empty hours? But you know, I do have a few new tours in mind. You could get a jump on the research."

"I could."

My words sounded like agreement (which they weren't) instead of desperation (which they were). Ella patted me on the shoulder and headed out of the office. "That's my Pepper! Jim was worried that you'd be upset, but I told him he was wrong. I knew you'd take the news well. Don't worry; nothing's going to happen anytime soon. Merilee isn't expected in town for a few more days. And isn't it just like you, wanting to get a head start on the research, working even when you don't have to? You're a credit to young women everywhere, Pepper. Why, I only wish my girls . . ."

Ella walked down the hallway, and her words faded. It was just as well, I knew what she was going to say. She only wished her girls would turn out as well as me.

Really?

I wondered if she'd feel the same way if she knew I'd turned out to be a broke cemetery tour guide whose job had just been whisked out from under her feet.

Oh yeah, and I talked to dead people, too.

No sooner had the thought occurred to me than I could have sworn I smelled cigarette smoke.

Something told me it was pink.

Chapter 3

Maybe it was the cigarette smoke that kick-started my brain and got me to thinking.

Maybe it was the fact that I didn't sleep a wink that night. After the day I had, I should have. Like a log. But every time I closed my eyes, everything I'd heard from Ella kept getting jumbled with everything I remembered about my visit from Didi.

Good news and bad news.

Pink chiffon and peach lipstick.

No work.

No money.

Oh yeah, and the Gift.

Was it any wonder that by the time I got back to Garden View the next morning, my nerves were on edge and my head felt as if it was going to explode?

But like I said, maybe it all worked in my favor. All that tossing and turning left me with lots of time to think, and think is exactly what I did. Even before I dragged myself to my desk and put away the Cool Whip container full of salad I'd brought for lunch, I had a plan.

It was simple, really. And brilliant.

I'd tell Didi that I'd changed my mind and that I would investigate her murder after all.

If, like Gus, she could pay for my services.

There was only one problem. Or maybe it's more accurate to say that there were two. Number one: Though I waited in my office all morning (and actually got some work done while I was at it), Didi never showed her ghostly face. And number two: I couldn't go looking for Didi on my own because she had neglected to mention her last name.

Not to worry. My stint as personal private detective to the city's most notorious mob boss had taught me a thing or two about investigating.

Unfortunately, a search of the cemetery's database didn't turn up even one Didi (though it did earn me some high praise from Ella, who thought I was doing something that was actually related to my job). Even then, I wasn't about to give up.

I did a little more thinking, dug a little deeper, and uncovered (figuratively, not literally—always important to make that clear in a cemetery) three Dionnes in our files along with six Deirdres and any number of Dees. I figured that any of them could have been nicknamed Didi, but, except for one who was a member of the Order of St. Francis (I was pretty certain Didi wasn't a nun) and another whose computer record mentioned that she was the granddaughter of slaves (that didn't sound like my blond, blue-eyed ghost, either), none of their birth or death dates meshed with what I remembered from my latest close encounter of the supernatural kind.

Didi had never come right out and said when she lived or when she died, but I was no slouch when it came to culture. I'd seen John Travolta in *Grease*. I knew the fifties when I saw them.

What it all boiled down to, of course, is that all that thinking and all that research led me absolutely nowhere.

Too bad, too. Because right then, a potential paying detective gig was looking like the best solution to my monetary problems, not to mention the only thing standing between me and those creditors who would start getting antsy when the bills from White House Black Market, Vickie's, and BCBG hit.

Damn.

At least if I had to be shackled with this Gift thing, it would be nice to be able to do something useful with it.

Like know how to contact Didi.

As it was, I didn't have a clue how—or where—to find her.

No one could ever accuse Ella of letting grass grow under *her* Earth Shoes. Just the day before, she'd dropped the bombshell about my forced hiatus, and already she'd put together a handy-dandy to-do list for me.

I glanced down at the yellow notepad that she'd given me right after lunch. *Take your pick*, it said at the top of the page in her characteristic curlicue handwriting and her trademark pink marker. *This will give you an opportunity to design a tour from start to finish and—bit plus!—once you've decided which of our residents to include on your tour, you can do all your research at home!* ☺

I noticed that *big* was spelled wrong, but I didn't

hold it against her. After everything she'd told me about *So Far the Dawn*, her involvement with the fan club, and the impending visit of über-author Merilee Bowman, I knew Ella was distracted. And I knew it was only going to get worse. Already that day, two of the local TV stations, a community newspaper, and the "Where Are They Now?" reporter from a celebrity gossip magazine had called the office. Needless to say, each and every one of them asked about Merilee.

With all the commotion, I couldn't think straight. And if I couldn't think straight, how was I ever going to be able to come up with a plan to shake Didi loose from whatever plane ghosts went to when they weren't haunting me?

Peace and quiet, that's what I needed, and I'll say this for my job: It isn't much in the chic and trendy department, it doesn't pay very well, and it sure never gives me the opportunity for much of a social life (not with the living, anyway), but peace and quiet are never far away.

As soon as I had the opportunity, I left the office. It was a warm spring afternoon, and the sun was shining, so in the great scheme of things, it wasn't much of a hardship to pretend I was going to scout the areas Ella thought would be good for new tours.

As I headed out the door and across the road, I made sure I read over the note on my clipboard one more time. Just in case anyone from the office happened to be looking out the window.

Here are some ideas for tours that I think would be terrific!

In the daylight, it was hard to read the pink

marker against the yellow paper, and I squinted at the rest of Ella's message.

Sports figures.

I thought not. The only thing I knew about sports was that I didn't like them.

I crossed off the first suggestion.

Cops and robbers.

Another topic I didn't want to consider. After all, every time I thought about cops, I naturally thought about Quinn. And when I thought about Quinn . . .

Maybe I'd better explain. Quinn Harrison, Cleveland Homicide detective. The kind of guy who makes words like *hot* and *hunk* and *hunka-hunka burning love* pale in comparison to his hot, hunky, hunka-hunka burning love reality. I met him when I visited the Cleveland Police Historical Society Museum looking for information about Gus. And Quinn and I . . .

Well, how can I say this delicately?

Quinn and I had this thing. This instant-attraction, sort-of-soul-mate, karma thing.

That is to say, he was hot for me. And I was just as hot for him. Like majorly. Except that the one and only time we'd had a chance to actually do something about all that heat, Gus had popped up right there in the living room of my apartment. Live and in color, as they say. Except that he wasn't. Live, that is.

Let me make this perfectly clear—I was not going to jump into bed with Quinn when I knew there was even the tiniest chance that Gus was watching.

And Quinn, well, he didn't understand why the

woman who was good to go only seconds before had suddenly put on the brakes.

How could I expect him to? I couldn't tell him about Gus. I couldn't tell anyone about Gus, at least not without looking like a full-blown nutcase. So I kept my mouth shut, and my relationship with Quinn (such as it was) fizzled in an instant. One painful, awful, terrible, will-regret-it-until-the-day-I-die instant.

I put a big X through *Cops and robbers* and pretended that the sigh I heard ripple the afternoon air didn't come from me.

I had been walking as I thought about all this, and I stopped in a pool of sunshine along the side of the road to get my bearings. Over on my right near the high stone wall that separated Garden View from the city neighborhood that surrounded it, a woman was visiting a grave. Her back was to me, but I didn't need to see her face to know what she was feeling. She was wearing a black dress and one of those old-fashioned hats with the big brims and a black veil that covered her face. Her head was bent, and she was staring at the grave at her feet.

I made sure to keep my distance. A few months of working at Garden View had taught me that some mourners wanted to be left alone. But more of them wanted to talk. About their lives. About the loved one they'd lost. About their pain. Honest, I'm not insensitive to all that angst, I just had enough of my own problems to deal with. I knew better than to get too close.

I skirted the section where the woman stood and checked the clipboard again.

Famous faces.

That didn't sound too bad. I flipped to the next sheet on the pad and read over the list of residents (Ella's word for the people buried at Garden View) she suggested for the tour. The first one was a bandleader from back in the 1940s, and I checked the section and grave number she'd listed against where I was, turned, and started out in the other direction.

The man's grave was in what we in administration called the "new" section of Garden View. Considering that the graves there dated from as far back as the 1930s, it wasn't all that new, but, of course, *new* is a relative term. A lot of the cemetery's three hundred or so perfectly landscaped acres were filled before the turn of the twentieth century. Back then, death was a big business, and the pomp with which a person was buried said a lot about that person's life. Since many of the people buried at Garden View were from the upper echelons of Cleveland society, pomp was the name of the game. The oldest part of the cemetery was a maze of artsy obelisks, gaudy mausoleums, and headstones taller than me.

By the thirties, though, death was viewed differently, and the poor folks who had to cut the grass by hand around all those obelisks, mausoleums, and headstones had learned a valuable lesson. In the new section, most of the gravestones were flat-to-the-ground and far easier to maneuver around on a riding mower.

I stepped over one headstone after another, checking against Ella's list for the number markers sunk into the ground as signposts. I only got turned around once, which isn't bad considering I was pretty new at this. As soon as I realized I was headed the wrong way, I swung to my right.

The first thing I saw was the woman in the black dress and the hat with the veil.

She was standing thirty feet or so in front of me, still with her back to me, still with her head down, and for a second, I thought I'd really screwed up and ended up right back where I'd started.

But I knew there was no way.

I glanced over my shoulder, back the way I'd come.

I looked toward the woman in black.

Only she wasn't there anymore.

"Damn." Not exactly the right thing to say in a cemetery, where everyone is supposed to be quiet and respectful, but hey, I figured if anyone had a good reason to swear, it was me. Something told me the whole Gift mojo had reared its ugly head again, and I didn't like it. Not one bit. I didn't need some other ghost meddling with my psychic whatever-it-was-that-made-this-Gift-thing-work. I had to leave my brain waves open for Didi.

I decided to do just that, forcing any thoughts of the woman in black out of my mind and dutifully looking for the bandleader's grave. Before I could determine if this was an effective strategy, I turned at one of the few tall, standing monuments in the section. It was a granite pillar nearly six feet high, and no sooner was I on the other side of it than I realized I wasn't alone.

My instincts told me to ignore the flutter of black I saw out of the corner of my eye. My brain advised against it. But I knew the drill. *Ignore them and they'll just bug you more.* It could have been my new mantra.

Fully prepared to tell this ghost to get lost, I spun around.

The woman in black had moved. She was draped artfully against the granite pillar, one arm behind her, the other pressed to her brow. Her hat was off, and sunshine glinted against her cropped, wavy blond hair.

"Didi!" I was so happy to see that it was her and not another somebody who was dead but not gone, I could have hugged her. I restrained myself. There was that whole chilled-to-the-bone thing to consider, not to mention another important thing I'd learned from Gus—the value of bargaining chips.

I told myself not to forget it and kept the boy-am-I-glad-to-see-you to myself. No use tipping my hand. "Didi, where the hell have you been?" I looked at the black satin sheath that skimmed her hips and thighs. "And how—?"

"Is this a blast or what?" Didi saw that I was examining her outfit. She touched a hand to her dress. "One of the few advantages of being dead. All the clothes I never could afford when I was living. It's like crazy, man."

"You mean like a heavenly Internet shopping site? Pick your clothes and click to select?" I liked the thought of that even if I didn't agree with Didi's choices. Her dress was nipped at the waist and snugged tight with a belt. It was pencil-thin, with above-the-elbow sleeves and a hemline that hit right below her knees. No wonder there was a fashion revolution of sorts in the sixties (if the kinds of clothes Ella still wore could be considered fashion). Dresses of the fifties were confining. Not to mention frumpy.

I reminded myself that I'd be looking pretty frumpy one of these days, too, if I didn't find a way to make some money to keep up with my excellent taste in clothing. "I was waiting for you to stop by the office today," I told Didi. "I wanted to talk to you."

She shivered like she was cold. "Too crazy over there for me," she said, which made me think that even though I hadn't seen her, maybe she had visited the office after all. "And besides, you looked pretty busy. I figured you didn't want company." She leaned forward and took a peek at the legal pad in my hand. "*Famous faces*, huh? You gonna include me?"

Call me skeptical. Or maybe I'm just pragmatic. I slanted her a look. "Are you famous?"

Didi tried for modest, but her grin spoiled the effect. "Only if you count being in the movies as famous," she said. "After all, I did appear in a picture with Kurt Benjamin."

"The Palmer guy?"

"That's right. He played Palmer in that other movie." She raised her chin and did a little primping. "It wasn't a huge part, of course, and I never really pursued my career. Hollywood . . ." She wrinkled her nose. "It wasn't exactly what I expected."

"So you came back here. And died."

Her smile faded. Her shoulders drooped. "That's right. And if you didn't know about my movie career, and you weren't going to put me on your tour, why would you want to talk to me? You made it pretty clear that you weren't going to help me."

"You're right, of course." I smiled in a way that I hoped looked apologetic. "But I've been thinking about it. Thinking about you and about how you asked for my help."

"You'll do it?" Didi's smile was as bright as the sunshine that spilled over us. "You'll help? I knew you would."

She was so enthusiastic, I hated to burst her bubble. But not nearly as much as I hated the thought of sleeping in the street.

"I'll help on one condition," I told Didi. "Gus may have mentioned it. About paying me for my services? If you want me to solve your murder—"

"Hold it right there! You've got it all wrong." Didi shook her head, and I could tell that she was trying to figure out the best way to explain things. She finally gave up and waved me closer. "Come on," she said, and she turned and walked away from the street and closer to the stone wall that marked the border of the cemetery. "I've got something to show you."

I followed along. All the way to a spot in the farthest corner. There was a tree a few feet away from where we finally stopped, and the sun didn't penetrate the sprinkling of leaves just opening on its branches. There where the northern section of the wall met with the eastern edge of the cemetery, the air was chilly and the shadows were deep. Moss blanketed one side of the tree, and it was obvious the grounds crew hadn't made their way over there for spring cleanup yet. The gravestones I stepped around were overgrown with grass and weeds.

"You're buried here?" I don't know why the thought bothered me, but it did. Maybe it was because Didi's cheery smile and vibrant personality didn't exactly jibe with this sad and forgotten corner of Garden View.

Maybe because I was way shallower than even I liked to admit.

My shoulders slumped. "You're telling me you weren't wealthy. You can't afford to pay me to find out who killed you."

Didi gave me a look, and in the dim light, I couldn't tell if it was one of understanding or disgust. I decided on understanding, simply because it was easier to deal with.

"It's not that I don't want to help you go to the light or wherever it is you're headed," I told her before she could contradict me and I was forced to deal with her disgust. "It's just that I've got some serious money problems, and my hours have been cut here at the cemetery thanks to that Merilee What's-Her-Name, and even if I wanted to, I won't be able to concentrate on finding out who murdered you if I've got to spend the next six weeks wearing an apron and asking folks if they want ketchup with their fries."

Didi made a face, and I realized she wasn't feeling disgust or understanding. Just confusion. "You're jumping way ahead of yourself, kid," she said. "Back up and take a deep breath. Who said anything about finding out who murdered me?"

"You mean—?" Now I was confused, too. "Are you telling me—?"

Didi pointed toward the grave at our feet. "Why don't you have a look?" she said.

I did just that.

Like I said, the light was dim and the graves were overgrown. I got down on my knees on the damp turf and made an effort to brush away the grass and weeds that nearly covered the stone. That didn't work, and I grabbed a handful of grass and clover. I pulled, and when that one clump gave way, I tossed it aside and grabbed another.

Little by little, I cleared the stone.

Deborah.

It was one of the names I hadn't considered, and at the same time I could have kicked myself for not thinking of it; I reminded myself that if I had, I would still be combing through the hundreds of Deborahs who were probably buried at Garden View.

Deborah Bow. . .

I grabbed another clump of grass.

. . . m . . . a . . .

"Bowman?" Still on my knees, I looked up at Didi, more confused than ever. "Bowman like in Merilee Bowman?"

Didi nodded. "You got that right. She's my sister."

I got to my feet and wiped my hands against my khakis. "Merilee Bowman, the famous author, is your sister. And you were murdered by—?"

As if the motion could clear both our thoughts, Didi shook her head. "I told you, this has nothing to do with murder. It's all about the book."

"*So Far the Dawn.*" What other book could we possibly be talking about? It seemed even the dead were caught up in the frenzy that had infected Ella and the rest of the known world. "So your sister wrote the book and you died and—"

"I died, all right. It's the other part you've got all wrong. Merilee didn't write *So Far the Dawn*. I did. And Pepper, I want you to prove it. Before that movie premiere."

Chapter 4

"No."

Talk about a mantra. Between the afternoon Didi told me she was Merilee Bowman's sister and the next day, I'd spoken the word no fewer than a hundred times.

"No, no, no. I told you, Didi, there's no way."

"But Gus said you were really good at this sort of thing."

I was supposed to melt under the warmth of the compliment. At least that's what Didi had planned. She didn't know that I was way beyond being schmoozed by the warm and the fuzzy.

After all, I'd been schooled by the best of them.

Nobody does hard-nosed like a Mafia don.

Just to prove how impervious I was to Didi's pleas, I got up from my desk. It was lunchtime, and I switched off my computer monitor and grabbed my purse and the brown bag I'd brought along with me from home. Peanut butter and grape jelly on white bread. Not exactly my favorite lunch (which was more in line with a Cobb salad and a glass of crisp Chardonnay at one of the darling little bistros over on Murray Hill) but I didn't have to remind myself that I had to learn to economize. Poverty was scratching at my door.

And the noise was getting louder by the second.

I twitched away the thought and headed across my office. For the third day in a row, the sun was shining (not a common occurrence in Cleveland in the spring) and there was a picnic table outside the back door to the administration building. I had plans. And while they might have included PB & J, they did not include listening to Didi for one more moment.

"Murder is one thing," I said to her. Again. "If you wanted me to find out who murdered you, I might be able to handle that. But fraud is a whole different ball game. Even if you could pay me . . ." I paused here to let the message sink in and to give Didi the opportunity to come up with some kind of solution to my thorny monetary problem. When she didn't, I sighed and went right on. "When I worked on Gus's case, I had help. Gus's help. I had no idea what I was doing. I was lucky I found out who killed him."

Lucky, of course, is a relative word, and if I had the sense, I would have remembered it. Luck didn't have anything to do with the weeks I'd spent dealing with mobsters, mistresses, and federal agents. Of course, it did say something about the fact that I'd managed to survive them all.

"It's not that I don't want to help you, Didi," I said, leaving out the part about how a little financial incentive would have made the *want* part more sincere. "It's just that I honestly don't know how. You're telling me that you wrote a book. A famous book. You're telling me that Merilee didn't. It makes my stomach hurt just thinking about how complex the whole thing is. Like I told you yesterday, I wouldn't even know where to start."

"But Gus says you're smart."

"Gus is a very good bullshitter."

"And he says you're clever."

"It's not something he ever told me when I was working on his case."

"Gus says you'd never let down a friend."

"And I didn't know we were friends."

The way I figured it, any self-respecting ghost should have taken the not-so-subtle hint and high-tailed it back to the Great Beyond. I guess Didi wasn't self-respecting.

When I made a move toward the door, she blocked my way.

"You're the only one who can help me."

I had heard the same argument from Gus right there in that office, and not that long before. I answered Didi the same way I'd answered him. "I can't help. I don't know how. I'm not—"

"A detective? Sure you are. At least that's what Gus says."

I didn't want to admit that what I was really going to say was *I'm not even sure I believe you.* I just wasn't ready to tell Didi that the story she'd told was a little too outrageous for me to accept at face value. So far, the only proof she had offered to support her claim of being the author of *So Far the Dawn* was her word. Call me cynical, but I didn't think that counted. Besides, I'd heard this song-and-dance before.

Take my word for it.

It was just what Dad had said when the news

broke that he was being investigated for Medicare fraud.

Take my word for it, Pepper. I didn't do it.

And when the evidence piled up that proved he did . . .

A shiver crawled up my back and settled on my shoulders. As heavy as a load of bricks.

I sidestepped my way around Didi and my own painful memories. "What I was going to say," I told her, lying through my teeth, "is that I'm not sure I know enough of the facts. I've never even read the book. I can hardly remember the movie. Except for the horses."

"You think I'm lying."

Maybe Didi was more perceptive than I thought.

Without confirming or denying, I stopped and looked her way. That day, she was dressed in a gray pleated skirt that skimmed the bottoms of her knees and a pink blouse with rolled sleeves and a D monogrammed over her heart. There was a touch of pink color on her lips, and just at that moment, a tear slipped down her cheek.

"Oh no!" I backed off and backed away, clutching my brown paper bag and my purse to my chest as if they could protect me from the guilty conscience that was sure to result from thinking that the ghostly waterworks were the result of my insensitivity. Not to mention my skepticism. "Don't pull that act on me."

Didi sniffed. "What act would that be?"

"That crying act."

"It's not an act." Where it came from, I don't know, but she touched a lace-edged hanky to her eyes. "You've shattered my hopes, that's all. You've destroyed my faith in the milk of human kindness. And Gus said you weren't that kind of person. He practically promised. He said you'd help, but here I am, getting the royal shaft. And there you are, being alive and young and pretty, and instead of appreciating everything you've got and everything you're able to do, you're a party pooper. And—"

"Enough, already!" I managed to not scream, but only because I didn't want to take the chance that someone in the outer office might hear me and wonder why I was in there talking to myself. "I'm sympathetic. Honest, I am. But I've got important things to worry about. Like how I'm going to buy groceries. I can't help you. I'm sorry, but really, I can't."

Just so she'd know I wasn't going to change my mind, I turned my back on Didi, opened my office door, and stepped into the hallway.

Out of the realm of the woo-woo and straight into chaos.

A wall of noise hit me, and I glanced around in wonder at the hallway that was usually empty and as quiet as the tombs that surrounded us.

There was a guy sitting on the floor right outside my office door. He had a TV camera slung over his shoulder and was shouting into a walkie-talkie, "Testing, one, two, three."

I heard a crackle and from the other end of the hallway, the reply from a woman I recognized as the tiny body with the big head with the bigger smile who sat behind the anchor desk on the six o'clock news.

"That's not good enough, Larry." Her perfectly arched brows dropped low; her perfectly bowed lips thinned into a frown. "We can't afford any glitches. Not with a story this big. I can't understand what you're saying. Talk more clearly, will you? Try again."

Larry did. His voice, each word spoken slow and loud, lapped over the sounds of a different camera crew setting up in the file room across from my office, the ringing of not one, but two of our phone lines, and the excited purr of conversation from down the hallway. I turned the corner to find everyone from Jim, the cemetery administrator, to Jennine, the woman who made the coffee and welcomed the grieving to Garden View so that they could choose a suitable site for their loved one's eternal rest, was out of their offices and milling around.

They were also all talking at once.

"What do you think, Pep?" Because I reported directly to Ella, Jim and I didn't often have the need to talk to each other. Aside from the fact that I knew he was quiet and not in the least bit flashy and that I'd heard he was married, had grandchildren, and was considered competent and professional by Ella (who would know competent and professional when she saw it), I barely knew the man.

Which made me wonder why he'd suddenly gone from calling me Ms. Martin to calling me Pep.

He didn't usually hop from foot to foot, either. He smoothed a hand over his navy and maroon striped tie, and I noticed there was a soup stain the size of a dime in the center of it.

Jim's hair was silver, his cheeks were red. His stomach sagged over his belt, and every time the TV anchorwoman looked his way, he sucked in his gut. When she went back to fiddling with her walkie-talkie, he let go a breath, hiked up his pants, jiggled the change in his pockets.

"You think this color will photograph well?" he asked me.

I realized he was talking about his tie, and I nodded. I didn't bother to mention the soup stain. "What's going on?"

Before Jim could answer, Ella came swooping out of her office. Today's outfit was a little red and yellow number that floated to the floor and had a matching jacket. With her chin up, her shoulders squared, and her eyes blazing, Ella looked like a middle-aged Wonder Woman.

She acted like it, too.

No sooner was she out of her office than she had everything under control.

"I've just heard," she said, and when the people in the hallway realized she was talking but they couldn't hear what she was saying, they shut up instantly.

Larry the cameraman jumped to his feet and flicked on his video camera. Anchorwoman elbowed her way to the front of the crowd.

"I've just heard," Ella said again, louder this time. "As of twenty hundred hours last night, Merilee was packed and ready to go. At precisely eight hundred hours this morning, she left her California compound. That's Pacific Time, of course."

There was a buzz of excitement in answer to the announcement.

It got in the way of me trying to figure out what this twenty hundred and eight hundred stuff was all about.

I didn't have time to work it out; Ella raised her voice again. "ETA is sixteen hundred hours, Cleveland time. She's coming in on her private jet. Don't know yet where she's landing, but I've heard from an informed source that until the premiere, Miss Bowman will be living at the family home."

"The one that's being turned into the *So Far the Dawn* museum?" When the anchorwoman poked her mike under Ella's nose, Ella nodded.

"Will she come here right from the airport?" someone else shouted from the back of the crowd.

"Not sure yet," was Ella's reply. "When I know—"

It was the *not sure* that did it. Certain there was nothing else to be learned for the time being, the reporter backed off and signaled to Larry to turn off the camera. The crowd went back to buzzing and humming and talking. The noise swelled, louder than ever.

I took the opportunity to close in on Ella. "Twenty hundred hours?" The skepticism in my voice said it all. "What the hell—"

"We're coordinating," Ella informed me. "All the chapters of ISFTDS. It's easier to work in military time. Helps keep everything straight and everyone on the same page. My gosh, Pepper! Can you believe it? Another few hours and Merilee will be right here in Cleveland." She drew in a deep breath and pressed a hand to her heart. "I can hardly think straight and my head is buzzing, I'm so excited!"

"Ella!" Jennine had left to answer a ringing phone, and she came back into the hallway, all giggles and motioning toward the waiting room and the phone on her desk. Her eyes were as big as saucers. "I've got network news on the phone. Stone Phillips! He wants to ask you some questions."

"Got to take this." Eyes twinkling, Ella patted my arm and went back into her office.

I headed for the picnic table outside, thinking that Stone Phillips and I had something in common. Because I had questions for Ella, too.

Like how the hell had she allowed everything to get so out of control that our usually peaceful office suddenly looked like the staging point for D Day?

And what would she say if she knew superstar Merilee Bowman had been accused of being a phony by her own dead sister?

There were two TV sound trucks outside the office door, a couple of SUVs that didn't look familiar, and a guy with a big-ass 35mm camera who raised it as soon as the door snapped open.

"Rick Jensen!" he called out. "*National Inquisitor*. Are you—"

"Anybody?" I hated to burst Rick's bubble, but there was no use in him wasting his film. I gave him a smile and a wave. "Sorry. I only work here."

Rick was a good sport. He shrugged and took a picture anyway. Probably on the off chance that I might actually prove to be somebody who was somebody.

I didn't stop to exchange pleasantries. Between Didi and the circus that was once my sort-of-normal work environment (except for the ghosts), my head was thumping like the bass line in a Metallica song. I walked around to the back of the building, hoping for a reprieve.

It was quieter than ever out there, and though like most people in their mid-twenties, I thrived on the stimuli of computers, DVDs, and iPod tunes (sometimes all at once), I closed my eyes for a moment, truly appreciating the silence. The picnic table was tucked in a secluded spot not easily seen from any of the grave sites. This was where Jennine and the other smokers came for their breaks. I turned up my nose at the lingering smell of their cigarettes, and just in case there was any stray ash around, brushed off the bench before I sat down. I massaged my temples with the tips of my fingers, willing away the tension and trying to convince myself that calories aside, really, peanut butter and jelly wasn't all that bad.

I'd just opened my brown bag and taken out my sandwich when I heard the unmistakable click of a camera shutter.

"Rick!" Honestly, didn't the guy have anything else to do? There had to be better things to take pictures of than me eating my lunch. "You really should save your energy for—"

I turned toward the sound.

Rick wasn't there.

As I had so many times over the past weeks, I wondered if I was losing it.

And reminded myself there was no way.

Was it my fault that Ella and the rest of the

Garden View staff had gone off the deep end and surrendered their usual levelheaded selves to Merilee madness?

Was it my fault the universe had decided to give me the Gift?

No. On both counts.

I knew for sure that these days, I was the only one around Garden View who wasn't nuts. Just like I knew the sound of a camera shutter when I heard one.

I looked around again, but there was still no sign of Rick, and he hadn't exactly struck me as the subtle type. Just as I turned to check out the area toward the side of the building, I heard the sound again. From the other direction.

This time four or five clicks in quick succession.

I slapped down my sandwich and spun in my seat.

I was just in time to see a man duck behind a tall monument commemorating all the past (and passed) Garden View board members.

A man who looked awfully familiar.

Before I even realized I was doing it, I was on my feet and on my way over there.

Which was no easy thing considering that my head was suddenly spinning and my knees were as jellylike as the gooey stuff stuck between my two pieces of lunch bread.

Overreacting?

No way.

Because I swear, the man I saw duck behind the monument had shaggy hair and wire-rimmed glasses.

Sure, he was wearing tight jeans and, under a

black leather jacket, a shirt that molded to a very toned chest. And sure, that wasn't the kind of outfit I'd ever seen him in before.

But I swear, the man who'd just taken my picture was Dan Callahan.

Another explanation is in order.

Dan is . . . well, I have to admit, I don't know precisely who Dan is.

I thought he was a nerd. At least that's the impression I got when I met him at the hospital where I went to have my head checked out after I'd bonked it on the front step of Gus's mausoleum.

Dan was the cute and cuddly type, the first guy who made me (and my hormones) realize that life without my rotten ex-fiancé, Joel Panhorst, might not be so bad after all. When it came to fashion, he was nowhere near as *GQ* as Quinn Harrison, but somehow with Dan, the un-chicness of brown pants worn with a navy shirt and sneakers didn't matter. He was adorable in an absentminded professor sort of way. Which sort of made up for the fact that he was absolutely obsessed with the brain scan study he was doing on behalf of the hospital.

I was looking for a personal relationship with Dan.

Dan, as it turned out, was looking to hook me up to machines with wires and buzzers to find out if what he called my "aberrant behavior" was in any way connected to my head injuries or my occipital lobe.

I told him to get lost, and I honestly thought he had.

Until the day he showed up out of nowhere and

used a couple of amazing Jackie Chan–type moves to take care of the hit man who was about to blow me away.

I was grateful. And confused. Especially after he kissed me and said goodbye.

Was it the last I'd ever see of Dan Callahan? I hadn't had time to think about it, but I suppose in my heart of hearts, I thought that it was. After an exit like that, anything else would have been anti-climactic.

Except for an entrance like this.

I got over to the monument where I'd seen the man with the camera, but except for some trampled grass that showed that someone had stood there recently, there was no sign of Dan.

"Shit." I looked around again, just to be sure. "Shit, shit, shit," I grumbled, and even though the sun was bright, I shivered. I turned to head back toward the picnic bench and the waiting PB & J.

And nearly slammed right into Didi.

"Don't do that to me!" I jumped back, well out of range of the iciness I knew would result if flesh-and-blood me happened to make contact with her ectoplasm. "Can't you clear your throat or something to let me know you're around? Sing a song maybe?"

"How about Elvis?" Didi swiveled her hips the way I'd seen Elvis do it in the old movies. It was no easy task considering how she was dressed.

"And why are you dressed that way, anyway?" I asked her, my brain segueing from one subject to the other so quickly, I didn't have time to explain myself. "Somebody die?"

Didi sniffed and tugged at the white gloves that

covered her arms all the way to the elbows. She straightened the hat that matched her brown and white striped dress. Like the last outfit I'd seen her in, this dress had a tight waist and a pencil-thin skirt that made swiveling—or pretty much anything else—something of a challenge. Over the dress, she wore a cropped brown jacket that was snugged tight with a belt.

"Have things gotten that uncivilized in the years I've been dead?" she asked. "A lady doesn't dress up just for funerals. She always dresses properly for a social call."

"I don't think I qualify."

"As a lady?" Didi squealed with laughter at her own joke.

I so wasn't in the mood.

I took another look behind the monument, and because things weren't any different there than they had been last time I looked—empty—I muttered my disappointment and headed back toward my waiting lunch.

"I meant as a social call," I told her when she fell into step at my side. "You don't have to dress up to come see me. I don't qualify as a social call."

"This isn't for you, silly." When we got to the road, she turned toward the small lot where staff members left their cars. Don't ask me how she knew which was which, but she walked right up to my red Mustang. "It's for the social call the two of us are going to make."

Before I had a chance to say, *No way, Jose,* the front door of the administration building opened and the news anchorwoman came out. So did her coworker, Larry. They backstepped their way toward the parking lot in front of Jim, who I knew had an appointment with the mayor that afternoon to plan strategy for Merilee's visit. Jim was followed by Ella. Ella was grinning (no doubt afterglow from her talk with Stone Phillips). She was followed by Jennine, who was reminding both Jim and Ella that there was a staff meeting scheduled for that evening so that we could all get on the same page and work like a well-oiled machine the day Merilee Bowman finally arrived at Garden View.

I took one look at it all and grabbed my car keys out of my purse. "Come on," I said to Didi. "Let's get the hell out of here."

Chapter 5

Though I was more than willing to get in my car and head out on the road—and away from the hullabaloo back at the office—I had no idea where Didi and I were going. From her place in the passenger seat, she provided the directions, telling me where to turn and making me wonder (in a purely academic sort of way, of course) how ghosts kept track of one-way streets and freeway extensions that, as far as I could tell, hadn't been around back in the days when Didi was.

I didn't ask. It didn't matter, and besides, I had all I could do to keep my mind on the road, what with Didi calling out the turns at the last second and urging me not once but twice to hurry through a light that had already turned red.

I explained about red light cameras and mailed-straight-to-the-home traffic tickets, and when my ghostly navigator told me to, I got onto I–77, the north/south freeway that cuts Cleveland in half, straight through its old industrial heart.

When it was time, I eased the car off the ramp and followed Didi's directions. We took another couple of turns and found ourselves in a part of town with narrow streets and postage stamp–size front lawns. On either side of us were rows of tiny houses that had—as we used to say in my world before my world fell apart—seen better days.

We cruised down a street where four houses were boarded up, one from a fire, the others (according to the signs posted out front) because of drug violations. I swerved around broken beer bottles that sparkled like jewels against the blacktop. I slammed on the brakes, then eased up again when a couple of teenagers, wearing jeans so big they looked as if they were about to fall off their skinny butts, zipped in front of the car on their skateboards, gave me the finger, then raced away again.

"There but for the grace of Daddy's six-figure income . . ."

I hadn't even realized I'd spoken the words out loud until Didi looked my way. "Six-figure what? What does your dad do?"

I didn't feel like a heart-to-heart, but it beat staring out the window at the old guy on the corner who was talking to himself. "My dad is . . . was"—I corrected myself—"a doctor." Enough said. "How about yours?"

Didi smoothed a hand over the skirt of her brown dress. "Daddy was a business executive. He took very good care of us." The light changed, and she looked out the window. "That doesn't mean that I didn't have any ambition. After all, I was an author. I had a job, too. Downtown. Got it the day after I graduated from West Tech High. It was at Howell, Michaels, and Roose. You know, the big law firm. I would have been supervisor of the steno pool if I'd lived long enough."

"Cool." I wasn't even sure what a steno pool was, but I figured supervisor was a good thing.

The light turned green, and we continued on our way. The next block was dominated by a huge brick building, old and abandoned. At the street alongside it, Didi said, "Take a right," and when I did, she told me to stop the car.

There was a parking place at the curb in front of a house where a rusted car sat up on cinder blocks in the middle of the lawn. Suddenly feeling awfully conspicuous in my shiny (and, thank goodness, paid for) Mustang, I eased my car into place, shut off the engine, and turned to my companion.

"Now what?" I asked.

Didi didn't answer. Her index finger tapping her top lip, she watched the house across the street.

Like so many of its neighbors, this house was small and weather-beaten. The front steps were lopsided, the roof looked as if it needed to be re-placed, one of the upstairs windows was cracked. Someone had made an effort to brighten things up. A couple of daffodils and some tulips that hadn't opened yet poked out of the soil near the porch.

Before I could ask again what we were doing there and what we were looking for, the front door of the house opened, and a teenaged girl stepped outside.

She was fifteen, maybe, though I have to admit, it was hard to tell. Her hair had been colored, and not professionally. It was a shade between black and brown with the sort of red overtones that make a girl look older and harsh. Not to mention cheap. The lack of professional styling didn't help. The girl's hair was spiked at the top and cut blunt at the shoulders. Her bangs were long and shaggy. They skimmed her pierced eyebrow.

Stepping off the porch, she unzipped the backpack she was carrying and reached inside for a pack of cigarettes. She lit one and took a long drag, then slung the backpack over her shoulder and headed down the street.

"Come on," Didi said, and when she did, she was already out of the car and standing at my window. "We've got to follow her."

Do I have to mention that I didn't want to?

Do I have to point out that I didn't have much choice?

Following the girl—even with a ghost—sounded like a better idea than sitting there waiting for that same ghost to return from I-don't-know-where. And it beat me trying to find my way back to the cemetery. We'd taken so many twists and turns, I didn't have a clue where I was.

I climbed out of the car and locked the door, tucking the keys in my purse.

"Why?" I asked, scrambling across the street to catch up with Didi. "Who is she? And why are we following her?"

"Her name is Harmony." When I walked a little too fast and got a little too close to the girl, Didi slowed me down, one arm stuck out in front of me. We waited while Harmony crossed a street before we started up again.

"She's a foster kid," Didi pointed out. "The family is good to her."

"They should offer some fashion advice." Harmony's jeans were riddled with holes, and the sunshine yellow halter top she wore with them was too small. Of course that bit of a fashion faux pas might very well have been planned. Though she had no boobs to speak of, the too-tight top showed off Harmony's nice flat tummy, her bellybutton ring, and the tattoo of a snake on her right shoulder.

"They don't have much money," Didi said, as if she needed to remind me. One look at the neighborhood would have taken care of that. "But she's a good kid. A hard worker."

"Why isn't she in school today?"

"She called in sick."

I slanted my companion a look. "And you know this how?"

Didi shrugged. Something told me it was the only explanation I was going to get.

After that, we followed the girl in silence. Across another street. Around another corner. There was a small grocery store up ahead, and I realized that it must have been later than I thought. School was already out for the day. There was a group of teenagers hanging around in the parking lot in front of the store.

"Hey, ass wipe!" One of the girls was big and broad, with a square chin and hair that had been braided and was pulled away from a face that might charitably be described as plain. She called out, and though Harmony didn't respond, I saw her slender shoulders tense. "What are you here for, a box of crayons?"

A couple of the other girls laughed. The boys they were with gave Harmony the once-over.

She walked right by them.

"Hey, Harmony. I'm talking to you!" The big

girl latched on to the strap of Harmony's backpack and dragged her to a stop. "You think you can avoid me by not showing up at school? Shit, you're dumber than I thought."

In one motion, the big girl spun Harmony around and reached inside her backpack. She pulled out a notebook and held it above her head, out of Harmony's reach.

Harmony was half the girl's size, and until that point, she had been stony-faced and silent. Now she lashed out. Her eyes blazing, she lunged at the big girl. The big girl was slow and lumbering. But she wasn't stupid. She dodged Harmony's every move, and when Harmony saw that she was getting nowhere, she kicked Big Girl in the shins.

"Fuck!" The big girl hopped around on one leg, and when the other kids laughed, she glared at them.

"It's mine," Harmony said, making another grab for the notebook. "Give it to me, Shayla. Right now."

"Give it to me. Right now." Shayla echoed Harmony's words in a singsong. She waved the notebook back and forth, careful to keep it just out of Harmony's reach.

And I had seen enough.

"Damn, but there's nothing that makes me madder than seeing somebody big and dumb pick on somebody small," I said, sauntering forward and making sure I acted like I knew what I was doing and like I belonged there.

Of course, neither was true, and if these kids thought it through, they would have realized it. But hey, I was older than they were by ten years or so. And because there were no tours scheduled at Garden View that day, I wasn't wearing the standard-issue khakis and white polo shirt. I was dressed in my own clothes—denim skirt, hot pink shirt, and a pair of darling Moschino Cheap & Chic pink polka-dot slingbacks that added another two inches to my height.

Needless to say, I made an impression. Especially in that neighborhood where they might know cheap, but they had no concept of chic. I was a princess in a sea of badly dressed (and poorly groomed, I might add) frogs, and just as I expected, the whole first-impressions thing worked like a charm.

Though she acted tough on the outside, Shayla was apparently a marshmallow in the middle. She wasn't going to take the chance that I was either a social worker or a cop. She took one look at me and chucked the notebook onto the pavement. She walked away, and the show over, their fun spoiled, her posse followed along.

"You shouldn't have done that." I was so busy feeling as if I was the David who'd whomped on Goliath, I almost forgot Harmony was there. I turned to find her glaring, not at Shayla, but at me. "I didn't need your help."

"You could have fooled me." I poked my hands in my pockets and rocked back on my heels, hoping it was a less assertive pose and thinking it might smooth Harmony's ruffled feathers. "Guess I got it wrong."

"Guess you did." Harmony stooped to make a grab for the notebook, but I was too fast for her. I scooped it up off the pavement before she could.

It had opened when Shayla tossed it down, and I found myself staring at a pencil drawing of flowers. Daffodils and tulips rendered in detail and with amazing skill. I had seen the genuine article, and I knew that in real life, the flowers were sad and stunted. In the drawing, they were transformed. I felt as if I could reach out and touch each silken petal.

I looked at Harmony in wonder. "Did you draw this? These are the flowers in front of your house."

She backed up and eyed me carefully. "How do you know where I live?"

I found you because of a ghost.

It was the first thought that sprang to mind, but of course, I couldn't say it. I shrugged instead and decided to play on the image I'd already established. "My name is Pepper. I check on foster kids." It wasn't really a lie. For reasons I still didn't understand, I was checking on *this* foster kid. "I just wanted to make sure that things were going well. You know. At home."

"With the Millers?" Sometime during her scuffle with Shayla, Harmony had lost her cigarette. She lit another one. "They're all right."

"They didn't worry about you not being in school today?"

She concentrated on taking a deep drag on the cigarette. "Doug and Mindy—the Millers, you know—they both work. They don't know I called in sick." She studied me through the thatch of brown/black hair that fell over her eyes. "They're okay people. They're not going to get in trouble because of me, are they?"

This, I couldn't say. Rather than doling out false hopes or hollow promises, I thumbed through Harmony's sketchbook. Page after page was filled with drawings, each of them emotionally charged. There was one of the house where she lived, and I could practically see the hopelessness of the neighborhood with every stroke of her pencil. There was another of a dog with a long snout and shaggy fur that made me want to scratch it behind the ears. There was even one of Harmony herself, and written underneath it in curling teenaged script were the words *Harmony in the Mirror*.

"You're really good." I flipped through a few more pages. At the back of the book was a drawing of Shayla. It wasn't a caricature; it was too precise for that. Still, it conveyed the big girl's personality perfectly, a cross between Baby Huey and the Jolly Green Giant. I smiled.

"Don't let her see that one." Harmony looked over my shoulder, and I realized that Shayla and her gang weren't gone, they'd just backed off. They were hanging around over near one of those Salvation Army drop-off bins, the kind that look like giant mailboxes. "I don't want to hurt her feelings."

"Why not?" I closed the notebook. "Shayla deserves to have her feelings hurt. She's a bully."

Harmony's eyes were blue. She looked away. "I don't have many friends," she said.

"And you want to hang with them?" I looked over my shoulder toward where Shayla and the rest of them were standing ten feet from the clothing bin, seeing who could light a match and toss it—still flaming—into the container. Luckily, none of them had very good aim. "They're jackasses."

Harmony wrinkled her nose. I guess there was nothing she could say.

I decided to change the subject and opened the sketchbook again. "You planning on studying art in college?" I asked.

Harmony laughed. Not like it was funny. More like I was the jackass this time. "Doug and Mindy can't afford to send me to college. They can't even afford to keep me with them after I'm eighteen and the state stops paying for my care. I'll get a job . . ." She shrugged. "I dunno. Somewhere."

It was on the tip of my tongue to tell her that she needed a better plan than that. After all, aside from the fact that at Harmony's age, my plans had been more in the ballpark of *rich husband* than *job*, we were both on the same road.

And I knew for a fact that it led to ruin.

Or at least to a dead-end job in the deadest of all places in town.

I hated to sound like Ella—honest—but I felt the first words of a lecture twitch against my lips. Shayla's voice stopped me.

"Hey, Harmony! Come over here, will you?"

"You're not going, are you?" I looked at the girl in wonder when she started across the parking lot.

"I told you," Harmony said, "I don't have many friends."

She snatched the sketchbook out of my hands and went to join the troop of her former tormentors, and that's when it hit me: the time I'd done pretty much the same thing.

Sophomore year in high school.

Tiffany Blaine and her buddies. The coolest, best-dressed, most socially influential girls at Beachwood High School, and I was dying to find my way into the inner circle.

Even when it meant sharing (a polite word for *cheating*) on the geometry exam.

"What do you think?"

The sound of Didi's voice snapped me out of my thoughts. I found her standing right beside me.

"About Harmony?" I shook my head. It was one thing caving in to the demands of the wrong crowd when you had Daddy's influence and Daddy's money to cushion the fall. It was another when you had no one but yourself. "She's headed for trouble."

"You think?" Didi stepped back and watched what was going on across the parking lot. Shayla and Harmony were talking, and I was poised and ready to jump in should the big girl decide to get physical again. Much to my surprise, the two girls came back across the parking lot together. Shayla's head was bent; she was saying something in Harmony's ear. They stopped at the door of the grocery store, and Shayla waited. Harmony walked in alone.

I went right inside after her.

I didn't want Harmony to know I was there, so I made sure I kept my distance. I trailed behind her, through the produce aisle, past the canned goods, all the way over to a section of the store that someone who'd never seen the inside of Saks had the nerve to label "Cosmetics."

In their dreams, I told myself, and watched around the corner of a display of Puffs as Harmony looked over the ninety-six-cents-a-bottle shampoo and the two-ninety-five nail polish.

She glanced toward the front of the store, and when another shopper came by, she reached for a bottle of conditioner and pretended she was reading the label. When that shopper disappeared, she went for the nail polish.

I knew she would.

It was the smallest thing there, and that meant it was the easiest to pocket.

Didi was nowhere around. Too bad. I wouldn't have minded a little input on the right way to handle this sticky situation. It struck me that like Harmony, I had nobody to fall back on but myself, and I trusted my instincts and followed Harmony to the checkout.

There were only two registers and one was closed, the lane blocked by a cart full of boxes of cheese crackers. The only way to the door was past a male clerk with a bad overbite and an eagle eye that looked Harmony up and down and stopped at the bulge in her jeans pocket.

His thin lips twitched into a predatory smile. He made a move to come around the counter.

I was faster.

Before he could step away from the register, I'd already plunked a five-dollar bill on the sticky conveyor belt (I didn't want to think about sticky with what) in front of him.

"Harmony," I said, startling the girl, who didn't know I was right behind her, "let me get that. Remember, I promised I'd pay for your next bottle of nail polish."

Harmony's spine stiffened. She reached in her

pocket, pulled out the nail polish and slapped it onto the counter.

"I changed my mind," she said. "This stuff is shit. I don't want it."

"But it's exactly the color you were looking for." I smiled and added the little lilt to my voice that guys always found so irresistible. It worked on the clerk (who was so busy staring at my chest, he hardly paid any attention to what Harmony and I were talking about). Lilt or no lilt, it didn't do a thing to cool the fire that shot from Harmony's eyes when she glanced over her shoulder at me.

"I said I don't want it," she hissed.

"And I said I'll be happy to pay for it for you."

She walked away.

I grabbed my five and followed.

"What the hell do you think you're doing?"

It was the question I should have asked, but Harmony beat me to it.

"What do you mean, what am I doing?" I was filled with my share of righteous indignation, and when we got as far as the row of gumball machines lined against the wall near the front door, I stopped, my fists on my hips. "I'm trying to save you from a criminal record, that's what I'm doing. Did you think you were going to get away with that?"

Harmony raised her chin and looked me in the eye. "I would have. And now . . ." She glanced outside. Shayla had been waiting by the door, watching. Her lip curled, she turned and left. All the other kids did, too.

Seeing them walk away, Harmony's shoulders slumped. "She said I could hang out with them," she grumbled, "if I could prove I wanted to bad enough."

It sounded so much like what Tiffany Blaine had said to me all those years before, it made my stomach bunch. "Shoplifting doesn't prove anything," I told Harmony, ignoring the fact that for me, cheating had proved to be my entrée into the in crowd. "You're going to get in trouble."

"Fuck off," Harmony said. She turned her back on me and walked away.

I had no choice but to follow her out of the store, but I made sure I stayed far behind. When it came to counseling skills, I was a zero; there was no use belaboring the point. I plunked down on the bench outside the front door of the grocery store and watched Harmony head back toward home.

"Too bad the kid doesn't have more to look forward to in her life."

Didi was right beside me.

"I was a fool to think I could make a difference," I admitted, and wondered if anyone who happened to glance my way thought I was talking to myself like the old guy I'd seen standing on the corner. "Nothing's going to change Harmony's life."

Didi's sigh rippled the spring air. "She'll try anything to show that she's worthy of Shayla's friendship, and when nothing works, she's going to turn to someone else for approval. I'm thinking that one tall, skinny boy. The kid with the dark hair and the little mustache. She'll get in trouble before she's a junior in high school. Guaranteed."

"You seem to know an awful lot about her."

"I know there's something that could make a difference."

I wasn't so sure, and I told Didi so. "Nothing's going to change her life."

"Money might."

I turned to my companion. "You're asking the wrong person about money."

"Am not." She smoothed her skirt and tugged at her gloves. "See, I know something you don't know."

I wasn't in the mood for games. I gave her a no-nonsense look.

She gave up without a fight.

"Harmony is my granddaughter," Didi said. "She's my daughter, Judy's, girl. Judy's dead now. Cancer. When Harmony was no more than five. The girl's father was a loser. That's why Harmony is in foster care. And she's headed down the same hopeless road as my daughter. No education. A mother too young. But you know, I could still make a difference in her life. You could make a difference in her life. If you prove I wrote *So Far the Dawn*, she'll collect the royalties. Then she'll never have to worry about money—or nosebleeds like Shayla—again."

Chapter 6

How big of a chump did Didi think I was?

Apparently, a pretty big one.

And apparently, she was right.

My heartstrings thoroughly tugged, my scruples outraged on Harmony's behalf, I agreed to do what I could to see that justice was done.

Too bad I didn't know where to begin.

The next day, I sat at my desk and drummed my fingers against the papers that sat on top of it in precarious piles like windblown snowdrifts. I'd come into the office early, raided the cemetery archives, and even spent some time doing Internet research. I Googled both "Deborah Bowman" and "Didi Bowman" and turned up nothing useful. I checked the Garden View database, and though many of our residents' files contained notes about their families or their former occupations, Didi's said nothing about either. If my latest ghostly nuisance was a mother (and thus, could have had a granddaughter), no one bothered to make mention of it. If she had ever been associated with the writing of *So Far the Dawn* . . . well, I couldn't find any evidence of that, either. And believe me, there were pages (and pages) of Internet sites devoted to the movie, the book, and its author.

Again, the little voice of doubt whispered in my ear.

It sounded like my dad.

I told it to shut up and glanced toward where Didi sat in the chair across from my desk. She was wearing the outfit she'd worn when I met her, and she adjusted the gauzy pink scarf that matched the bow around the neck of the appliquéd poodle on her skirt.

"If you wrote the book, how come you never told anyone?" I asked her.

"I did." She frowned. "I told plenty of people."

"Then why didn't they come forward when your sister published it?"

She shrugged.

It wasn't much of an answer, and it didn't do much to bolster my confidence. I tried another avenue of questioning.

"Why can't Harmony just talk to Merilee and ask for money?"

"Merilee doesn't know Harmony exists."

"I could tell her."

"It wouldn't make a difference." Didi rose and walked to the other side of my office. When she spoke, she kept her back to me. "My family didn't disown me or anything, but they were very unhappy," she said. "You know, when I got into trouble. Oh, they let me live there in the Ohio City house, me and Judy. But things were never the same between us. They barely spoke to me. And poor little Judy, they treated her like she was dirty."

It took me a moment to figure out that I'd heard Didi use the expression before. *Getting into trouble* was obviously mid-twentieth century code for *pregnant*. "Nobody cares about stuff like that anymore," I told Didi. "When Merilee connects with the only daughter of the only daughter of her only sister, I bet she'll get all warm and fuzzy. And when she finally kicks the bucket, Harmony will inherit a bundle."

When Didi turned to me, she rolled her eyes. "Harmony won't inherit one red cent. Merilee's will leaves everything to the Grand Order of the Grand Daughters of the Grand Army of the Republic. No one can make her change it."

I wasn't buying it. After all, I had been raised in the upper middle class. Growing up, I'd heard plenty of stories about money, and often they were based on someone being pissed at someone else who didn't leave the first someone a big enough piece of the pie. "Harmony could contest the will."

"She could," Didi admitted. "If she was smart enough. Which she'll never be if she never goes to a good school. And if she can find a lawyer who will believe her when she tells him that she's not only the great-niece of a famous author, but the only surviving relative, too. Which she won't, because let's face it, Harmony doesn't exactly look like the type who has tens of millions of dollars coming to her."

"Tens of millions?" I gulped down my surprise. "You mean we're talking that kind of money?"

Didi pouted in an oh-poor-me sort of way that made me think she'd used this tactic before. "Don't worry," she said, tears suddenly watering down her voice. "You'll get some of that money. It's all you care about, anyway."

I bet the bowed pink lips and the tearful blue eyes worked plenty good on suckers who were susceptible to that sort of thing. Just like I bet that in Didi's lifetime, she'd found plenty of suckers to use them on.

Bad news for her, I was not one of them. Besides, she got me all wrong. I had to defend my reputation and my motives.

I jumped to my feet. "That is so not true," I said. "It's not the money I'm thinking about. At least not in the way you think I'm thinking about it. Sure, I need money. And sure, I'd love to be paid for working on your case. But what I was thinking is that if there's a lot of money involved—"

"There is." She nodded.

"And if Merilee was underhanded enough to steal your manuscript—"

Didi's top lip quivered. "She did. She waited until I was dead, then published it under her name."

"Then if she's got that much at stake—"

"She does."

"Will you let me get a word in edgewise here?"

Unfortunately, I didn't have a chance to speak that edgewise word. No sooner had I screeched the question than I realized that my office door was open. Sometime while I was talking to Didi, Ella had walked in. By the time I realized it, I was already emphasizing my point by stabbing one finger into what must have looked to her like an empty corner of my office.

I scrambled to come up with an explanation that sounded even half plausible.

I shouldn't have wasted my brain cells.

Because Ella didn't even notice.

How could she when her eyes were glowing, her cheeks were crimson, and her breaths were coming so fast, I thought she'd stroke out right there on my office floor?

"Ella?" Instinctively I moved forward, one hand out to catch her when she collapsed. Which I was pretty sure she was about to do.

Only she didn't.

Instead, Ella grabbed my outstretched hand with both of hers. "The limo just pulled in," she said, and she jumped up and down. Like a kid on Christmas morning. "Come on, Pepper. You want to be part of this historic event, don't you?"

She didn't give me the opportunity to respond. Out in the hallway, the sounds of excited voices rose to fever pitch. Then they stopped cold. Silence descended. Both Ella and I knew what it meant.

The door of the administration building had opened.

Merilee Bowman had arrived.

Ella gulped in a breath. She dragged me into the hallway and through the crowd. We ended up at the front of the reception line.

I don't know what I expected. Mink, maybe. Or at least a Kate Spade bag and a pair of really kicky little shoes.

Instead, the woman who stood inside the front door was dressed in a drab brown suit and a white oxford cloth shirt that was buttoned all the way up her scrawny neck. The shoes? Brown loafers. Enough said.

Her hair was the same color as her suit and her shoes. It was shot through with gray and cut short, like a man's, and it was so thin, I could see her scalp. Except for a touch of color on her lips— mauve, which did nothing for her sallow complexion—she wasn't wearing a speck of makeup.

Believe me, if I had tens of millions, I would have made a little more of a fashion statement.

Like a deer in the headlights of an eighteen-wheeler, the woman blinked at the crowd assembled in the office reception area. She sniffled and swallowed, and the scent of menthol was as thick around her as the paparazzi I could see outside the open door. They scrambled, not to get into the office but to jockey for a place closer to the limo parked right outside. It was as big as a boat and so shiny, the morning sun glinted off it like sparkling stars.

I noticed that Dan Callahan—or at least the leather-and-jeans-clad photographer I'd seen the day before and thought was Dan—wasn't in the pack.

"I'm Trish Kingston, Miss Bowman's secretary," the scrawny woman said, and I gave myself a mental slap. Of course! This woman was forty, maybe. Too young to be the famous author whose not-so-famous sister had died way back in the fifties when they were both adults. Trish scraped her palms over her brown skirt and extended one bony hand. She didn't so much shake Ella's as she clung to it for dear life. "Everything's ready, isn't it? Everything's perfect? Please tell me everything's just the way we discussed it on the phone."

Ella's smile was beatific. "It sure is," she said, and Trish breathed a sigh of relief. A wave of menthol washed over me.

Ella looked past the secretary and out the door toward the limo. "Is she happy to be here?"

"Happy?" Trish repeated the word as if she wasn't quite sure what it meant. Her slender shoulders rose and fell inside the boxy brown jacket. She worked over the lozenge in her mouth as if the harder she sucked it, the better she'd be able to think. "I dunno. It's kind of hard to tell with Miss Bowman. But if you're ready . . ." She glanced around at the assembled crowd of Garden View employees before she looked over her shoulder to where the extra security guards the cemetery had hired for the occasion had set up a barrier and were busy keeping the eager reporters and photographers behind it.

Ella raised her chin. She looped one arm through mine, and like it or not, I found myself front and center as we processed outside to greet our guest of honor.

We arranged ourselves in a phalanx outside the door. As soon as I untangled myself from Ella, I scrambled over to the side next to Trish Kingston and let Ella and Jim take center stage. Didi, I noticed, was nowhere to be seen.

Before I had a chance to think about it and what it meant, the limo driver popped out of the car and walked over to the back door. He opened it and stood aside.

Ella held her breath.

Jim sucked in his gut.

Trish mumbled something that sounded like,

"Oh please, God, don't let anything go wrong."

And Merilee Bowman stepped out of the car.

Okay, all that stuff I said about fashion statements? I take it all back. Even with tens of millions, I couldn't have made a fashion statement like Merilee Bowman made a fashion statement.

It was ostentatious, that's for certain, what with the robin's egg blue picture hat and the matching suit and alligator pumps.

It was flashy, or at least the golf ball–size diamond she wore around her slender neck was.

It was over-the-top. Just like the smile she aimed at the photographers all around us who clicked picture after picture.

The effect was lost on no one. Except for Trish, still muttering a prayer—this time to St. Jude, who I knew from my father's mother (a great believer in divine intervention) was the patron of impossible causes—a reverent hush fell over the crowd. There was no doubt about it: We were in the presence of royalty.

Big points for Ella, though. She may have looked as if she was about to swoon at Merilee's feet, but she kept her cool. She stepped forward and reached for Merilee's hand, and I guess I was right about the whole royalty thing, Ella bobbed a little curtsy.

"Miss Bowman . . ." Her voice failed, smothered beneath the excitement that clogged her breathing. Ella had to start again. "Miss Bowman, I'm Ella Silverman. I'm community relations manager here at Garden View and president of ISFTDS. Welcome."

Merilee's skin was porcelain. Her eyes were the same shade of baby blue as Didi's. From beneath her hat, I saw a sweep of silvery hair. She accepted Ella's homage and held on to her hand long enough to assure a good photo.

"We are honored to have you here," Ella said.

"Of course you are." Merilee smiled, and something told me that if she hadn't been busy making sure that the photographer who darted forward for a picture didn't get exactly the right shot, she would have patted Ella on the head.

Like a dog.

Have I mentioned that I'm a redhead?

I know, I know . . . there's the whole stereotype thing. Redheads are hot-tempered. Redheads are quick to judge. Redheads don't give anyone the benefit of the doubt.

Well, put me in a pigeonhole.

Because it's all true.

In my case, anyway.

All it took was that one moment and the hint of condescension that wafted around Merilee the way the smell of menthol did around Trish, and the bubble of Merilee's celebrity burst. At least for me. Free of the spell that seemed to have entranced everyone else, I crossed my arms over my chest and stepped back, watching as Ella introduced Merilee to Jim and the rest of the senior staff.

Had this elegant, silver-haired egocentric stolen Didi's manuscript and taken the credit for Didi's work?

For the first time since Didi told me her tale of woe, I wanted to believe it. And not just because I wanted to help Harmony or because I was hoping to share in a little chunk of those tens of millions of dollars.

But if I had learned anything from my investigation into Gus Scarpetti's death, it was that nothing is that easy. Especially when it comes to private investigation for the dead.

It didn't matter whether I liked Merilee or not (and as I watched her bask in the adoration of her fans and accept it as if it was her due, I decided that I definitely did not). I had to look at the situation objectively. After all, it was Merilee's name on the covers of all those millions of books, not Didi's. It was Merilee who had the credentials, too. From what I'd learned during my research earlier that morning, nobody knew the American Civil War like Merilee did. She had been trained as a librarian, and early on in her career had taken an interest in the War Between the States and had made it her mission to learn everything there was to know about it. Even before *SFTD* was published, she was considered an expert.

But I had also learned something else: Though she dangled the promise of *someday* in front of her millions of fans, Merilee had yet to produce another book.

Did that mean anything in terms of my investigation?

Sure. If I believed the gossip on the dozens of chat boards I'd looked over that morning, it meant:

(a) Merilee was really dead and the woman who would be attending the premiere in Cleveland was a body double.

(b) Merilee couldn't write another book because *SFTD* was the greatest book ever written and she couldn't compete with herself.

(c) Merilee was an alien who had been sent to this planet to prove that Earthlings are culturally imperfect. After all, who but a member of some super-human race could have produced a book that was perfect down to every last period and comma?

And

(d) She was working on it. At least that's what the "letter to our loyal members" signed by Ella on the ISFTDS Web site said. Merilee was a perfectionist and she was working on not just another book, but a *SFTD* sequel. When she was satisfied that it was good enough, she'd let the world—and the dozens of publishers clamoring for the rights with their pens poised over their checkbooks—know.

I was chewing over all this as Ella, Jim, and the superstar in question made their way down the line toward me, and it occurred to me that this was, in fact, the most salient argument to support Didi's claim.

Merilee had made a boatload of money on her first book. Why on earth didn't she bust her ass to write another one?

"And this, of course, is Pepper. She's the tour guide here at Garden View." Ella got around to me sooner than I expected. I shook myself out of my thoughts and found Merilee Bowman directly in

front of me. She was waiting for me to bow and
scrape and kiss her ring, but I decided a more
direct approach might better serve my purpose.

"So," I said, "when *are* you going to publish a
So Far the Dawn sequel?"

At my side, Trish Kingston blanched and urped.
I think she swallowed her lozenge. Ella closed her
eyes, and I could tell she was praying for patience.
Jim realized the photographers were nearby again.
He sucked in his gut.

Merilee took my question in stride. She smiled
in a grandmotherly sort of way and reached for my
hand. She gave it a gentle squeeze. "I'm so pleased
you're anxious to read the sequel," she said. Her
voice was soft and as cultured as sour cream. "So
many of my dear, dear fans have asked me that
question over the years and I can only tell you
what I've told them. When it's ready." Her eyes
twinkled like the diamond at her neck. "When it's
ready," she said again, louder this time and in a
singsong voice that fooled those around us into
thinking she was sharing a secret. "Please remind
me." She patted my hand. "When it comes out,
remind me, and I'll sign a copy just for you."

She snapped her fingers, and out of nowhere,
Trish produced a business card and pressed it into
my hand. It was damp around the edges and it featured a photo of Merilee—in color—along with a
post office box address in California and a line
that told me to drop Merilee a line anytime. *I love
to hear from my many, many fans!*

I pocketed the card, and when the crowd moved
forward, I was swept along with them.

"Your parents' mausoleum isn't far," I heard

Ella tell Merilee. "But we'd better drive. That should help keep everything orderly. You can drive over in the limo, and we'll follow in a staff car."

"The flowers?"

The question was meant for Trish, and she scrambled to the front of the crowd to provide the answer. "Ordered," she said. "Red roses. Pink orchids. White fuchsia."

Merilee's back was turned to the photographers when her top lip curled, and she grumbled a question meant only for Trish's ears. "How the hell can fuchsia be white?"

Trish didn't get the joke.

I did, but I wasn't laughing.

We looked like a funeral, the limo in front and a long line of cars behind it. I had gotten separated from Ella, and I rode over to the Bowman family grave site with the guys from the grounds crew. I waited until they were out of the Jeep and headed toward where everyone—including the photographers and three television crews—waited in front of a pink and gray granite mausoleum. It was, in fact, the only mausoleum nearby. We were in the new section, not far from Didi's grave, and there where the gravestones were simple rectangles flush with the ground, the mausoleum stuck out like a sore thumb. I'd seen it before, of course, but I'd never paid much attention except to wonder who had the balls to dress a grave like a two-hundred-dollar-an-hour whore in a section where every other burial was as modest as a nun.

Now I knew. Merilee. She was the one responsible for the spires, the stained glass window, and the weeping angel who sat atop the whole shebang like the bride on a macabre wedding cake.

Didn't it just figure?

I had already started to join the group gathered around the door of the mausoleum when I realized Didi was walking beside me. She was dressed in black again. Her face was covered with a long black veil. Her stockings had seams up the backs of them.

Call me a softie, but I was uneasy thinking that Didi and Merilee's parents were spending their eternity in the Garden View equivalent of the Taj Mahal while Didi herself was tucked away in a dark, mossy corner. I scrambled to come up with some small talk, but Didi beat me to it.

"My parents were originally buried back near my grave," she said, her voice devoid of emotion. "Until Merilee decided that wasn't the impression she wanted to make. She had this mausoleum built twenty years ago, and she paid a fortune for it. What do you think?"

"I think you should know that I wasn't talking about the money I'd like to earn for taking your case," I said, and even I was surprised that the tiff I'd had with Didi back in the office was still on my mind. "When I said I didn't know we were talking tens of millions, it wasn't because I suddenly saw dollar signs flash in front of my eyes. What I meant is that's an awful lot of money, and the more money that's involved, the more dangerous this investigation is likely to be. If Merilee did steal your book, she's going to fight like hell to make sure no one uncovers the secret."

"Of course, silly." Didi clicked her tongue. "I could have told you that."

We were on the fringes of the crowd, and I knew I couldn't chance another comment. I watched Trish disappear along the side of the mausoleum and reappear carrying an urn that was as tall as she was and twice as wide. It was filled with red roses, pink orchids, and the infamous white fuchsias.

Staggering under the weight, Trish made her way to where Merilee waited, and with Trish walking backwards and Merilee looking regal and serious, they marched to the door of the mausoleum. With a grunt, Trish lowered her burden to the ground, and Merilee touched her hand to the closest flower petal.

"My family was very dear to me," she said. She paused when a camera flashed. "It's a privilege for me to be able to visit them here today. My dear mother, Louise, and my dear father, Gerard. I have so many fond memories of them and of my wonderful years here in Ohio."

"Are you glad you came back, Miss Bowman?" A reporter called out the question from the back of the crowd.

Merilee touched a hand to the diamond at her throat. "I've been so fortunate in my life. It's such a privilege to be able to give back to the people who supported and encouraged me all those years ago. If only . . ."

I heard a sniff, and I thought for a moment that Merilee was going to show some honest-to-gosh emotion, but as it turned out, it was only Trish.

She unwrapped another Halls and popped it in her mouth.

"If only my parents could see me now." Merilee's smile was bittersweet. "They'd be so very proud. They were the ones who told me to always follow my dream. I did, and it has taken me to wonderful places. Family." She sighed. "My dear mother and my dear father. That's what's really important in life. Success, money, achievement—none of it matters as much as my dear, dear family."

"Will you be back to visit them before you leave town?" a reporter called out.

"Will you ever publish your memoirs and tell us what it was like during those years you wrote *So Far the Dawn*?" another one asked.

It wasn't that I was feeling left out, I just didn't like the fact that all this talk about Merilee's dear, dear family had left out one vital bit of information. "How about your sister, Didi?" I made sure I talked loud enough for everyone in the crowd to hear me. "You gonna visit her grave while you're here? You know, the plain, ordinary grave that's over there in the shadows?"

Ella's eyes went wide.

Trish gulped and coughed when the lozenge got stuck in her throat.

Merilee's expression hardened to stone. Her eyes narrowed, she scanned the throng in front of her, and hey, who could blame them? They may never have heard of Didi Bowman, but these reporters were no dummies. They knew aggravation when they saw it, and not one of them could risk getting on Merilee's bad side. The crowd parted in front of me like the Red Sea before Moses, and Merilee's blue eyes met mine. "What did you say?" she asked.

There was nothing to be gained from cowering behind the phalanx of photographers so I stepped forward. "I asked about your sister." I looked toward the reporters to fill them in. "Her name was Deborah. Deborah Bowman. Aka Didi. She died right here in Cleveland, back in the fifties when she was pretty young. I don't think a lot of people know about her, even though she's buried not far from here. Her grave, it's not nearly as fancy as this one." I glanced back toward the guest of honor. "I just wondered, you know, if you were going to visit her, too."

I had to give Merilee credit. I knew she was surprised—and not in a good way—because I saw those elegant hands of hers curl into fists. But in just a moment, she was once again as cool and as calm as ever. "Of course I'm going to visit my dear, dear younger sister," she said, turning the smile of a dowager angel toward the cameras. "The very next time I stop at Garden View. Which brings me to an announcement I thought I'd save for another time. I've been thinking about my own mortality. Well . . ." She blushed on cue. "After all, a woman of my age must. I've decided that while I'm here in Cleveland, I'll be meeting with the wonderful folks here at Garden View to design and plan my own mausoleum."

This was news. To the reporters. To the photographers. To the Garden View staff. They all reacted just as Merilee knew they would.

The reporters tripped over one another asking questions about the mausoleum's placement and design.

The photographers fought to get to the front of the crowd for the best picture.

Ella smiled as if she'd just been handed a million bucks, and I swear, Jim was so happy, his shirt buttons just about popped.

Any and all thoughts of Didi were lost in the excitement.

"Sorry." I said it to Didi, but when I turned to her, she was already gone. It was just as well. I might as well have been talking to myself.

The place had gone gaga, and no one would have paid the least attention to me even if I'd stood on top of the nearest headstone and declared that I could see and talk to ghosts.

Of course, that wasn't why I suddenly felt awful, like my credit card had been rejected at Saks.

I could see the writing on the wall, and call me paranoid, but something told me that Merilee could, too.

With the promise of a series of visits from the world's most famous author, the stage was set. From now until Merilee got her robin's egg blue self back on a plane and headed home, Garden View was going to be a zoo. There would be no time for tours. I didn't need it spelled out. I knew that no tours equaled no tour guide.

Which meant that as of right then and there, I was officially out of work.

I knew it was coming, but the reality hit harder than I expected. Rather than risk anyone knowing it, I decided to walk back to the office. I'd already started that way when I felt a chill shoot up the back of my neck.

Like someone was watching me.

I turned to find Merilee not three feet away, those cold eyes trained on me. "I don't like surprises," she said.

That made two of us.

As I went to my office to collect my things, another thought struck.

It looked as if Merilee had the last laugh after all.

Chapter 7

I was officially on vacation, and if I was smart, I would have stopped worrying about Didi and Merilee and how I was going to pay for my rent and my groceries and started working on my tan.

I would have, too, except that the day after Merilee showed up at the cemetery, it began to rain, and three days later, it still hadn't stopped.

I was stuck in my apartment, and frankly I was bored.

I could have gone shopping, of course.

Only I couldn't afford clothes or, for that matter, the gas to get me to the mall.

I could have called a friend for lunch.

But funny how that works . . . most of my so-called friends had lost contact the day the slammer door slammed behind my dad.

I could have cleaned or caught up with laundry or even turned on the TV to see what was happening on the soaps, but let's face it, except for the daytime dramas, none of that stuff was much fun. And as for the soaps . . . well, I had no doubt that if I turned them on, I would have seen multiple glamorous people having multiple wild love affairs. The only thing that would have accomplished was to make me wonder what was wrong with me that I couldn't even get one *un-wild* love affair going. And that was just plain depressing.

That left me with two choices: the cemetery, where I could collect some of the research materials I needed for the "Famous Faces" tour, and Didi.

Fortunately, it was the old two-birds-with-one-stone theory. Unlike Gus, Didi had yet to follow me home. Which meant that I had to go looking for her. Naturally, that meant a trip to Garden View.

My windshield wipers slapping out the minutes, I drove the few blocks from my apartment and up Mayfield Road through the heart of Cleveland's Little Italy. When the cemetery was established in the middle of the nineteenth century, a call went out for stonecutters to provide its monuments, its mausoleums, and its bridges. There was a skilled workforce—ready, willing, and able—in Italy, and the workers moved into the surrounding neighborhood and brought their families and their culture with them. The rest, as they say, is history, and these days, the neighborhood featured fabulous Italian restaurants, gorgeous art galleries, and trendy boutiques. Of course, my days of being able to afford to patronize any of them were history, too.

I guess that's what I must have been thinking about as I headed to Garden View. That would explain why I almost missed the turn into the cemetery.

Or maybe it was because though I'd worked

there for a couple of months, I had never seen a few dozen people milling around outside the gates. A group of them was huddled in plastic ponchos and holding a WELCOME, MERILEE! sign. When they saw my car, they darted forward. One look, of course, told them I was not the superstar they were waiting for, and their expressions reflected their disappointment. They scurried back to the sidewalk to stand next to costumed Civil War re-enactors and vendors who had set up their wares under plastic tarps and were selling everything from *So Far the Dawn* T-shirts to posters that featured Merilee's dear, dear smiling face.

When I got to the gate, Nate, one of my favorite fellow employees, stepped out from the shelter of a wooden guardhouse. I slowed my car and pressed the button to roll down my window. "What's going on?"

Nate was a tall, thin African American who was nearing retirement. He had a grizzled face and an eagle eye that served him well in his job with cemetery security. He was swaddled in an orange slicker, and when he shook his head, raindrops flew in every direction. "I don't understand it," he said. "They've been out here for days. Ever since that Miss High-and-Mighty stopped by. I guess they figure she's going to be back and they don't want to miss her."

I looked at the mob gathered at the gates. "And the city's okay with this? Jim approved it? Ella doesn't mind?"

"What can anybody do? City gave 'em a permit. I suppose they figured it was better than having to arrest everybody for trespassing. You know and I

know, they're not going to go away. In the mean-
time, I got to stand out here and make sure they
don't get in the way of any funeral processions or
of anybody here to visit their loved ones." As if he
didn't understand any of it—that made two of
us—he shook his head again, and again raindrops
flew in all directions. "You, of course"—he
grinned—"are welcome anytime."

"Thanks, Nate." I eased my foot off the brake.
"Want me to bring you some coffee on my way
out?"

"Got a thermos!" He pointed over his shoulder to
where he'd been standing. "But thanks, anyway."

I waved goodbye and headed for the office, no-
ticing as I did that there were more visitors than
usual in the cemetery. Considering that it was a
weekday, that seemed odd. Considering that it was
raining, it was odder yet. Until I realized that many
of them were wearing hoop skirts and poke bon-
nets. Or Civil War uniforms.

Ghosts?

My heart skipped a beat, and for one crazy
second I worried that this whole Gift thing had
gotten way out of control.

Until I saw that many of the women in their long
dresses were carrying cameras. And a couple of the
guys in uniform were listening to their iPods.

More reenactors.

I breathed a sigh of relief. It wasn't too hard to
figure out that they weren't as interested in the
dead as they were in the living. Like the folks outside the gate, they were hanging around hoping for
a glimpse of their idol.

Surprisingly, though, none of them were gathered

at the Bowman mausoleum. In fact, the only one I saw over there was Rick Jensen, the photographer who took my picture a few days earlier. I waved. He didn't see me. I continued on to the parking lot closest to the office.

There were no surprises there. The usual group of paparazzi was waiting around. With one exception. I didn't see the Dan who might not have been Dan.

I didn't see Didi anywhere, either, and rather than go looking for her in the rain, I decided to pop into the office.

The first person I ran into was Ella. Her outfit was the same color as the leaden clouds outside. Gray skirt. Gray jacket. The only thing that jazzed it up was her sparkling pink earrings and the strings of multicolored beads around her neck. She smiled. "You're here to work on the new tour."

"Yeah." For once, it was the truth—even if it wasn't the whole truth. "I have to pick up some things in my office. That's okay, isn't it?"

She patted my arm. "*Mi casa es su casa*," she said, and laughed. "You know you can stop in anytime, even if you're not officially on the payroll. And actually, I'm glad you came by today. I've got some fabulous news."

I wrinkled my nose and looked around warily. "Don't tell me Merilee is hiding out somewhere nearby."

She thought I was joking. "Now, Pepper, don't you be that way. Miss Bowman isn't used to the glare of the public spotlight. That's why she acted a little funny the other day. She's really a very gracious and kind person."

Good thing I was busy opening my office door and switching on the light—I didn't have to agree or disagree. Inside the office, I rummaged around on my desktop for the notes Ella had provided for the new tour. I gathered some books from the shelf across the room, grabbed a map of Garden View, and got set to leave.

Ella was waiting just outside the door. "It's all going so well," she said, and even after I flicked off the overhead lights, her smile lit up the place. "And today we've got another opportunity to shine. Merilee is going to be interviewed on Channel 5. The noon news. They've asked me to come along. Want to join us?"

I looked down at the jeans and open-toed heels I'd paired with a tank the color of coffee and a lightweight sweater of the same shade. "I'm not exactly dressed for TV."

"Don't worry about that. You won't be on camera. Come on, Pepper. It will be a blast," she said. Which made me wonder about her definition of fun. "Merilee's giving them three minutes. Really, that's a long time for news, a whole segment. Then they've got me scheduled for one. You know, to talk about everything ISFTDS has planned for the summer. The museum opening and the costume gala and the book discussion groups we've scheduled at local library branches." She gave me a wink and a playful elbow to the ribs. "While I'm at it, I'm planning to put in a good word for Garden View, too. Things are working so smoothly here." We were walking down the hallway by then, and she glanced around and beamed her approval.

"Between our usual security staff and the extra help we've hired, we're taking care of all the traffic inside the cemetery," she said. "And the city police are handling the crowds outside the gates. Everyone's working together and everything is falling into place. The publicity we're getting from all this is invaluable. The mayor has already called to thank us. The press is saying nothing but nice things. There is no way in the world we can't spin this into the PR coup of all times. Why, if it keeps up—"

"Ella!" Her face pale, her voice tight, Jennine screeched around the corner from the outer office. "Ella, you won't believe what just happened. Somebody found that photographer, Rick Jensen, over near the Bowman memorial. He's on the ground and he's bleeding. It looks like he's been mugged!"

When we got over to the pink and gray granite mausoleum, Rick Jensen was sitting up on the ground. Robert E. Lee stood next to him. The general had a cell phone in his hand.

"I called 911," the reenactor told us. "They said they'd be here pronto."

From Rick Jensen's ashen complexion and the blood that was trickling from the wound at the back of his head, I'd say pronto was a good thing.

"Oh my goodness!" Her face screwed into an expression of concern, Ella wrung her hands and paced back and forth in front of the injured photographer. Seeing the blood and the way Rick's eyes were glazed over, I knew her maternal instincts had kicked in. She was torn between administering first aid and a little comfort and the thought of what getting down on the wet ground with Rick would do to her outfit—and her impending TV appearance.

I saved her the trouble and knelt down next to Rick myself. "What happened?" I asked him.

He pressed a hand to his forehead. "Like I told this guy . . ." He looked up at Robert E. Lee. "One second I was standing here waiting to see if I might get lucky and Miss Bowman might come by so I could snap some pictures, and the next second, wham. Something hit me on the back of the head."

I glanced around. There was a foot-long piece of marble on the ground nearby. It looked like the tip of an angel's wing. I knew one of our angel statues wasn't far away, and something told me that when I checked, I'd find that her wing had been broken.

"Did you see anyone?" I asked Rick.

He made an attempt to shake his head, but it must have hurt. He closed his eyes and took a deep breath. "Not a soul. And I didn't hear anything, either."

"Did they take your wallet?" This question came from Ella, and I couldn't blame her for being concerned. News of a robbery inside the cemetery would damage all that good PR she'd worked so hard to establish.

Rick patted his pants pocket. "That's the funny thing," he said. "My wallet's here. So is the cash I'm carrying. A couple hundred bucks. The only thing missing is my camera."

I'm not sure why that struck me as odd, but I guess after hanging around with the local mob, I was beginning to think like one of the bad guys. If

I had gone to all the trouble of clunking Rick on the head, I would have left the camera and gone for the cash. After all, cash didn't leave a telltale trail. Sure, the camera could be pawned, but why take the chance? Hot merchandise was evidence, evidence that could eventually be used to pin the crime on the perp.

Leaving Rick in the care of Ella and the general, I rose to my feet and walked around the perimeter of the mausoleum. Nothing looked unusual, except for the flowers Merilee had left three days earlier. When she presented them, I could have sworn she'd left them directly in front of the mausoleum door. Now the urn was moved to one side. There were holes in the arrangement. Like some of the flowers were missing.

I turned back to Rick. "Have you been here every day?" I asked him.

"Just about." From out on the street, we heard the sounds of an ambulance siren. Help was on the way, and if these paramedics were as efficient as the ones who'd come to help me the day I bonked my head on Gus Scarpetti's mausoleum, I knew they'd get Rick loaded onto the ambulance and to a hospital in no time flat. If I was going to learn anything from him, I had to do it fast.

"Has anybody been messing with these flowers?" I asked.

"Anybody? How about everybody?" The ambulance pulled up, and two paramedics jumped out.

They hadn't turned off the siren, and I hurried closer to Rick because I didn't want to miss a thing he said. "Everybody who?"

"All those crazy Merilee Bowman fans," Rick

said. "They keep coming by, snipping flowers. You know, taking souvenirs."

"And you took pictures of them while they were doing it?"

"Sure. Some of them. Not that any of the photos are worth anything. I just thought, you know, that I might be able to do a little freelance business. That there might be some newspaper somewhere that might want to do a piece on how crazy fans can be." Rick gave me what was almost a smile. "Lucky thing Miss Bowman never did show up, huh? When that creep took my camera, he didn't get any pictures that were valuable."

I wish I could have been as sure as Rick was that the assault at the Bowman memorial didn't net the mugger anything important, but no matter how many times I tried to work it through in my head, I always ended up exactly where I'd started: It all seemed just a little too convenient.

The flowers had been messed with.

Rick took pictures of the folks messing with the flowers.

Rick's camera was missing.

Of course, though my logic was flawless and my reasoning impeccable, none of it meant squat.

At least not to me.

And none of it did diddly in terms of proving that Merilee Bowman was not the author of *So Far the Dawn*, either.

And that—I reminded myself—was what I was supposed to be doing.

"But of course it was difficult."

Merilee's voice seeped through my consciousness

and interrupted my train of thought. I looked across the TV studio to the set where she was being interviewed. This afternoon's appearance was a first of its kind, according to Ella. On our way downtown to meet up with Trish and Merilee, Ella had pointed out that Merilee was as shy as a spring violet and had only agreed to this interview because it was an opportunity to publicize the *SFTD* museum, and thus help with the fund-raising.

That afternoon Merilee was resplendent in a red silk suit. Her silvery hair was swept up and away from her face. Since she was sans picture hat, I had the opportunity to take a good look at her for the first time.

If I squinted and used my imagination, I could see the resemblance between Didi and Merilee. Both their eyes were blue. Both their complexions were flawless.

But that was pretty much as far as my imagination was able to take me.

Sure, at seventy-seven, Merilee was years older than Didi, who, according to her headstone, had entered into her not-so-eternal rest at the tender age of twenty-four. But even without the added years, it was hard to believe the two women were related.

Didi's figure was lush; Merilee was as skinny as a green bean.

Didi's lips were full; Merilee's were thin, and even the coating of scarlet lipstick she'd slathered on before the cameras rolled couldn't keep her mouth from looking like a slash against her pale face.

Didi was the liveliest dead person I'd ever met. She was bubbly and friendly and sometimes even funny.

Merilee was none of those things. Sure she was elegant. Hell, she had money, and money could make even the plainest woman look like a queen.

But underneath it all—the silk and the diamonds and the ego that knew no bounds—that's exactly what Merilee was—plain. A plain little librarian who was obsessed with the Civil War and who just happened to have written the world's most famous book.

Maybe.

I told myself not to forget it and turned my attention back to the interview.

"Anything of any real value is always difficult to accomplish," Merilee was saying. "I remember staying up nights, worrying about what Opal would say to Palmer. Wondering how Palmer would react. These characters, you know, they take on a life of their own. Before long, even the person who created them comes to think of them as real."

"As so many millions of your readers have!" The reporter, a perky thing with blindingly white teeth and blond hair, scooted to the edge of her chair. She leaned forward, her eyes bright. "When can your fans expect another book?"

"When it's ready." In a whisper, I repeated the words along with Merilee.

"How did you know she was going to say that?" Ella bent her head close and whispered.

I shrugged in reply. "Call me psychic. Why hasn't she finished another book?" I asked Ella. I figured as president of the fan club, she might have the inside track. "If this is writer's block, it's the longest lasting case on record."

"Shhh!" A woman with a clipboard, who was standing between us and the set, turned and put a finger to her lips.

Chastised, Ella stepped back. I knew I wouldn't get another word out of her. In front of us, the director gave the reporter the high sign to wrap things up. After a commercial break, it would be Ella's turn to go in front of the cameras. I watched her smooth a hand over her skirt and comb her fingers through her hair. She was nervous, but I had confidence in her. Ella was always cool under fire.

Not so Trish Kingston. In my one and only encounter with her back at the cemetery, I'd learned that Trish was as jumpy as a cricket on a hot sidewalk. She was afraid of Merilee, and who could blame her? Miss Congeniality, Merilee was not. Yet when I looked around, Trish wasn't toeing the edge of the set as I expected her to be, waiting for Merilee's next orders, hanging on Merilee's every word.

In fact, Trish was nowhere to be seen.

It was curious, and I was curious about it. I gave Ella an encouraging pat on the back and carefully stepped over camera cables and around light stands, heading out in search of Trish.

I found her in what I'd heard the TV folks call the greenroom, the place guests waited until they were told it was time for them to go in front of the cameras. She was lounging in a plush recliner, and I did a double take when I saw her.

Trish was dressed in a navy and red plaid skirt and matching jacket.

I recognized the pricey as well as the dumpy. My mom had always shopped at Talbot's.

Trish's scrawny legs—and the navy pumps on her feet—were stretched out in front of her, and she had a can of Coke in one hand.

"Hey, Trish." When I smiled and waved, she opened her eyes, and I realized that she'd been napping. "Just thought you'd like to know that Merilee's interview is almost over."

"Yeah, whatever." Trish stretched and sat up. The smell of menthol wafted through the room toward me. She drained the last of the Coke in the can. "God, maybe we can get out of here now. I always thought TV studios would be, you know, interesting."

"Me, too." There wasn't much else to say. Aside from asking who this person was and what she'd done with the scared-of-her-own shadow Trish I'd met at Garden View. Knowing I wouldn't get an answer, I stepped back into the hallway.

And smacked right into Merilee.

"Sorry." The apology was automatic. After all, how sorry did I have to be? I was the one walking backward. Merilee was the one going straight ahead. She might actually have noticed me if she didn't look so distracted.

I moved out of the doorway and let her into the greenroom. Call me a rubbernecker. Like a witness at the scene of an especially gruesome accident, I was anxious to see what was going to happen between Merilee and the new and improved Trish.

What I saw was Merilee take one look at Trish and open her mouth. I could just about read the biting words that were ready on her lips.

But instead of speaking them, she swallowed hard. A small, nervous smile flickered over her lips. "Are you ready to leave?" she asked Trish.

"Hell, yes." Trish hoisted herself out of the chair and thrust her Coke can in Merilee's face. "Get me another soda first."

Merilee jumped as if she'd been slapped, and I braced myself, waiting for the tirade. Instead, Merilee held out her hand for the can and headed across the room to toss it into the trash, her teeth clenched around her question.

"Regular or diet?"

I guess I must have dreamed about the whole weird situation between Merilee and Trish that night. That would explain why I woke up the next morning thinking about Coke cans and cameras and a frump who turned into a plaid-clad shopping princess right before my eyes.

I was making coffee and still shaking away the memory when my phone rang.

"Pepper, it's Ella."

I could tell from the tone of her voice that something was very wrong.

I sat down at my kitchen table. "What?"

On the other end of the phone, I heard Ella gulp. "I have bad news," she said. "Very bad news. Trish Kingston is dead."

Chapter 8

Considering that Ella was in the business of death, she was awfully upset by Trish's passing.

Considering that I was in the same business and had the added bonus of knowing that dead didn't always mean gone, I still couldn't blame her.

It was one thing spending forty-plus hours a week surrounded by the dearly departed when they were simply names on headstones and notations in a database. It was another when, the last we'd seen her, Trish was alive and well.

Even if she had been acting as if aliens had taken over her body.

On my way to the cemetery, I stopped at Starbucks for a cup of the jasmine tea Ella loved so much, and once inside the office, I nodded hello to Jennine, who was busy with a grieving family, and hurried to Ella's office to get the tea to her while it was still hot. I set the cup down on the desk in front of her and watched her blow her nose.

"I know this is ridiculous." Ella's voice was watery. Her nose was raw. Her eyes were the same shade of red as the beads on the bracelet she was wearing that day. "I mean, I hardly knew the woman, but still, this is such a shock. And what a shame! Especially when everything was going so well."

No sooner were the words out of her mouth than Ella's face went ashen.

"Oh my gosh," she moaned. "I didn't mean that. Not the way it sounded. I only meant—"

"I know." I didn't. Not for sure. And I wasn't very good at offering comfort, but at the same time I figured it was the right thing to say, I also knew this was the perfect opening to bring up the subject of Trish's odd behavior the day before. "I bet you meant that you weren't talking about *SFTD* and the premiere and all that stuff. You meant that things were going well for Trish personally."

"Exactly." Ella nodded and blotted the tip of her nose. "She told me. Just yesterday as we were leaving the television station. She told me that things were looking up for her."

Ella's office was larger than mine. She had two guest chairs. I dropped down into the one closer to the window that looked out at the section of Garden View where Didi was buried. "Really? She said that? Didn't it strike you as a little odd?"

Ella sniffed. Confused, she wrinkled her nose.

I sat back. "Think about it. When Merilee and Trish were here at the cemetery, Trish looked like a *Queer Eye* guest *before* the guys got to her. And one look from Merilee practically melted her on the spot. Yesterday at the TV station . . . well, I can't say she looked like she stepped out of *Vogue*. Nothing could make Trish look that good. But she was dressed differently. More stylishly. Sort of.

And definitely more expensively. She was acting strange, too."

"Was she?" Ella scrubbed her hands over her face, and I remembered that I was the only one who'd witnessed the odd exchange between Merilee and Trish in the greenroom. "I noticed her clothing, of course. I just thought . . ." She shrugged. "I don't know. I guess I just figured it was a side to Trish that we hadn't seen."

"I'll say." I'd wound my carrot-colored hair into a braid before I left the house, and I fingered the end of it, thinking. "Don't you wonder why?"

"Why we hadn't seen that side of her?" Ella popped the lid on the cup and breathed in deep. I could practically see some of the tension melt away from her, and I was glad I'd taken the time to stop for the tea. She took a careful sip. "I guess we just didn't know Trish long enough to know what she was really like. And now . . ." The memory of Trish's untimely end negated the positive effects of the jasmine tea. Ella's eyes filled with tears. "We'll never have a chance to know her well. What a shame. She was my age, you know. Or at least close to it. That's when it really hits hard. When it's someone you know and they're the same age as you." She heaved a sigh, and the white blouse she was wearing with a relatively conservative purple skirt rose and fell along with the strings of orange and red beads that hung around her neck. "So unexpected."

When Ella called with the news of Trish's death, she'd been too upset to say much about exactly what had happened. And I'd felt a little ghoulish pressing her for details. But of course, I was curious. "How did she die, anyway?" I asked Ella.

She blinked and swiped at the tears that trickled down her cheeks. "That's the really sad part," she said. "Trish was trying on her gown. For the costume gala that will mark the opening of the museum. And from what I heard, it sounded positively beautiful! Gold silk with a trimming of . . . well, I guess none of that matters now. Anyhow, what happened . . ." Ella shook her head, the gesture not one of uncertainty as much as it was of despair. "Well, nobody knows how it happened for sure, but somehow, she tied the laces on her corset too tight. By the time Merilee heard a few muffled gasps and found her, it was too late. She suffocated."

"From wearing a corset?" The question burst out of me along with a laugh. One look at the shock on Ella's face and I knew both were inappropriate. I swallowed down the rest of what I was going to say (which was something in the line of *How stupid could the woman be?*) and nodded solemnly. "Merilee must be knocked for a loop. What's she going to do now that she doesn't have Trish?"

Ella rose from her seat. But not before she looked at me out of the corner of her eye. Like there was something she was uneasy about.

"What?" I got up, too. Sure, Ella was my boss, but I was a whole head taller than her. I figured if I had the height advantage, maybe she'd come clean. "There's something you're not telling me."

Ella's smile came and went. "It's something good."

"If it was something good, you'd look happy."

"I am happy. I mean, not about Trish or anything, but, Pepper, you should know that this is a golden opportunity for you. And it will take care of your financial problems. I've been worried about you, you see. Worried about how you were going to get through the summer without your regular paycheck. That's why when the opportunity came up . . ."

The opportunity had already come up. The opportunity to make a few bucks. If I could prove that Didi wrote *So Far the Dawn*. If Harmony ended up coming into those tens of millions and was willing to toss even the tiniest percentage of it my way.

I was pretty sure this was not what Ella was talking about.

I barked out a laugh. "What did you do, offer my services as a secretary to Merilee?"

Ella didn't say a thing. She didn't have to. She turned as red as her beads, all the way from her chin to her forehead.

"No, you didn't." The words came out of me in a whoosh of horror, and I backed away. From Ella and her sick sense of humor. From the very thought of spending the better part of my summer with the author from hell. "You're trying to pull a fast one on me. You're joking. Please tell me you're joking."

Ella didn't confirm or deny. Instead, she gave me her Mother Knows Best smile. "It's a perfect arrangement," she said. "Think about it. You need money and Miss Bowman needs—"

"A punching bag? A whipping boy? A Trish clone to grovel at her feet?"

Ella's lips pinched. Her shoulders were rigid. "Trish wasn't a groveler. But she was respectful. Who wouldn't be? Merilee is a star. Don't forget that, Pepper. She's earned the right to be treated with a certain amount of dignity."

No way was I hearing this right. "I'm too smart to get sucked into that nonsense," I reminded Ella and myself. "I'm too much my own woman to bow and kiss Merilee's ring. And in case you haven't noticed—and boy, I hope you've noticed, because if you haven't, I'm doing something really wrong— I'm much too well dressed to take Trish's place."

Buying some time—and maybe thinking about using the window as a means of escape—I spun away from Ella. Lucky for me I wasn't very quick on my feet. One step farther and I would have walked smack into Didi.

"This is perfect!" Didi's eyes glowed with excitement. "This is exactly the opportunity we've been waiting for."

"No." I was talking to Didi. And to Ella. Just so they'd both know it, I turned back around. "No," I said again.

"But why not?"

The question may have come from Ella. Or it might have come out of Didi's mouth. It was hard to tell because Didi was suddenly standing right behind Ella, and they were both talking at the same time.

"It's the answer to our prayers," Didi said.

"It's the solution to your problem," Ella reminded me.

"It's the perfect way for you to investigate," Didi told me. "You'd have the inside track."

"Up close and personal." Ella smiled. "How lucky you are to have the opportunity to establish that kind of relationship with Miss Bowman. And don't deny it, Pepper!" She wagged a finger at me. "You're a closet fan. No matter what you say. I'd read about it, of course, but even I'd forgotten that Merilee had a sister. And who knew that she was buried here at Garden View? That alone makes me think that you're the ideal candidate for this job. You care about the family. You know their history."

"You sure do!" Didi grinned. "What a way to help me out."

"And you'll really be helping me out," Ella said. "After all, if I can handle this and get Merilee the help she needs, it will make me look like a miracle worker."

"It will be perfect," Didi commented. "Especially since I heard someone around here say that Merilee's staying at our old house."

Both their voices bounced around inside my head, warring to see which would make me feel guilty enough to cave. I couldn't stand it anymore. "What difference does it make where Merilee is staying?" I shrieked.

Ella wasn't following my train of thought. Who could blame her? She didn't know that I was carrying on two conversations at the same time. She eyed me warily. "Merilee's staying in the family house," Ella said, and behind her, Didi smiled and nodded. "As far as I can tell, that doesn't make any difference to anybody except maybe to you. But it can't be more than twenty minutes between the Bowman house in Ohio City and your apartment.

You can pop back and forth every couple of days to check the mail, or I can pick it up on my way into work. Miss Bowman, of course, isn't used to being on her own. She'll want you to stay there with her."

"Perfect!" Didi chirped.

"Not a chance in hell," I said.

"Oh, come on, Pepper!"

This comment came from both Ella and Didi at the same time.

I grumbled a curse, flopped back down in Ella's guest chair, and dropped my head in my hands. "Why?" I groaned. "Why is it so important?"

Ella, being rational, thought the question was for her. She hurried over and sat in the chair next to mine. The better to have a heart-to-heart with me. "Merilee's doing us a tremendous favor. *Us* being ISFTDS, of course. And *us* being Garden View. Look at all the fabulous publicity we've gotten." She frowned. "Well, except for what happened to that poor photographer and now to Trish." She shook away the gloomy thoughts. "But don't forget all the good stuff. There's been plenty of positive press. And none of it would have been possible without Merilee. She's been gracious and kind. And she's being generous, too. She's even donating personal mementos to the museum. One of them is her first, handwritten draft of *So Far the Dawn*."

"Well, doesn't that just take the cake!" Didi perched on the arm of the chair where Ella was sitting.

Gift or no Gift, Ella must have sensed her presence. As if she was suddenly cold, she chafed her hands over her arms.

Didi was too angry to notice. Or to care. "The nerve of that Merilee," she growled. "How can she say she has the first handwritten draft when I was the one who handwrote the first handwritten draft in the first place?"

"How can she?"

I was echoing Didi's question. Like Ella could know that? Her face scrunched up. "How can she donate the manuscript? Well, it's hers, of course. But I see what you mean, Pepper!" She grinned and pointed a finger my way. "How can she bear to part with something so valuable and so personal? That just proves it, doesn't it? It just proves that in your heart, you're as much an *SFTD* lover as the rest of us. You know how difficult it will be for Miss Bowman to give up something so wonderful. But don't you see, just the fact that she's willing to donate the manuscript to the museum proves what a terrific person Merilee is."

"How can she have the draft?" I asked the question again, and at that point, I didn't care what Ella thought I was talking about. I needed answers and I needed them fast. Before I could get talked into something I knew was the mother of all bad ideas.

Didi pouted. "She's had fifty years to copy it," she said. "And besides, whatever she says she has, it's not going to matter. Not once you're in the house."

"Why? What's in the house?"

Ella eyed me carefully. As if she was worried about my sanity. "What's in the house is what's in most houses," she said. "Except for the museum on the first floor, of course. Upstairs are the bedrooms, and you'll have your own and your own bath. I haven't been there myself, but I've heard the restoration is fabulous. You may have your own sitting room, too."

"Not what I meant." I looked away from Ella and toward Didi.

"It's the manuscript," Didi said. "The real original, handwritten copy of *So Far the Dawn*. My original, handwritten copy. Merilee never knew it existed. I hid it, you see. In the attic. Right before I died. I knew it wasn't smart to have only one copy so I kept one in my bedroom. That was the one I typed to send to publishers in New York. The other one, I tucked away. Just in case, I don't know, just in case there was a fire or something and the typewritten one got damaged or destroyed. If it's true and the house hasn't been lived in since then, the manuscript should still be there, right where I left it. And finding it . . . that will be as easy as pie. Like I said, it's in the attic. There's a loose floorboard right under the windows that look out at the front walk. Tip up the board, lift it up, and voilà! That would prove everything once and for all, wouldn't it? The original manuscript. No way can anybody believe Merilee after they see it."

This was making too much sense. I can't say I was happy about it. "Why didn't you tell me this before?"

Ella rose. "I just found out myself, Pepper. After I heard about Trish. Miss Bowman called to say what a terrible inconvenience it all was and—"

"How much?" I got up, too. Not because I felt I had to challenge Ella, it was just that with her standing, I couldn't see Didi. "We've never discussed my fee. Not in dollars and cents."

"You know Harmony will be generous."

"You know Miss Bowman will be generous."

"Come on, Pepper. It's the only way."

"Please, Pepper. It would be such a help."

I was being tag-teamed.

By the living and the dead.

I tried one more desperate attempt to ignore their pleas.

"It's not going to work," I told both Ella and Didi.

"Of course it will." Ella smiled and rounded her desk. She picked up the phone and even before she hit the buttons, I knew she was calling Merilee with the news.

"We're all set now, kiddo." I turned at the sound of Didi's voice. Just in time to see her walk through Ella's office wall. The next thing I knew she was outside the window. She waved. "See you at home!"

I've never liked history.

I know that might seem like a weird statement considering that back in college, I majored in art history, but the art history thing . . . well, it wasn't because of the history. Or, for that matter, because of the art.

Truth is, I found out early on in my college career that art history wasn't as impossible as some other subjects, like chemistry or biology. It wasn't as boring as English, either, with all those useless similes and metaphors. Besides, I never intended to actually do anything with my education. Art history was a means to an end. It was all about doing what was expected (as in getting through, degree in hand), making the right contacts, finding the right man.

All of which I'd done.

None of which had made even a little bit of difference when the expected changed overnight into the unexpected. As for the right contacts and the right man, I may have mentioned before that they turned out all wrong.

But back to the history . . .

Like it or not, my job as tour guide at Garden View meant that I had history thrust in my face every day. I knew more about the city of Cleveland, its residents, and, yes, its history than I could have ever thought possible. Way more than I ever wanted to know or cared about. That's why when Ella mentioned that the Bowman family home was located in Ohio City, I was able to make sense of the whole thing.

Back in the day (and don't ask me when, I only know that it was a long time ago), Ohio City was just that. A city of its own. The area is just west of downtown Cleveland, right across the Cuyahoga River that splits the city in two. Eventually, of course, the inevitable happened. Cleveland gobbled up Ohio City and it became just another of its many neighborhoods.

These days, Ohio City is an odd mix of Victorian mansions, pricey condos, light manufacturing, charming restaurants, and not-so-charming rundown houses with boarded-up windows and cracked sidewalks. As I drove around looking for the Bowman home, I was reminded of Harmony's neighborhood. Except that Harmony's side of town was—and always had been—home to the workingman. In other words, utilitarian was the name of the game. Ambience definitely was not.

On the other hand, Ohio City had once been where the movers and shakers lived. Obviously, some of them still did. On every street, at least a couple of grand old Victorian mansions had been lovingly restored to perfection.

I stopped my car in front of one of them and got out to watch as a team of workers put a sign in place on the front lawn:

SO FAR THE DAWN MUSEUM

Looked like I was in the right spot.

The background of the sign was marine blue, the same color as half the turreted house behind it. The other half of the house . . . well, let's just say that when the workers who were scrambling over the property finally got around to painting it, it would do the old house a world of good. From what I could see, the Bowman family home had spent the last however many of its years as a gray and grungy hulk. Its front steps sagged and its shutters hung off the windows like the skin around a middle-aged woman's eyes.

Once the work was finished, though, it was clear that the museum would be a showplace. The house had a wraparound front porch, a stained glass window on the second-floor landing, and—from what I could see—a garden in the back that hadn't been touched in years. Even as I watched, a team of workers was stepping through the thigh-high weeds, assessing the damage and talking about what could be saved and what would have to go.

Go.

The single word was like a beacon in the night, and not for the first time since I'd agreed to Ella's plan, I thought about chucking the whole thing.

I could go.

Now.

I should go.

Now.

Before I had to deal with Merilee.

Except that dealing with Merilee was exactly what I needed to do if I was ever going to prove Didi's claim to the *So Far the Dawn* throne.

Right?

Doubts filled me, and though I tried to ignore them, there were too many. Instead of dwelling on them—and making my stomach any sicker than it already was—I reminded myself that if I could get in and find the manuscript Didi said was in the attic—fast—I could just as quickly tell Merilee the Merciless that I'd changed my mind and I was quitting.

It was that thought and that thought alone that gave me the courage to get a move on. I got my suitcase out of the car and headed up the front walk.

Not as easy as it sounds, considering that there were boards and paint cans piled everywhere along with a whole bunch of scaffolding that was being assembled and, oh yes . . .

More reenactors.

When a fellow in a Union cavalry uniform tipped his hat and made a showy bow, I nodded hello. I sidestepped a woman in a wide hoop skirt who was chatting on her cell. Across the street there was a vacant lot, and someone had set up a small white pup tent. I glanced that way, watching as three Confederate soldiers sat outside the tent playing cards with two guys in Union uniforms.

One of the Union officers looked awfully familiar, shaggy hair, wire-rimmed glasses, and all.

I dropped my suitcase and did a double take, automatically stepping in that direction.

"Dan?"

"Why, no, ma'am." The cavalry officer standing nearby thought I was talking to him. He stepped forward and looked me up and down. "My name's Joe, but I'll tell you what, if you want me to change my name to Dan, I'd be willing. But only if you'll meet me for a drink later."

"No. Thanks." I turned to him and offered what I hoped was an apologetic smile. "I didn't mean you. I was talking about that man across the street." I turned back that way. "The one playing—"

There were three Rebels playing cards with one Union officer now.

Do I need to point out which of them was gone?

Baffled, I shook my head. "Shit."

Joe chuckled. His eyes were wide with pretended amazement. "Ma'am," he said, "this is the year of our Lord eighteen hundred and sixty-three. No proper lady talks like that!"

"I've got news for you, Joe." I grabbed my suitcase and headed up the front steps, carefully stepping around cracked boards and a box of spilled nails. "I'm no proper lady. You want proof, stick around. Something tells me that before I get out of here, I'm going to be using plenty of four-letter words."

Chapter 9

Of course I didn't realize I was being delusional.
Not at the time. That's what makes a delusion delusional, right?

When I stepped inside the Bowman home, I actually expected some sort of welcoming committee.

Who could blame me?

After all, I'd agreed to fill in for Trish on short notice and, let's face it, that automatically put me into the above-and-beyond category. Add to that the fact that Ella had done the seemingly impossible and found someone—anyone—willing to put up with Merilee for the better part of the summer, and I was thinking that a brass band and a dozen roses would have been just about right.

Short of that, I was ready to settle for Merilee waiting to greet me at the door with one of the construction workers (preferably a cute, muscular one who was not currently attached) to carry my suitcase to my room.

No wonder I was surprised when I pushed open the front door and there was nobody around.

"Hello?" I set my suitcase down on the marble

floor of the entryway and leaned forward, peeking into the rooms beyond. Ahead of me was a hallway that led to the back of the house. It was cut in half by a stairway. To my left was what must have once been the living room and, across from it, a room of similar proportions with built-in china cabinets in two of its corners. The ceilings were spanking-new white, and the chandelier at the top of the staircase gleamed like it was a recent addition. The walls were papered in high Victorian kitsch: maroon and purple flowers against a black background, accented with green vines and gold leaves. There was scaffolding, paint cans and lumber stacked all around. Between that and all the vegetation going on, it was hard to see a clear way through to anywhere. Even when I thought I could, I found the path blocked with furniture and museum displays covered with white canvas tarps.

Like shrouds.

Of course I made the connection instantly, and I can't say I was especially happy about it. Me and the whole life-after-death thing . . . well, I guess I was just predisposed to think that way.

"Hello?" Don't ask me why I bothered, but I tried again, convinced that if only they knew I was here, someone would make an effort to acknowledge my presence and remind me that what I was doing was fabulous and phenomenal and that he (or she) would be forever grateful. "Anybody here?"

"You Pepper?"

The sound of a man's voice came at me from out of nowhere, and I jumped and gulped down a gasp of surprise. I took another look around, just in time to see him step onto the landing at the top of the steps.

The man in question was tall and broad. He was dressed in a dirty blue denim shirt and jeans that were torn at the knees and frayed at the bottoms. Like a worn blanket, his face was creased in a thousand places. His salt-and-pepper hair (more salt than pepper) was long and stringy. It was pulled back in a ponytail.

Okay, so maybe my imagination was working overtime, what with me thinking I'd seen Dan Callahan across the street and all. Still, when the man moved out of the shadows and positioned himself to look down at me over the railing that ran the length of the landing, I have to admit, my stomach clutched. The stained glass window was directly opposite from where he stood, and the red light filtering through it stained his hands.

Was it a simile? Or a metaphor?

Either way, it sure looked like blood to me.

I forced my morbid thoughts and my gaze away from his hands just in time to see him lean forward and study me from behind thick tortoiseshell glasses. From where I stood, his eyes looked as if they were two sizes too large.

"Yeah. I'm Pepper." My own voice sounded small and breathless. I told myself it was because of the tall ceilings and not because I was anxious.

"Miss Bowman, she says you're staying up here." The man jabbed his thumb over his shoulder. "First door on your left."

I smiled. And waited for him to come down the steps to take my suitcase.

He didn't.

Smile or come down to take my suitcase.

Realizing he wasn't going to, I hoisted the suitcase myself, threaded my way through the maze of construction materials, and climbed the stairs. The closer I got to the man, the stronger the smell of cigarettes became. Believe me, even when I got to the top of the steps, I kept my distance—from him and from the nasty smell—but even so, I felt as if we were too close. I skirted him and got my bearings.

Like the entryway downstairs, the landing led in two directions. To my right, the hallway was carpeted and the walls were papered (more flowers and vines). The smell of Pine-Sol and lavender wafted out at me, and, grateful for the reprieve from the stench of nicotine, I inhaled deeply.

The breath caught in my throat when I turned the other way. No carpeting there. No flashy wallpaper, either. I eyed the stained and pitted floorboards and the chipped plaster walls.

"You sure Merilee said left?" I asked the man. "It doesn't look like this part of the house is finished yet."

"First door on the left. Miss Bowman says."

I swallowed my misgivings and stepped that way. I'd quibble with Merilee later about the renovations (or lack thereof) in my temporary quarters. For now, getting away from this man and from the stink of cigarettes was top priority.

My hand was already on the doorknob when he spoke again. "Name's Bob," he said.

"It's nice to meet you, Bob." Years of Easter at the country club, Fourth of July at the yacht club, and Christmases spent with the social-climbing

contingent of my social-climbing family down in
Florida had taught me to lie with a smile on my
lips. I turned to Bob and hey, I may have been a
smooth talker, but there was only so far I was willing to go when it came to making nice with weird
old guys. As if they were made of Velcro, all ten of
my fingers clung to the handle of my suitcase. The
better not to have to shake Bob's hand. "Do you
work here?"

Bob sucked on his lower lip. He was staring at
the front of my shirt, and for the first time since I
packed my bags and headed for Ohio City, I wished
I'd chosen to wear something other than a lime
green tank.

His gaze flickered down to my hips and back up
again. "Live here," he said. "Always have."

"You're the one who's kept the house for the
Bowmans all these years." I nodded, confirming
what I'd heard from Ella about how the house had
never left the possession of the family. I didn't
bother to mention that from the look of my side of
the landing, Bob hadn't kept things too well. After
all, if he'd been here since Didi's days, he might
prove to be a valuable source of information.

I opened the door to my room. "I guess that
means we'll be seeing each other around," I said, a
clear indication that—at least for me—our conversation was over.

Bob stepped forward. "She died. Right here, you
know."

Was Bob a mind reader?

The question flashed through my brain, and
hard on its heels, the name fell off my lips.

"Didi?" I asked.

Like I'd sucker punched him, Bob jerked back. He narrowed his eyes and looked at me hard. "What do you know about Deborah?"

It actually might have been fun to watch Bob's face when I told him my newest best friend was a woman who'd been dead for fifty years. But like I said, I couldn't afford to alienate him. At least not until I found out what he knew. About the Bowman sisters. And about *So Far the Dawn*.

"I'm a fan," I said. I stopped myself on the verge of a shrug. No use calling any more attention to my chest. "A fan of Merilee's. I've read everything ever written about her. About *So Far the Dawn* and how she wrote it right here in this house. About her family, too. Of course I've heard about Didi. I know she died young. I didn't know it was right here in the house."

Bob shook his head. His ponytail twitched across his shoulders. "That was the Lorain/Carnegie Bridge. Not here. Deborah didn't die here."

"I thought you said—"

"It was that Trish. The one who smelled so bad. Like cough drops." His nose wrinkled, he turned and stalked down the steps. "That room you're staying in, that's where she died. Just a couple of days ago."

"Great."

Now that I was alone, the sound of my own voice echoed from the high ceiling and bounced back at me from the bare floor. I shivered.

Not that I was scared, I told myself. There was no reason for me to be.

Except for the fact that I was here at the request of a ghost who wanted me to prove that Merilee had built her reputation—and her considerable fortune—at the expense of her dead sister, and that if I did, I'd ruin one of the great legends of American literature . . .

And the fact that I'd be spending the next however many days in a decrepit house with a guy weird enough to make my skin crawl and that my new boss made Cruella De Vil look like a candidate for sainthood . . .

And the additional fact that I was staying in a room where a woman had recently lost her life and that I knew beyond the shadow of a doubt that just because ol' Trish was dead didn't necessarily mean she was gone . . .

Except for all that, what did I have to worry about?

If there was any good news in all this, it was that my room didn't smell like menthol. I should know. Before I even put down my suitcase, I looked over every inch of it, sniffing as I went, convinced that if I found—or smelled—one trace of Trish, I was out of there.

The bad news was that my home away from home was a twelve-by-sixteen box with one window. It looked out at an alley. The wallpaper that had once been—maybe—dotted with pink carnations, hung in shreds and was a uniform and unattractive shade of gray. The floor was bare. The bed was squishy. When I tried to put my clothes in the one and only dresser in the room, the drawers stuck and refused to open until I gave them a healthy smack.

There was no attached bathroom, and at the

same time I knew in my head that I shouldn't have expected one in a house this old, I dreaded the thought of a trip down the hallway in the middle of the night.

I wondered where Bob slept.

"Find the manuscript and get out." I gave myself the pep talk as I tucked my clothes away.

"The manuscript is in the attic." I gathered up my shampoo, conditioner, and makeup and headed out to find the bathroom, reminding myself of everything Didi had told me. "If you can get your hands on it—"

As I neared the door that led from my room into the hallway, the toe of my sandals caught on a rough spot in the floor. For a second, I lost my footing. I didn't fall, but I didn't hang on to what I was holding, either. The shampoo and conditioner went one way. A bottle of Happy went the other. A brand-new tube of Pretty in Pink landed on the floor and rolled. Before I could get to it, it disappeared under the bed.

"Damn," I mumbled and stooped to pick up what I could, then knelt and gingerly lifted the ruffled skirt that covered the mattress. I peeked under the bed.

It was too dark to see anything.

"Double damn." I grumbled and reached out my hand, carefully feeling around, and when the only things I got for my effort were dust bunnies, I lay on my stomach and stretched some more, groping through the dark and the dust. Finally, my fingers connected with something. I grabbed and pulled.

It was not a tube of Pretty in Pink.

I sat back, blew a strand of hair out of my eyes,

and examined the roll of duct tape I'd retrieved.

It hadn't been under the bed long. I could tell because in comparison with the rest of the room, the roll of tape wasn't dusty. It didn't belong to any of the construction workers, either. I could tell that because . . . well, all it took was one look at my room to figure that out. No one with an eye for remodeling had set foot in this place in a long, long time.

Which meant that the duct tape might have belonged to Trish.

Which really didn't interest me in the least.

At least not as much as a new tube of lipstick did.

I tossed the tape aside and felt around under the bed some more. This time I was successful. The Pretty in Pink in hand, I sprang to my feet and set out to find the bathroom.

Another room that needed a whopping dose of TLC.

I set my cosmetics on the sink and took a gander at the pitted linoleum and the hole in the wall that provided an unobstructed view of the claw-footed bathtub—and anybody in it.

"Find the manuscript fast," I reminded myself, and as funny as it seemed, the thought gave me courage. I told myself not to forget it, combed my hair, and checked to make sure there was no dust lurking anywhere on my clothes.

Sure that I was together and as ready as I was likely to get, I went in search of Merilee.

As it turned out, I didn't need to worry about my hair or my makeup. When I found Merilee, she was in her study, sitting behind a huge mahogany desk and writing in a notebook. She didn't even bother to look up.

I toed the threshold and wondered how to announce myself, and while I did, I took the opportunity to check out the room with its rich paneling and its plush Oriental carpet. Every lamp in there glittered. The empty bookcases that took up all of one wall and the tables on either side of a burgundy-colored, uncomfortable-looking sofa gleamed.

No doubt, a cleaning crew had just finished with the room. After the musty odors on my side of the house, I basked in the lemony scent of furniture polish.

Which is why the undertone of smoke in the air struck me as odd.

I glanced toward the fireplace. Two huge oil paintings hung above the mantel. One of them was of a woman with flashing blue eyes and cascades of golden hair. Her gown had a wide skirt and a tight waist. It was the color of sapphires and cut low enough to show off her shoulders and her slender neck.

The other picture was of a dark-haired man with a bushy mustache. He had the hint of a smile on his lips and a naughty twinkle in his eyes. He was wearing a blue uniform.

The mantel itself was chock-full of knickknacks, china figurines of women in gowns (one was the same deep blue as the woman's in the picture) and men in old-fashioned clothing. It didn't take much of an imagination to figure out that they represented characters from *SFTD*. Like the rest of the room, they were as clean as can be, and the oak mantel itself was sleek and glossy.

I guess that's why the small pile of ashes in the hearth looked out of place.

"It's too warm for a fire."

I didn't need to worry that Merilee had heard me. She was so deep into whatever she was deep into, she never budged.

Of course, that didn't mean that no one answered.

"We never had a fire." Didi's voice was breathless. It bounced over the words. "Mother said it was too dangerous. A house down the street burned down, you know. When I was little. After that, Mother never allowed a fire."

I turned just in time to see her materialize. She was wearing a plaid skirt and a white blouse. Her hair was in pigtails. She was jumping rope.

I rolled my eyes. Enough said.

"Don't like the little-girl look, huh?" Didi laughed, and in the blink of an eye, she was back to normal. At least as normal as a ghost can be. "Hey, you can't blame me for trying to relive my childhood. This is where I grew up."

"And it's where you wrote the book, right?"

"Of course it's where I wrote the book." Merilee's voice came at me from across the room. "If you'd been paying attention, you'd know that."

I turned toward her and forced an enthusiasm I didn't feel into my voice. "I was just kidding. I'm sure Ella told you, I'm a huge fan."

"Of course you are." The desk was piled with books. Merilee closed one of them and set it aside. She took off the glasses that were perched on the end of her nose and put down her pen, studying me intensely. It didn't take a detective to figure out that she still hadn't forgiven me for mentioning Didi back at Garden View. She might have accepted me as Trish's replacement, but no way was she going to make this easy.

"Cleveland had an especially interesting place in the Civil War," she said, her voice as crisp and clipped as if she was giving a lecture. "But then, if you're a fan, no doubt you know that, too. I'm sure we'll have plenty of opportunities this summer for some lively discussions, you and I. We can talk about the increase in petroleum refining and the growth of the railroads during the war years."

I could hardly wait.

"And then, of course . . ." Merilee aimed a laser look at me. "There's Elizabeth and Kurt. Since you're such a huge fan, I expect you'll have plenty of questions to ask about them, too."

The names were vaguely familiar.

Which didn't make it any easier to make small talk when I didn't know who we were small-talking about.

"Psst." Didi's whisper was close to my ear. I don't know why. It wasn't like Merilee could hear her. "The paintings." She tipped her head in that direction. "Elizabeth Goddard is the blond bombshell in the blue dress. She played Opal in the movie, and they were lucky to get her. At the time filming started, no one knew she was knocked up. Another couple of months and there was no way she could have been Opal. And Kurt." One hand on her heart, she stared up at the picture of the man with the mustache. "He was Palmer. Their first choice was Gable but let's face it, he was too old, and not half the actor Kurt was. For a while, they even talked about giving Cary Grant the part. Imagine!"

I smiled across the room at Merilee. "Can't wait to hear what you have to say about Elizabeth and Kurt," I told her. "I mean, that whole thing about Elizabeth being pregnant and no one knowing it. That must have caused quite a stir. And Cary Grant as Palmer!" I laughed as if I actually knew who this Cary Grant guy was and why the idea of him playing Palmer was so funny. "Imagine!"

"Yes. Really. Imagine." Merilee's expression soured. She didn't like to lose. But then, she'd pretty much told me that back at Garden View. Merilee didn't like surprises. Wouldn't she get a big one if I could prove Didi wrote *SFTD*?

I decided now was as good a time as any to start.

Doing my best to sound interested like a fan might be interested and not like a private investigator might be interested, I closed in on her. "So tell me about when you were writing the book. I mean, it must have been so much work. And you had a full-time job, too, didn't you?"

"That's right. I was a librarian. Cleveland Public. In the reference room of the main library downtown."

"Which explains why you know as much as you know."

I meant it as a compliment, but Merilee didn't take it that way. She frowned, and an unattractive blotch stained her neck and crawled into her face. Her voice broke with emotion. "It's taken me sixty years to learn everything I know. And it has nothing to do with the library. It's because of work. Lots of hard work. I don't just make things up and say they're real and people believe it. I never write about anything unless I have documented proof. That's what history is all about. Proof. Not stupid, made-up stories. It's about facts and figures and . . ." She gulped in a breath, and even she must have realized she was a little too caught up in the whole thing. Her chin quivering, she clutched her hands together and got ahold of herself.

"You know," she said, "I'm considered the foremost expert on the subject of the Civil War and its effects on Northern industrialization."

"Something else we'll have to talk about sometime," I told her.

When hell froze over, I told myself.

"That's sort of what I was thinking about," I said. "I mean when I mentioned what it must have been like for you to write the book. It must have been very difficult. Did anyone help you?"

Her perfectly arched eyebrows did a slow slide up her forehead. "Are you saying—"

With the flick of a wrist, I waved away the very idea that I might have offended her. "I just mean that it can't be easy keeping all that information straight. And thinking of things to happen in a book. How do you fill all those pages?"

"Research." Merilee tapped one finger against the cover of the book closest to her. "It's all about research."

"But it's all so amazing. Where did you get your ideas? Did you brainstorm with anyone?"

Merilee made a sound that reminded me of sandpaper on stone. Maybe it was a chuckle. "Like who?"

I shrugged. "I dunno. How about your sister, Didi? Did you ever brainstorm with her?"

Whatever emotion Merilee betrayed while she was preaching about railroads and petroleum, she shut it off completely. The look she trained my way was pure venom. "You seem obsessed with my sister, Didi. Really, Miss Martin, if you told Ella Silverman that you'd take this job only because you thought it was a way to serve some sick interest in my unfortunate sister—"

Another shrug. I hoped it looked casual. "I'm interested in you and in your book. So naturally I'm interested in Didi, too. Besides, I'm going to include her on a tour I'm getting ready at the cemetery. 'Famous Faces.' That's what Ella wants to call it. I figure as long as Didi's one of our residents, we might as well include her."

This time there was no doubt that the sound that came out of Merilee was a laugh. Even if it was a malicious one. "You've got to be kidding me! Didi, a famous face? My sister, Didi? What's she famous for, being the biggest tramp on the west side of Cleveland?"

This was not something Didi had ever mentioned, and at the same time I made a mental note to ask her about it, I strolled closer to Merilee. "I wasn't thinking personally, I was thinking professionally. You know, because of her movie career."

"Deborah? In the movies?" Merilee snorted and reached for another book. "You haven't been listening, and I'll tell you something here and now. If you don't listen, we're not going to get along at all this summer. Remember, I said that research is important. Obviously, you've got yours all wrong. My sister was never in the movies."

"But she said—"

I swallowed down the rest of my words.

"I must have been mistaken," I told Merilee. And myself. "I thought before *So Far the Dawn* was filmed, she appeared in a movie with Kurt Benjamin. It was a bit part, sure, but it was still a part."

"It would have had to have been before *So Far the Dawn* was filmed. Because by the time the movie was made, Didi was dead. And if she was in a film before that . . ." Merilee rose and flattened her palms against the desktop. "My sister never left Cleveland for more than a couple of days at a time. She was never in Hollywood, and I know for a fact that she was never in a movie with Kurt Benjamin or with anyone else. Research, Pepper. Don't forget. Research is important. If you did yours about my sister, you'd know that she was the biggest liar this side of the Mississippi."

I wasn't naive; this was something I had considered. But after meeting Merilee—not to mention Harmony—I'd put aside my doubts in favor of proving that Merilee herself took the prize when it came to lying.

Just thinking that I might be wrong . . .

My stomach got queasy. If I was spending my summer in this hellhole for nothing . . .

I took a breath and got a grip.

"Well," I said, "then we could always include Didi on the tour because of the murder. That sort of makes a person famous whether they want to be or not, doesn't it?"

"Murder?" Merilee's shoulders went rigid. "Whatever are you talking about? What murder? Whose murder? You don't think Didi was murdered, do you? I swear, you've got all your information all wrong."

Merilee swept past me and out the door.

"If you'd done your research, Pepper, you'd know that my sister Didi wasn't murdered. She jumped. Off the Lorain/Carnegie Bridge."

Chapter 10

Was Didi the biggest liar this side of the Mississippi?

If the things Merilee said—about Didi's lack of a film career and her manner of death— were true, then, yeah, it was looking that way.

But since I couldn't find Didi, I couldn't ask her. And even if I asked, could I put any faith in her answer? If she admitted to being a liar, then I couldn't believe anything she said, right? Not even the stuff about how she was a liar. And if she told me Merilee was full of it, I wouldn't know if that was because it was true or because Didi was making it up.

It was like someone's sick idea of a riddle, and I thought about it the rest of the day. The results were predictable: a splitting headache.

After all, if Didi was lying about being in movies and about being murdered (not exactly insignificant subjects), then she might also be lying about *So Far the Dawn*. And if she was lying about *So Far the Dawn*, I was wasting my time. And if I was wasting my time . . . well, if I found out I was wasting my time, I was going to be royally pissed.

On the floor of the study, I sat back on my heels and brushed a curl of hair out of my eyes, stretching in an attempt to relieve the tightness in my neck. The muscles in my lower back were bunched, and my arms felt like they were going to fall off.

These pains, I couldn't blame on Didi.

Aside from spending hours considering the possibility of her being a dirty, rotten liar, I'd also unloaded box after box that Weird Bob dragged up from the nether regions of the house and deposited in front of me with a gleam in his eyes and a lecherous smile on his lips.

Now I knew why the bookcases in the study had been empty.

"Who the hell drags an entire library of books across the country with them?" I grumbled. No one answered me. It was nearly seven in the evening, and Merilee had gone to dinner with the mayor. I was alone in the house (except for Weird Bob, but that was something I didn't want to think about).

I sized up the stacks of boxes I'd already emptied and glanced toward the other stack—a little bigger—that had yet to be touched. "Doesn't Cleveland have perfectly good libraries?" I asked, my voice hollow in the empty room. "Isn't the Internet chock-full of information about the Civil War? Is Merilee completely out of her mind?"

This, I couldn't say, and besides, what did it really matter, anyway? Until I cleared up a few things with Didi, I wasn't qualified to say who was crazy and who wasn't.

Maybe they both were.

I plucked the last book (*The Emergence of*

Modern Economies in the Turbulent Years of the American Civil War) out of the box in front of me and jammed it onto the shelf with other books that sounded equally dull.

"That's it!" I stood and dusted off my butt. "No more books. Not tonight. And if Her Majesty doesn't like it—"

"I'm the one who doesn't like this. Not one bit."

Remember how I said I was alone in the house?

I remembered it, too. That's why the sound of a voice that wasn't Didi's caused me to spin around.

"Reenactors." There I was, grumbling again, and frankly, my dear, I didn't give a damn if the man and woman (he in a Union uniform and she in a blue gown) who stood near Merilee's desk heard me. Bad enough I had to worry about Bob. Worse if the new security system he assured me was state-of-the-art wasn't efficient enough to keep out the freaks.

"You shouldn't be here." I stepped toward them, chin high, and with a copy of *War, Petroleum and Iron: The Industrial Consequences of the Fight for Confederate Sovereignty* in one hand. Just in case I needed to bonk someone. Or bore them to death. "The museum isn't open yet. You can't just waltz in here. It's trespassing, or breaking and entering, or something."

"It's ridiculous." The woman tossed her head. Her cascade of golden curls glittered in the evening light that streamed through the window on the far wall. She looked down at the notebook that sat on the top of Merilee's desk. "It's insulting!"

"It's karmic justice. That's what it is." The man

stood with his back to me, but I could tell from his voice that he was probably smiling. At least he sounded mighty pleased with himself. "It's about time she realized there's more to be gained from using the talents of a real thespian than there is from calling on a two-bit ham."

"Ham!" The woman's blue eyes sparked. "I'll have you know, I trained on the stages of London and New York and—"

"Yeah, yeah, yeah." The man waved away her protest. He turned and perched himself on the edge of Merilee's desk.

That's when I saw that he had a bushy mustache.

And a face that looked awfully familiar.

I glanced over my shoulder to the portraits that hung above the fireplace.

I turned the other way and took a closer look at the woman. It was the same gown, all right, sapphire blue and cut low to show off her slender neck and shoulders.

The blood drained out of my face and left me feeling chilled.

"Oh no!" I waved one hand, as if that alone could dispel the possibility that I was seeing what I was seeing. "No way you two are here. I've already got my quota of ghosts. One at a time. Take a number. Wait your turn."

"What the hell are you jawing about, sister?" The golden-haired woman who I knew must have been Elizabeth Goddard—at least when she was alive—gave me a sneer of epic proportions. Her New Jersey accent didn't exactly tally with her elegant gown or her angelic face. "Can't you see we're having a conversation here?"

"I can see it, all right. And I don't like it. Not one bit." I closed in on them, pointing to the door. "Out! Only one investigation at a time. Only one dead person at a time. I can't help either one of you."

"But you're living and you can see us." Kurt Benjamin sounded puzzled. He gave his companion a quizzical look. "Is she the one I've heard about? The one with the—"

"Gift? Yeah, that would be me." I answered before Elizabeth could, and let me just say for the record, I wasn't very happy about it. Kurt, who according to Ella had died only recently, had already heard of me. Or at least of my special skill. Apparently word was getting around on the Other Side.

"Can't you two find someplace else to hang out?" I asked them. "I really don't have time for your problems right now."

"It's not you we're here to see." I have no idea how these things work, but in the blink of an eye, Elizabeth had a long silver cigarette holder poised between two fingers. She perched it between her lips, took a drag, and let out a stream of smoke. "It's Merilee."

"Technically, it's the sequel to *So Far the Dawn*." Kurt glanced down at the desk. "You know, she's working on it."

This was not news, and I told them so. "She's been working on it for fifty years. Seems a little odd, don't you think?"

Elizabeth snorted. "She's probably trying to

figure out exactly the right, excruciatingly painful way to kill off Palmer! The son of a bitch wore out his welcome pretty much right after he walked into the first scene of the movie."

"Opal would have been nothing without Palmer!" Kurt's accent was more refined. Like he came from old money. His voice carried all the oomph of a Shakespearean actor, center stage. "Without Palmer—"

"Without Palmer, Opal would have lived happily ever after with that Hanratty fella. And I would have won the Oscar I deserved. But no!" She drew out the last word, emphasizing her point. "Nobody had a chance to find out what a really good job I did in that movie. They were too busy watching you chew up the scenery. I was great. The movie could have been great. If you hadn't turned it into melodrama with all your huffing and puffing!"

"Melodrama?" Kurt stood and threw back his shoulders. "Honey, when they coined the word *overplayed*, they were talking about you. Those wide eyes and that trembling lower lip!" It was his turn to snort. "That's not acting. The only real acting you've ever done was when you spread your legs on the casting couch and pretended you enjoyed it."

Elizabeth finished her cigarette. Don't ask me what happened to it, but when she set down the holder, it wasn't on the desk. "Are you still sulking because you didn't get a chance at me?" She laughed. "News flash, sweetums, you were never in my ballpark. Not as a man and certainly not as an actor. Like strutting around with your chest puffed out is acting. Talk about milking a scene."

Kurt stepped forward and they stood toe to toe. "Talk about stepping all over my lines!"

"Talk about histrionics!"

"As if you could even spell it."

"As if you know what it means."

"As if—"

I knew I had to end this before somebody got hurt.

"Hey! Guys! You two want to take a deep breath?" Both Elizabeth and Kurt looked at me in wonder, and I felt the blood rush into my cheeks. "Okay, so you can't breathe. How about a time-out, then? Take a time-out. Both of you. If you're here to see Merilee, she's not home. So why don't you go wherever it is you go when you're not haunting a house and I'll let you know when she shows up."

"We're not waiting for Merilee. Not technically." Elizabeth rolled her eyes.

"We're waiting for her to get to work again." Kurt looked down at the desk. "You know, so she can turn the page. So we can find out what happens next."

Elizabeth groaned. "He thinks he's going to have a bigger part."

"She thinks the world can't go on without Opal."

"He thinks he's hot stuff."

"She knows she's a has-been and that she doesn't stand a chance to—"

"Stop it! Both of you!" I clapped my hands together. That got their attention. "Number one, the sequel isn't written yet, and number two—and this is pretty important so pay attention—it doesn't matter who has the biggest part. Neither one of you is going to be in a movie if a movie is ever made. Get it? You've gone on to the great curtain call in the sky. You're dead!"

Kurt smoothed a hand over the front of his uniform. "That doesn't mean we don't have our pride," he said. He gave his costar a sidelong look. "Or at least I do. But then, I had a career I could be proud of."

Elizabeth threw back her head and laughed. "Yeah, you went right from *So Far the Dawn* to a series of B monster movies!"

"And you went from *So Far the Dawn* straight to the bottom of a bottle."

"Yeah, well, if I drank, I had my reasons."

"Your bad acting being one of them?"

"*Your* bad acting being one of them. Why, if you didn't try to upstage me, people would still remember my understated performance in that scene where I help the escaped slaves find safe passage to Canada."

"Understated? Is that what you call it? The way I remember it—and my memory is excellent, by the way—the *New York Times* said, 'Miss Goddard apparently did not get enough sleep the night before the climactic scene was filmed. Like a sleepwalker, she—'"

"Baloney!" Elizabeth propped her fists on her hips. "They wouldn't know good acting if it hit them over the head. They said yours was—"

"Refined and elegant." Kurt's smile was radiant.

"Which only proves they didn't know what they were talking about."

"Which only proves that you—"

"You're doing it again." I didn't know if ghosts could actually do damage to each other, but I didn't want to find out. I stepped between the two of them. "Listen, both of you. You're waiting for Merilee to come home and get back to work. I can do you one better. How about if I turn the pages of the manuscript for you. Would that work? Then you can see what you want to see and get the hell out of here."

Elizabeth and Kurt exchanged looks.

"Exactly what I was going to suggest," he said.

"In your dreams!" She laughed and looked my way. "Let's get going, sister. I can't wait to show this star"—the way she said the word, it wasn't a compliment—"that Merilee really is going to get rid of Palmer in the next book."

"All right. Okay." I rounded the desk. "Only before we look at the manuscript, I need your help."

"Us?" Kurt shot daggers at Elizabeth. "You can't be serious. What could we possibly do for—"

"You can tell me about when the book came out. The original book." Merilee's notebook sat in the middle of the desk. It was closed. I put my hand on the cover, just to let these two dueling ghosts know that I wasn't kidding. Their answers were the price of my cooperation. "Back when the book was published, did you think Merilee really wrote it?"

Elizabeth rolled her eyes. "We didn't know her then," she said. "No one did. Not until the book came out and caused a sensation. Then, of course, everybody knew her name! I never even met Merilee until she came to Hollywood when the movie was being filmed. Before that . . ." She tossed her head. Her golden hair gleamed. "Before that, I had my career to worry about. I was an ingenue." She said the word like it was something special, and when I didn't react because I didn't know what the hell she was talking about, she made a face at me.

"In-gen-ue. It's French, honey. It means I was young and a very hot property. Oh yeah, back in those days, I had more important things to worry about than who wrote what book."

"Yeah, like who on earth would ever hire you after your horrendous reviews in *Henry IV* on Broadway." His artistic sensibilities offended, Kurt shivered. He looked my way. "Of course Merilee wrote the book. Her name is on the cover, isn't it?"

"You're listed in *Who's Who* as an actor, aren't you?" Elizabeth thought this was very funny. She laughed until tears ran down her cheeks. When she got ahold of herself again, she looked at me through narrowed eyes. "What you're saying is that you don't think she wrote it."

"What I'm saying is that I don't know." There was no use beating around the bush. Not with these two. It wouldn't get me anywhere, and besides, maybe they knew something that could help. "I've heard from Merilee's sister, Didi. She says she wrote the book."

Elizabeth lit another cigarette. "Don't know Didi."

"Never heard of her," Kurt said.

"Are you sure?" I looked at him hard. "She says she was in a movie with you."

He grinned, and as much as I hate to admit it about a dead guy, I could see why the millions of women who'd seen his movies had fallen in love with him. Kurt Benjamin had a twinkle in his eyes that said S-E-X. That must have been very appealing to women back in the Stone Age fifties. He was good-looking, too, even if he did have that goofy mustache.

He glanced over my body before he looked me in the eye. "My dear, I've been in movies with plenty of people. If she was a bit player, I might never have known her name."

"But I need to know if she's lying about this."

He smiled an apology. "Can't help you. She might have been in one of my movies. She might not have been."

I was getting nowhere fast, and I scrambled to come up with the right questions, hoping something these two knew might help. Maybe if I concentrated on what—if the clothes they were wearing meant anything—must have been the highlight of their acting careers, I might get somewhere.

"What about when you were filming the movie? *So Far the Dawn*, I mean. When you were filming the movie, was there anything about Merilee that made you think maybe she didn't know as much as she should know about the book?"

Kurt shook his head. "It wasn't that she knew too little. It was that she knew too much. She complained to the set designers and the costume folks a lot. The lamps weren't authentic to the period. The clothes weren't right. She even said something about the shoes I was wearing in the scene where I see Opal off at the train station." He bent his head close to mine and whispered, "Should have taken the opportunity while I had it and given her a push."

Elizabeth sneered.

Kurt got back to the matter at hand. "Merilee said a Union officer would never wear those kinds of shoes. Those were the kinds of details she was obsessed about."

"And you never thought that was weird?"

"I never cared enough to think about it." He gave his broad shoulders a twitch. "That's not what I was there for."

"And what difference does it make, anyway?" Elizabeth chimed in. "She was the author of the book and you know how weird writers can be."

"As weird as actors?" Neither one of them got the joke, so I didn't belabor the point. Trying to decide the best way to move ahead, I flipped open Merilee's notebook.

"Chapter fourteen," Elizabeth said. She moved closer to the desk. "That's as far as we've gotten."

I found the right page. Merilee's handwriting was neat, even if it was a little cramped. Because I didn't want either one of these ghosts to get too close, I read the text out loud.

Palmer arrived at the house.

"Aha! See there." Kurt scooted closer. "The chapter starts with Palmer. She likes Palmer better."

"Shut up," I told him, and went back to reading.

He climbed the stairs. He knocked on the door.

Knock. Knock. Knock.

No one answered, and he went back down the stairs. As he did, he thought back to the Panic of 1857 and how it had increased unemployment in Cleveland by twenty-five percent.

Things had improved since then. The war had been good to Cleveland.

"You're kidding me, right?" I looked from one ghost to the other. "People consider this great writing?"

"The first book was better," Kurt admitted. "It had more depth."

"More emotion," Elizabeth added.

"More than none," I mumbled. I thumbed through a few more pages.

This plot didn't thicken. In fact, as far as I could see, it never got past the watery stage. I read through a stilted conversation between Palmer and someone named Betty and a description (not all that descriptive) of a house that sounded a whole lot like the one we were standing in. A few pages after that, the notebook was blank.

I'm not one to criticize. After all, I'd barely made it through college composition. But even I could have done better. Especially if I had fifty years to do it.

I flopped into Merilee's desk chair. "I'm more confused than ever," I admitted to Kurt and Elizabeth. "I might not know best-selling material when

I see it, but I know this stuff sucks. If it's nothing like the first book—"

"You mean you've never read it?" Elizabeth's outrage was evident in her question.

"You've never seen the movie?" Kurt was just as stunned.

"I've seen the movie. All right?" I slapped a hand on the desk, just to emphasize my point. "It's about guys in uniform and women in gowns. And horses."

"And the book?"

There was a paperback copy of *SFTD* on the desk, and I eyed it—and its well over eight hundred pages—warily. "It might not look that way to you right now," I said, "but I've got a pretty busy life. I've got more important things to do than read some silly old book."

"Then how," Kurt asked, "can you possibly make a judgment about who might have written it?"

Damn, but I hate it when ghosts are right.

I grumbled my surrender, grabbed the book, and headed for the door. As long as I was stuck in Merilee's little house of haunted horrors, I might as well do some reading.

Chapter 11

I know it doesn't sound like it, but I had a plan.
Really.

Before I went up to the attic to look for the handwritten manuscript Didi swore was stashed away there, I was going to wait until Merilee got home. Then I was going to wait some more. Until the wee hours of the morning, in fact. I wanted to be sure she was in her room and fast asleep. In my mind, this made a whole lot more sense than taking the chance that she would show up—the mayor on her arm—and find me rummaging around in places I didn't belong.

And hey, who was I kidding? I wanted to wait until Weird Bob was asleep, too. No way did I want to bump into him in some dark hallway.

If the manuscript really did exist and I could get my hands on it, my troubles were over. I'd grab it and run, and not to worry, I'm not a complete philistine. I was planning on leaving ol' Merilee a not-so-fond farewell note. It was the least I could do to thank her for making the last twenty-four hours of my life miserable.

And if the manuscript wasn't there?

At the time I considered this—again—I was hunkered down in the overstuffed chair that sat in one corner of my room. I was wrapped in a tattered quilt, and I shifted uncomfortably beneath it. The possibility of Didi's story being nothing more than fiction was something I really didn't want to think about. At least not until I had all the facts in front of me. (Or not in front of me, which is where the facts would be if the handwritten manuscript didn't exist.)

Until then, I had to keep my mind distracted, and the conclusions I was all set to jump to firmly grounded.

It was, after all, the way a real private investigator worked.

The good news in all of this was that at least I had something to keep me occupied.

That something was *So Far the Dawn*. I'd begun reading the book as soon as I walked out on Elizabeth and Kurt and settled myself in my room. Like a first-time sushi eater, I'd been cautious, starting with a nibble, just to see if I could get a sense of either Didi's or Merilee's voice there in the pages. No one was more surprised than I was when that nibble turned into a bite, and the bites into gulps.

By the time I heard the limo deposit Merilee at our front door, I was into chapter two. When I noticed her footsteps on the stairs and heard the squeak of the door on the other side of the landing as it closed, I had already finished chapter four.

The next time I looked at the clock, it was close to two, and I was well into chapter seven, the heretofore mentioned-to-the-point-of-tedium scene where Opal is leaving for her wedding in Baltimore and Palmer is none too happy about it.

Okay, time to come clean. As much as I hate to admit it, the more I read of the book, the more I hoped Merilee wasn't the author.

I didn't want her to be associated with anything this delicious.

I know, I know ... admitting that I actually liked the book that launched a million crazy collectors and nearly as many wacky reenactors was something like confessing that I watch the Lifetime Channel (which I don't) or that I think movies that deliberately set out to make women cry aren't lame (which they are).

But honest to gosh, I couldn't help myself.

I couldn't wait to find out what was going to happen next.

So Far the Dawn was soap opera between two covers. It was salt and vinegar potato chips. It was chocolate in all its most enticing forms.

The book was trashy and decadent. It was pulp fiction at its worst—and its best. It was melodrama. Pure and simple.

And I couldn't stop.

Of course, I knew I had to eventually. After all, I had to do what I had to do. So when Opal stepped onto that train, I sniffed (not that I was crying or anything) and forced myself to close the book.

I set it down and bent my head, listening closely.

There wasn't a sound in the big old house.

"Showtime," I told myself. I twitched off the quilt and reached for the pink cardigan I'd left on one corner of the bed. It was spring, but the nights were still chilly. Obviously, no one had thought to turn on the heat. Or maybe it just didn't work in my half of the house. I slipped on the sweater, then my sneakers, and grabbed the Wal-Mart bag I'd left on the top of my dresser.

Remember, I said I had a plan. On my way to Ohio City, I'd stopped and bought a flashlight. Armed with it but reluctant to turn it on until I was safely in the attic, I inched open my door and stepped into the pitch-black hallway.

I'd already checked out the lay of the land, and I knew the location of the door that led up to the attic. Of course, finding the right door when all the lights were on wasn't the same as finding it in the dark.

In the dark, the old house seemed bigger, emptier, and spookier than ever. The floorboards groaned, and after each step I took, I paused, just to be sure no one had heard me. When no lights flicked on and no one came running, I continued on. One hand on the wall to anchor myself, I inched my way down the hallway, and when I got to the door that led to the third floor, I took a deep breath and wiped my damp palms against my jeans.

As ready as I was ever likely to be, I opened the door and turned on my flashlight. I started up, one creaking stair at a time.

As it turned out, the attic was huge. It was just as cluttered as the first floor. And way more dusty.

I slid the beam of my flashlight over boxes and trunks and furniture covered with old sheets. I sidled between stacks of packing crates and stopped dead when I ran smack into one of those old dress forms that look like a woman's body—minus the head. She swayed and tilted, and good thing I have quick reflexes, I grabbed her by the shoulders right before she crashed to the floor.

Like a million tiny fairies dancing in the shaft of light, a puff of dust rose up from the dress form. I sneezed.

And froze.

I waited for a minute.

Nothing.

I waited for another minute.

Still nothing.

If either Merilee or Bob had heard the sound in the attic, neither one of them was heading up to investigate.

Reminding myself to be quick and more quiet than ever, I whispered the directions I'd gotten from Didi, my voice muffled by the head-high wall of boxes on either side of me. "The windows that look out over the front sidewalk. The board below the windows is loose and if you lift up one corner . . ."

I arced the thin beam of light around me, heading in the direction I thought was the front of the house, carefully threading my way between one of those mirrors on a swivel stand and an old metal storage closet taller than me. Just on the other side of it, I found the window and breathed a sigh of relief.

There were no boxes piled nearby, and I was grateful. At least I didn't have to move anything.

I'd just knelt down for a closer look at the floorboards when I heard a sound from across the attic.

Like the tread of a footstep.

I held my breath, listening for I don't know how

long. When I didn't hear the sound again, I told myself my imagination was on overdrive and the sooner I got out of the attic and back to my room, the better.

With that it mind, I ran my hands over the floorboards.

Just as Didi said, one of them was loose. Just as she assured me it would, when I pressed on the corner of the loose board, it tipped up. Just as she told me to, I wiggled it out of position and looked beneath it.

There was a twelve-by-twelve space below the floorboards. Just as Didi promised. And just as she'd described it, it was big enough to hide a manuscript.

Trouble was, it was empty.

In spite of the way I sometimes act, I'm not stupid. I'd known all along that this was a possibility. Still, facing the reality of the empty hiding space, and the fact that it meant that Didi's claim to authorship of *So Far the Dawn* was as close to fiction as she'd ever get, made me feel as if all the air had been sucked out of the room. I struggled to catch my breath and listened to the words that echoed inside my head.

You actually believed me? How naive can you be?

The voice was my dad's. No big surprise there. My reaction, however, was.

Though I'd spent close to two years dealing with Dad's lies and the maze of legal troubles (not to mention the social pariah-ness) caused by his selfishness and his greed, I guess I had yet to come to grips.

A tear slid down my cheek.

I wiped it away, sniffled, and scrubbed a finger under my nose.

That's when I realized my hands were clean.

All right, I know I just said I wasn't stupid, but honest to gosh, I'd been so busy concentrating on Didi's directions and the thrill of finding her hiding place, it never occurred to me when I knelt down that the floor was bare.

I mean, really bare.

I arced the beam of my light over the boards.

Not two feet away, the floor was coated with dust. But here near the window, it was clean. As if something had been piled here and that something had been moved.

Someone had been here before me.

I was so busy thinking through this new discovery, I didn't pay any attention to the catlike sound behind me. Not until it was too late, anyway.

The next thing I knew, I heard a thump and then a crash. I jerked upright and aimed my light across the room, but it was already too late.

The last thing I saw was the metal storage cabinet. It was falling. And it was headed right at me.

I knew what it felt like to be knocked out. After all, that's how this whole Gift nonsense started in the first place. After I got knocked out from knocking my head on Gus Scarpetti's mausoleum.

That time, I'd come to my senses in the ER of the hospital.

This time . . .

The sound of a groan penetrated the fog that filled my head. It took me a couple of seconds to realize the noise was coming out of me.

I opened my eyes to total darkness. I knew I wasn't dead because I could feel my cheek pressed to the attic floorboards. My stomach was flat to the floor. My legs were asleep, and I tried to move them. I wasn't worried until I realized I couldn't.

I tried my arms, and this time had more success. I swept my left arm over my head at the same time I groped around for my flashlight with my right hand. I didn't find the flashlight, but I did figure out why I couldn't see anything. There was something soft and warm over me. Something that felt like an animal.

It's not every day you wake up and feel as if you're being smothered by a Wookiee. With a screech, I plucked at the thing. My hand closed around fur and something that felt like silk lining.

"Fur coat," I told myself with a little hiccup of relief, and just to prove it, I pulled the coat off me and flung it as far away as I could.

That's when I saw that it was already morning.

Pale gray light seeped in at the windows, and for the first time, I was able to take a look around and assess the damage. Instantly, I saw why I couldn't move. My legs were pinned by the metal storage cabinet. I twisted out from under it and sat up, my back to the wall, pushing my hair out of my eyes and realizing how lucky I'd been. When the cabinet fell, it didn't hit me in the head. Instead, whatever had been stacked on top of it had come down on me. The fur coat had kept me warm all night. The wooden box that lay next to me (open and empty) was what must have conked me into unconsciousness.

Nothing was broken. I knew that for a fact because I flexed my arms and legs and everything was working, even if it all was a little stiff. Still, a night on the attic floor hadn't done much for my looks or my mood. The taste of dust filled my mouth, and when I swiped one hand over my face, I felt grit dig into my skin. A deep pore cleansing was in order. ASAP.

So was a change of clothes. The left knee of my jeans was ripped. The right strap of my tank top was torn. There was a smudge of dirt across my pink cardigan.

And none of that was as disturbing as the questions that bounced through my head.

When the cabinet came down, it made one hell of a noise. Hadn't anyone heard it? And if so, why hadn't they come to see what was up?

There was only one way to find out. I dragged myself to my feet.

As anxious as I was to get out of there, I couldn't avoid the whole private investigator thing. On my way across the attic, I stopped to check out the spot where the cabinet had previously stood. In my dazed and confused state, I had yet to question what caused it to fall or if the sound I heard (or at least I thought I heard) right before it tumbled had anything to do with the mishap. Now, in the anemic morning light, I saw that the floor nearby was scuffed, the dust kicked into little mounds.

As if someone had stood there and pushed.

My blood went cold, and another barrage of questions assaulted me.

If someone tipped the cabinet over on me on purpose, was it to scare me?

Or kill me?

I glanced around, but there was no sign of anyone there now. Still, I wasn't taking any chances. I bolted across the attic, heading downstairs in search of answers, coffee, and a long, hot shower.

Not necessarily in that order.

I might have opted for the shower first, but the moment the attic door closed behind me, the aroma of coffee enveloped me like a wonderful, caffeine-laden cloud.

Dirty face and torn clothing be damned. I hurried to the kitchen to find a good, hot cup of java.

What I found instead . . .

Well, how can I possibly express the mix of horror and embarrassment I felt when I walked into the kitchen and found Quinn Harrison in there pouring himself a cup of coffee?

At five eleven, with a 38C bust and hair the color of fireplace embers, I'm not exactly easy to forget.

Still, I swear that when Quinn heard me out in the hallway and looked over his shoulder just as I saw him and froze in the doorway, it took him a second to register that he knew me. But a second isn't very long, and I could tell exactly when the truth dawned.

That would have been when his jaw tensed and his shoulders went rigid.

"Well, look what the cat dragged in." He took a sip of his coffee, examining me over the rim of a mug that was decorated with pink roses and the letters ISFTDS in flowing script. "Don't tell me, let me guess. You missed me so much, you tracked me down all the way here."

"I didn't miss you." I lied, but hey, like I should feel guilty? I was dirty, disheveled, and feeling like shit. Better I should lie to the man who topped my would-like-to-jump-his-bones list than look like a complete loser. I tried not to limp when I crossed the room.

Keeping my distance—from Quinn and from the uncontrollable urges (see the above reference to jumping his bones) that swept over me whenever he was around—I reached for a mug and filled it with coffee.

"And I didn't have to track you down anywhere," I told him almost as an afterthought. "I work here. In fact, I'm living here for the summer."

"You're kidding me."

I was in the process of rummaging through the cupboards in search of sweetener, and I made a face at him. "Do I look like I'm kidding?"

He glanced from the tips of my sneakers to my ripped jeans, and from there to the top of my head. Big points for him, he didn't ask why I looked as if I'd spent the night on the floor of the attic. He was more the cut-to-the-chase type. "You look like hell."

"Thank you very much." I finished with the cupboards and tried the drawers of the baker's rack that stood next to the stove. "Which explains why I'm getting a cup of coffee." I ransacked one drawer and started on another. "Want to tell me why you're here?"

Don't ask me where he got it, but he held up one of those tiny bags of sugar. "This what you're looking for?"

Okay, so it wasn't sweetener and the calories

were empty. I wasn't in a position to argue. I plucked the sugar out of his hands, ripped the bag open with my teeth, and dumped the contents into my cup. "Were you going to make me beg?" I asked him.

I had meant it as one of those—what do you call them?—rhetorical questions. But Quinn took it at face value. He set down his coffee, cocked his head, and leaned back against the countertop, his arms crossed over his chest. "I'll tell you what," he said. "I'm kind of liking the sound of that. You begging, that is. Does this scenario have anything to do with you being down on your knees?"

Have I mentioned that Quinn is gorgeous?

Of course I have. I can't possibly talk about Quinn and leave out the gorgeous part. Gorgeous is as much Quinn as his take-no-prisoners attitude and the wardrobe that came from a place where cops shouldn't be able to afford to shop.

Today was no exception. Navy suit. Crisp white shirt. Red tie. All of it expensive. All of it designed and tailored to make the most of the chipped-from-granite chest, the lean and stubborn chin, and the dark hair that was so thick and wavy, I had spent more than one night dreaming about running my fingers through it.

None of which meant I was going to crumble.

At least not this early in the game.

I pretended I had no idea what he was talking about. Just like I tried to convince myself that what he was talking about didn't make me tingly all the way down to the tips of my toes. Instead, I reached for a spoon and stirred my coffee. "You haven't explained why you're here."

"What can you tell me about Merilee?"

I shrugged. So what if the broken strap of my top slid down my arm and made the front of the tank dip just a bit? For all he'd put me through, Quinn deserved a little torment. I saw him glance at my chest. He was tormented, all right. It cheered me right up.

"Merilee is my boss," I said.

"What about the cemetery?"

"I'll be working at the cemetery again. As soon as Merilee leaves town."

"And how did you get the job here?"

"What, you don't think I'm qualified?" I had to give myself credit. Even I knew I wasn't qualified, but still, I made it sound like I was offended.

"Oh, I'll bet you're plenty qualified." Quinn reached for his coffee and took another sip. "But you're talking about being qualified to work here at the museum, and I'm talking about . . ." His grin was hot enough to smoke the angels out of heaven. "Well, never mind."

The smile I shot back at him was tight around the edges. Maybe because I was tired. Or maybe there was just so much grit on my face, I couldn't manage anything more sincere. "Only if we're talking about me working as Merilee's secretary for the summer," I told him.

Though he tried to corral it, Quinn couldn't control the fleeting expression that crossed his face. It looked like worry to me. But then, I'd had a rough night. And finding him there in the kitchen had been something of a shock. Maybe I was just imagining it.

"So . . ." His expression blank again, he took

another sip of coffee. "You haven't told me what you know about Merilee."

"You haven't told me what you're doing here."

"And what about that Bob guy? Not exactly the kind of person I ever pictured you working with side-by-side."

"My sides and Bob's sides have never been side-by-side," I told him. "And never will be." I shivered. "He gives me the willies."

"That's the first thing we've agreed on since—"

Since the night we almost ended up in bed together.

I knew that's what Quinn was thinking.

Quinn knew that I knew that's what he was thinking.

Which is why I decided it was time to change the subject.

"Merilee is a royal pain in the ass," I said. "Why do you care?"

He shrugged. "Maybe I don't. Maybe I'm just thinking that it may not be just dumb luck that you're here."

"Nobody said it was dumb."

"I didn't mean you."

It was as close to an apology as I'd ever get from him, and I knew it. I finished my cup of coffee. If Quinn had made the coffee—and I hadn't seen anybody else around, so I had to assume he had—it was another thing to add to the list of things he did (or probably did) better than any other man alive.

"Call me crazy . . ." No one ever would. Quinn was a lot of things, but crazy wasn't one of them. "But I'm thinking you're not just here because

Merilee needs a secretary. I know you too well for that, Pepper. You have a way of sticking your nose where it doesn't belong."

"You don't know me well at all," I reminded him. "And why do you care if I'm here, anyway?"

He looked me up and down. "Maybe because you obviously ran into some problems. And from the looks of things, I'd say it was just recently."

"It's nothing." I waved away his concern, mostly because I knew it was professional and not personal. "I was up in the attic and I got attacked by a Wookiee."

He raised his dark brows.

I sighed and confessed. What choice did I have when he was giving me that penetrating tell-me-everything-you-know look? "I was up in the attic and a storage cabinet fell over on me. There was a fur coat on top of it."

"The Wookiee."

I nodded, confirming his theory.

"Storage cabinets don't fall over by themselves."

"I didn't get hurt." Just to prove it, I dance-stepped across the kitchen. "Everything's in good working order."

He gave me another quick once-over. "I have no doubt of that. What were you doing in the attic?"

"Looking around."

"Minding your own business?"

"Don't I always?"

"Not if hanging around with the local mob means anything."

"It doesn't." That much was true. My investigation of Gus's murder was done with. My hanging-around-with-the-mob days were over. "I'm here as a favor to Ella, my boss, who just happens to be the ringleader of the crazy SFTD fans," I told Quinn. "That's it. Honest."

"Is there a reason I don't believe you?"

"I don't know what you believe and what you don't believe. And honestly, I don't really care." I poured another cup of coffee. "If you want to stay here and drink coffee all day, be my guest. Right now, the most important things to me are a shower and a change of clothes." I headed for the door.

"You haven't put it together yet, have you?"

I didn't know what he was talking about, and honestly, I doubted that it had anything to do with Didi and the missing manuscript that may not have been missing because maybe it never existed in the first place.

But I couldn't take the chance.

I stopped and turned to him. "What?"

"You don't think I stopped by just to see you, do you?"

"Is it that impossible?"

"It is, because I didn't know you were here."

"Which means—"

The *chunk* I heard inside my head was the pieces falling into place. Slowly, I admit. Then again, I had a good excuse for the fact that my brain was moving at a snail's pace. I had recently been knocked out. I had spent the night on a hard wooden floor. I'd been ambushed by a man I wasn't expecting to see and a whole lot of wants/needs/desires that I had hoped to never have to grapple with again.

At least not with this man.

"Trish died," I said. "Here. Just a couple of days ago. And you're with—"

"Bingo!" Quinn grinned. It was not a happy expression.

"That means—"

"You got it." When Quinn's cell phone rang, he set down his coffee cup and reached for it. "You're working here as Merilee's secretary. And apparently, no one told the new secretary what really happened to the old secretary. She didn't just die, Pepper. She was murdered."

Chapter 12

A sour taste filled my mouth. It had nothing to do with Quinn's coffee.

When he walked out of the kitchen to take his phone call, I was left there trying to absorb everything I'd just heard.

The news of Trish's murder put a whole new spin on what happened in the attic the night before. Not to mention the little detail of me staying in Trish's room.

The room where she died.

"Chocolate chip? Or peanut butter?"

My grim thoughts were interrupted by Didi's pleasant chirp.

I turned to find her standing at the stove in a pencil-slim dress, heels, pearls, and an apron. She had a quilted oven mitt on each hand, and she held out a cookie sheet toward me. "Chocolate chip?" She glanced toward the left half of the tray and two rows of steaming hot cookies dotted with gooey chocolate morsels. She looked at the right half. "Or peanut butter?"

"How about the truth for a change."

The tone of my voice told her I wasn't kidding

around. She set the cookie sheet down on the stove and just as had happened when Elizabeth discarded her cigarette holder, the cookie sheet instantly disappeared. So did the oven mitts when she yanked them off. "What are you talking about?" she asked.

I barely contained my sigh of frustration, but there was nothing I could do to control the wave of exasperation that churned through my stomach along with a healthy dose of anger. "Well, we could start with your movie career. Or should I say your lack of a movie career?"

Can ghosts blush? I guess so, because a pink flush raced across Didi's cheeks. She wrinkled her nose. "There was no harm in telling you I'd been in the movies," she said. "I was just . . . I dunno . . . Just fooling around. It's fun to pretend, don't you think?"

"Not when you pretend you were murdered."

"Oh, no!" She went on the defensive, stepping back and shaking her head. "I never told you I was murdered."

"You never told me you weren't."

"You never asked how I died."

"I never thought—" My words came out too loud. I looked toward the hallway, and when I still heard Quinn's baritone hum on the phone, I lowered my voice. Decibels notwithstanding, I was plenty pissed. "Don't pull that on me. I shouldn't be expected to know how this stupid Gift thing works. Gus was murdered, and I was able to see him. When I saw you, I figured you must have been murdered, too. I thought you showed up so that I could investigate. I even told you I'd look into your murder. More than once. You never said I was wrong."

"No, but I did tell you I didn't want you to do anything but find out the truth about my book."

"And you never mentioned that you killed yourself."

"What difference does it make?" Didi's shoulders slumped. Her voice wavered. She untied her apron and slipped it over her head. It, too, vanished the moment she set it down. "Dead is dead."

I couldn't argue with that.

I couldn't afford to get sucked in by the pathetic trembling in her voice, either. Rather than think about what awful thing could have brought her life to the brink of despair, I stuck to the matter at hand.

"And then there's that original handwritten manuscript," I said.

Didi's face brightened. "You found it?"

I didn't need to answer. My expression said it all.

"You didn't find it." Her smile disappeared like magic. Just like the cookie sheet and the oven mitts had. "You don't believe it was ever there."

Too irritated to keep still, I threw my hands in the air and did a turn around the room. "What am I supposed to believe? You've been telling me stories, Didi. And sucker that I am, I've been more than willing to believe them. Then the truth comes out and smacks me in the face. Your movie career, the way you died, the manuscript. Sorry if I'm jumping the gun here, but I'm thinking that pretty soon, I'm going to need hip boots to wade through your lies. Maybe if I could find something in *So*

Far the Dawn that sounded like you—"

"You're reading it?" Didi's smile was radiant. "Do you like it? I mean, really, tell me. Is it the best book ever? Have you gotten to the part where—"

"I've gotten to the part where Opal is leaving for Baltimore," I confessed. "And what difference does it make what I think of the book? I'm not reading it to be entertained." Not exactly a lie since I never dreamed I'd actually like the book. "I'm reading it in the hopes of finding the truth. I don't see you in those pages anywhere."

"You don't see Merilee, either."

I couldn't deny it. "You're right. It's just that I thought maybe there would be some hint of your voice. I was thinking that maybe the way you describe things in the book would sound like the way you talk. That one of your characters would sound just like you."

"That's not what writing is all about." Didi waved away my theory. "It's not like writers take their own lives and just plunk them down on paper. It's fiction, silly. I made it all up."

"But if your voice was there—"

"What about what's not there?"

I wasn't sure what she was getting at, and it was Didi's turn to be frustrated. She gave me a penetrating look. "How far have you read?" she asked.

"I told you. Opal is leaving for Baltimore."

"That would be . . ." Didi narrowed her eyes, thinking. "About page 147."

As far as I remembered, she was just about right. I nodded.

"So tell me, in the 147 pages you've read, have

you seen one mention of the unemployment rate in Cleveland in 1857?"

"No, but—"

"Have you read anything about the petroleum industry here? Or the way steel is manufactured? Or"—she shuddered—"economics?"

I knew where she was headed with this. "No," I said again. "And you're saying—"

"I'm saying that all you have to do is look at that so-called sequel Merilee is writing—"

"I already have." I dropped into the closest kitchen chair. "You're right. What I saw in her notebook is nothing like what I read last night. I just thought that some editor somewhere—"

"Please!" Like she smelled something bad, Didi sniffed. "No amount of editing could turn her sow's ear into my silk purse. I'm right, aren't I? Admit it Pepper, I'm right."

"You're right."

"About what?"

I'd spoken to Didi, but it was Quinn who answered. He walked back into the kitchen. "I mean, not that I'm arguing or anything," he said. "After all, I usually am right. I just wondered what you think I'm right about."

"Not much of anything as far as I can tell." It wasn't true, but it sounded hard-assed, and sounding hard-assed, well, it was better than throwing myself at his feet and begging him for a second chance at the date we'd once set up for a candlelight dinner at Pietro's. I'd stood him up—sort of—but only because Gus's son, Rudy the Cootie Scarpetti, had made me an offer I couldn't refuse for the same night.

"I was just thinking that you were right about Trish," I told him. It was better than trying to explain that he was standing at the door, I was sitting in a chair, and there was a woman between us who'd been dead since before either of us was born. "Nobody told me she was murdered." A new thought struck and I groaned. "Great, now I feel bad about thinking how stupid she was to get smothered by her own corset."

"The corset story isn't entirely wrong." Quinn took another few steps into the kitchen. "As a matter of fact, the coroner believed her death was an accident. Until he completed his autopsy. That's when he determined that the angle was all wrong. Those things . . ." Quinn wiggled his fingers along his back. "What do you call them?"

"The laces? On the corset? You mean the things that tie at the back?"

"Yeah, that's it. They left marks on Ms. Kingston's skin. And the coroner could see that the angle was all wrong. Ms. Kingston may have started out tying that corset, but someone else finished the job. That someone else kept pulling tighter and tighter. Until Trish Kingston couldn't breathe anymore."

I didn't want to think about the way the murderer must have squeezed all hope out of Trish. Just like he squeezed out all her air. I pictured her up there in my bedroom, as limp as a rag doll, powerless to save herself. Helpless. Blue.

A shiver snaked up my spine, and I knew I'd better concentrate on the facts at hand.

"I guess all that makes sense. Look." I got up from the chair and put my hands behind my back, pretending to tie a pretend corset. "There's only so far I can reach around to my own back. And if I was tying a corset like this . . ." I went through the motions, approaching the matter scientifically.

Apparently Quinn's mind was on something other than science. When I looked his way, his eyes glimmered. "Is there something I should know about you and corsets?" he asked. "Looks like you know your way around sexy lingerie pretty well."

"Maybe I do." There was no harm in dangling him along. "Maybe I'm wearing a corset right now."

He stepped closer and looked at my cleavage. "Oh, I don't think so. Though I will admit they have a certain appeal, corsets are stiff and old-fashioned. Something tells me if you were wearing one, the view wouldn't be nearly as nice."

"You're slipping, detective. That almost sounded like a compliment."

Quinn reached for my arm. "It was a compliment. As a matter of fact—"

His cell rang.

Quinn gritted his teeth. "Duty calls," he said, and he left the kitchen again.

"He's a dreamboat!"

I didn't need Didi to remind me.

"Yeah. A dreamboat who keeps floating away."

She chuckled. "That's funny. But listen, kiddo, you can't expect him to stay around when you treat him the way you do."

I'd been staring at the spot where Quinn had recently been, enjoying the scent of his expensive aftershave. I turned to Didi. "Excuse me?"

"Come on, honey, lighten up." I had the feeling that if she could, Didi would have elbowed me in the ribs. "You're young. There's plenty you don't know about getting a guy."

"And you do?"

She winked. "Sure I do. I had a baby, didn't I? And just so you know it wasn't some kind of stupid accident, the baby's father, he wasn't my first. I knew my way around. I had experience. You know, of the romantic kind."

"You mean sex."

She blushed again. "We weren't as blunt back in my day."

"We're plenty blunt now."

"That's your whole problem." When I looked at her in wonder she rolled her eyes. "You've got to keep some mystery in a relationship. That's how you get a man. And you've got to let him have his way. Tell him he's right even when he's not. Give in."

"No thanks." I'd heard enough. It was time for that shower. "Don't forget, this is the twenty-first century. Women aren't doormats."

"Maybe that's why so many of them are unhappy."

It was my turn to roll my eyes. "Oh please! Are you telling me I should let Quinn be the boss?"

"If you want to get him in bed."

"That's not how it works."

"You know this, right? That's why you've been to bed with him."

It was a low blow, and besides, it wasn't true. "The reason I have not been to bed with Quinn," I told her, "is because your friend Gus Scarpetti interrupted us. If it wasn't for him—"

"If it wasn't for him, you would have had yourself a one-night stand. Is that what you're looking for?"

Heck, yes!

I opened my mouth to tell Didi this when another question bounced through my head.

Was it *all* I wanted from Quinn?

I snapped my mouth shut again.

"Just what I thought." Didi turned away from me, then whirled around again just as quickly. She was back to wearing the apron and the oven mitts. "Take some advice from Mom," she said. "If you're looking for a little backseat bingo . . . let's face it, you can find any guy for that. But that one . . ." She looked toward the hallway. "He looks like he's too good to let slip through your fingers. You're going to need to be more careful, Pepper, if you intend to keep him around. Be a lady. Let him open doors for you. Ask for his opinion. You know, about things women don't understand like money and politics. Tell him—"

"Thanks but no thanks," I told Didi, and grabbing another cup of coffee, I headed out the door.

By this time, Quinn was nowhere to be seen, and I guess it was the fact that he hadn't stuck around to say goodbye that sent my temper soaring. That, and Didi's half-baked advice to the lovelorn.

I grumbled to myself, and the way I saw it, I had every right.

After all, I was an intelligent, modern woman. I knew what was what when it came to relationships. My love life wasn't so pathetic that I needed advice from a dead woman.

Was it?

*   *   *

"These need to be addressed." With an imperious wave of one perfectly manicured hand, Merilee indicated a stack of white boxes that hadn't been on her desk the night before. "By hand."

The boxes reminded me of the ones my wedding invitations had been delivered in. If they did contain invitations and if there were two hundred invitations to a box like there had been in the boxes that had arrived from my wedding planner . . .

"All of them?" The question squeaked out of me.

When I'd walked into the study, Merilee had been busy writing. Something fascinating about how iron ore was smelted, no doubt. She slapped her pen down on her notebook. "Are you that stupid?" she asked, but she didn't give me a chance to answer. "Of course all of them. They're the invitations to the costume gala at the Renaissance Hotel. You know, the party that will mark the opening of the museum. It's the biggest thing to happen in this town since the opening of the Rock and Roll Hall of Fame. People are clamoring for invitations." She picked up her pen, indicating that our conversation (such as it was) was over. "Best handwriting."

"The only kind I ever use." I smiled.

She didn't notice because she never looked up. "And finish with the books and get rid of those boxes, too." She waved toward the bookshelves and the boxes I'd begun to unpack the night before.

Call me crazy, but unpacking books sounded more appealing than worrying about my best handwriting. I started that way.

"Not while I'm in here working. How could I possibly concentrate?" Merilee's exasperation dripped from her every word. "You can do that tonight. If you're not too tired, that is."

I'd taken a shower and changed my clothes, so there was nothing in my appearance to make Merilee suspect my adventure in the attic the night before. Which made me wonder if maybe she had heard some of the commotion after all.

"I don't need much sleep," I told her. "As a matter of fact, last night—"

The sigh she heaved was of epic proportions. "Do you see me working here?"

I did. But I didn't move, and Merilee looked at me over the rims of her glasses. "Is there anything else?"

"Yeah. As a matter of fact, there is." I piled the invitation boxes in my arms. "You can tell me why you didn't mention that Trish was murdered."

As if I'd slapped her, Merilee jumped. "How do you— Oh, that policeman. Yes, well." She set down her pen and scooted back in her chair, her hands clutched together on the desk. "I couldn't tell you. Because I didn't know myself. Not until that nice policeman arrived here this morning." She glanced toward the doorway, but I was one up on her. I knew that Quinn was already gone. "I hope he doesn't make a nuisance of himself," she said.

Funny, I was kind of hoping he did.

Not that I was going to share that little fact with Merilee.

Instead, I watched her face, hoping something in her expression would help me make sense of the situation. "Aren't you worried? She was killed. Right here in the house. Doesn't that make you nervous?"

"Those reenactors have been in and out. And the workers . . ." Her lip curled at the very thought. "There are some who don't speak English, you know."

"Always a good indicator of guilt." The irony was lost on Merilee, so I decided to stick with facts. "You're the one who found her, aren't you? What did you see when you got to the room?"

"See?" She looked at me as if, like so many of those workers, I'd suddenly started speaking another language. "I saw Trish. That's what I saw. Trish, lying on the floor right there next to her bed. She was breathing her last. It was . . ." Merilee's voice bubbled with emotion. She looked away, and when she looked back, her expression was blank, as if she'd built a wall around her feelings. No way was she going to let me see beyond it. "Are you happy now? You've made me remember a particularly disturbing event. I'll never be the same."

"Neither will Trish."

"Perhaps you *should* get those empty boxes out of here before you begin the invitations. I'll need them again when I leave for California, so we want to put them somewhere nice and safe. How about where they came from? Downstairs in Bob's workshop." Merilee picked up her pen and started to write. Her smile was sleek and as sharp as a knife. "Don't forget to wash your hands before you touch any of the invitation envelopes."

I knew a brush-off when I got one. Just like I knew there was nothing to be gained from pressing her any further. Besides, whether Merilee realized it or not, I had learned a couple of useful things. I was pretty sure that Merilee had heard the noise in the attic the night before and that she knew I had something to do with it. She just hadn't cared enough to see what it was all about.

And I'd learned that she didn't want to talk about Trish.

Call me crazy, but I didn't think it was because the memory of Trish's grisly death offended Merilee's sensibilities. As far as I could see, Merilee didn't have any.

I set down the invitations and grabbed a few of the empty boxes, wondering as I did what all this meant in terms of Trish's murder. And how (or even if) any of it affected my investigation.

"Who would want to murder Trish, anyway?" I grumbled the question to myself while I traipsed through the hallway and into the kitchen, juggling the boxes and opening the basement door. "She wasn't worth murdering."

I realized just as I said the words that because of the Gift thing, Trish might actually have heard me.

"Sorry," I said, clumping down the steps. "But it's true. I hope you're having more fun there on the Other Side, because I'll tell you what, over here, you were just about as exciting as oatmeal. You were as meek and as mild as—"

But she wasn't. At least not that last day at the TV station.

Now more than ever, I wondered what the change in Trish meant and if the comment she'd made to Ella about how things were turning around for her could have had anything to do with her death.

Except Trish's murder wasn't what I was supposed to be investigating.

"Sorry," I told her again. I set the boxes down on the basement floor and kicked them across to where there was a door with a sign on it that said, BOB'S WORK ROOM. KEEP OUT. "It's not that I don't care, but that's what the cops are for. Don't worry, Quinn's on the case. I don't know a whole lot about him, but I know him well enough to know he doesn't give up. He'll solve your murder."

By the time I was finished with this weird monologue, I was at the door of the workroom. I half expected it to be locked, but when I tried the knob, it turned in my hand.

"Bob?" I inched the door open, and when there was no answer to my inquiry, I breathed a sigh of relief. No Weird Bob to deal with. I felt along the wall for a light switch, flicked it on, and stepped inside.

The room was exactly as advertised. I was in the basement, and there were no windows. The only light in the place came from a fluorescent fixture that hung over a worktable. The cement-block walls were covered with shelves, the shelves were chock-full of old glass jars that were filled with things like screws and nails and bits and pieces of wire. The place was hardly bigger than my bedroom, and at the same time I wondered why Merilee had thought it was a good spot to store the boxes, I knew I wasn't a total jerk. I couldn't just drop the boxes and leave. Weird or not, that wouldn't be fair to Bob. I'd have to stack them in one corner.

One of those huge plastic garbage cans stood at the far corner of the workbench, and I wouldn't have given it a second glance except as I nested one box into another, I saw something caught under the lid and hanging over the side. The something in question was long and curling and shiny.

I stopped and set down the boxes. I myself did not own a camera, but if I did, it would be digital. High-tech yearnings aside, I knew a lot of people still used 35mm cameras, and 35mm cameras required film.

If Bob was a photographer, I didn't want to know what kinds of pictures he took. Still, I was curious, so curious, I plucked the film out of the garbage can and held it up to the light.

No wonder Bob had trashed it. What images I could see were blotchy and distorted, and most of the film was completely blank.

As if it had been exposed to the light.

"Junk," I mumbled to myself, and convinced of the fact, I lifted the lid to put it back where I'd found it.

That's when I saw that there was a camera at the bottom of the garbage can.

This did not look like junk, and just to make sure, I fished it out of the trash can.

The camera looked to be expensive, and as far as I could tell, it was in perfect shape. I turned it over in my hands, and the light glinted off the words engraved on the bottom of the camera.

"Rick Jensen," it said. "*National Inquisitor.*"

Chapter 13

Lucky me, I had plenty of time to try and unravel the mystery of how Rick Jensen's camera had ended up in Weird Bob's workroom.

Like the whole afternoon while I addressed gala invitation after gala invitation. And the entire evening when I finished unpacking Merilee's traveling library and stashed almost all the boxes in the basement. I say *almost* because one of them never made it into the workroom. I squirreled away the camera and the exposed roll of film in that one and tucked the box in my closet.

By the time bedtime rolled around, my hands were cramped, my brain was fried, and I was no closer to figuring out an answer to this little mystery.

"Why would Weird Bob mug Rick Jensen and steal his camera?" I asked my own reflection in the mirror that hung over the dresser in my bedroom. By now, I knew not to be surprised when someone else answered.

This time, that someone else was Didi. Though I couldn't see her reflection, her voice came from right behind me.

"Who's Rick Jensen?" she asked.

I spun around, all set to explain. I would have done it, too, except I was too shocked. I pointed at Didi's head.

"What the hell are those things?"

She touched a hand to the pink plastic cylinders lined up in rows along her scalp, her hair wound around them. "They're rollers, of course, silly. You know, to curl my hair. You don't use rollers?"

I looked at the rollers and the plastic picks that were poked through each one and then wedged against Didi's scalp. "There's no force on earth that could make me do that to myself. Besides, my curl is natural. So is the color."

"Lucky you." She peered into the mirror, and though I couldn't see her there, she checked her roots. Satisfied, she plunked down on my bed. She was dressed in plaid pajamas and fuzzy slippers the same color as her rollers. "Aren't pajama parties the best?"

"I didn't know we were having a pajama party, and besides, they call them sleepovers these days."

Didi giggled. "Then aren't sleepovers the best?"

"Not when you're sleeping over in this house of horrors." I slipped out of my jeans and grabbed the flannel lounge pants at the foot of the bed. When I saw Didi staring at my butt I did what any self-respecting woman would do. I got defensive. "What? What's wrong?"

"Those are underpants?"

It was my turn to laugh. "Underpants? You sound like a second grader. Yes, this is underwear. It's called a thong."

"Guys must love them."

Guys weren't something I wanted to think about because thinking of guys made me think about Quinn and thinking about Quinn . . .

I slipped into my lounge pants, tugged off my tank and bra, and pulled on a loose T-shirt. "The only guy I care about right now is Weird Bob. What do you know about him?"

"Bob is . . ." Didi shrugged. "Bob is Bob. He's always been here. You know, helping around the house. Fixing things, cutting the grass."

"He's related?"

"To us?" Didi shook her head. "He lived across the street when Merilee and I were kids growing up. He's a couple of years older than us. When Merilee left for California, Bob sold his house and moved in here to keep an eye on things."

"And he's been here ever since." This did nothing to help me figure out why Bob would go all the way to Garden View to steal a camera and then throw it away. I wracked my brain for the right questions that might lead to some sort of helpful answers. "Does he know?" I asked Didi. "I mean about you and *So Far the Dawn*? Does Bob know you wrote the book?"

She squeezed her eyes shut, like she was thinking hard. "He may have seen me working on it," she finally said. She pointed in the direction of the empty lot across the street. "He lived over there. You know, back when there was a house on that property. Our bedroom windows were right across from each other, and that's where I wrote the book, in my bedroom. I worked on it in the evenings when I got home from work and at night, before I went to bed. I used to see him looking out his window toward our house. A lot. You know, just watching."

I didn't know, but I could imagine, and imagining it . . . well, it gave me the willies.

I pushed the thought to the back burner. "Okay, so if Bob didn't know, who did? You said you talked about the book."

"Sure I did. I talked about the book to plenty of people."

"Like . . ."

"Like Susan Gwitkowski. She was my best friend. We worked in the steno pool, and we had lunch together every day. She'd ask how the story was going, and I'd tell her what I'd written the night before."

"Then why didn't she say something when Merilee published the book?"

There was that shrug again. Not that Didi's stonewalling mattered. No sooner had I asked the question than I knew the answer.

"You'd lied to Susan Gwitkowski, right? Just like you lied to me. About stuff that didn't really matter. Then when something really did matter, when the book was published and Merilee was praised as the Second Coming, Susan must have figured you'd been lying about the book like you did about everything else. That Merilee really was the author and that you'd just been pretending."

"It's possible."

It was more than possible. I knew it because Didi wouldn't look me in the eye.

Just like Dad never would.

Here was another thought to throw me for a loop. Rather than deal, I grabbed my facial cleanser, my toothbrush, and my toothpaste and headed for the bathroom.

When I got back, Didi was standing at my window.

"There is someone else," she said. "Someone who knows for sure. He'll tell you I wrote the book." She looked at me over her shoulder, and I wondered why she didn't sound—and look—more excited. "I mean, if he'll talk to you."

"And you kept this little tidbit to yourself all this time, why?"

Didi turned and sat back down on the bed. "I thought you'd find the manuscript I put in the attic and then it wouldn't matter. I didn't want to involve him."

"Because . . ."

"Because I based Palmer on him. You know, the hero of *So Far the Dawn*."

"And . . ."

"And I told him about it, of course. I mean, he was a special person and I was so happy to be able to do something special for him, and I knew he'd be happy, too, to think that I'd put him in a book, and every woman who read the book would fall in love with Palmer, and no one would know that Palmer was really him. No one but us. It was our little secret, and that made it so exciting. I even dedicated the book to him."

I flipped open the paperback copy of *SFTD* that was on the table near my bed and read the words on the first page.

To my dear parents. And in memory of all the courageous men and women who fought to keep this Union whole.

I looked up at Didi. "Yeah, right. You dedicated the book to him all right."

She jumped to her feet and spun to face me. "That's Merilee's dedication. Not mine," she said, and though I can't say for certain what righteous indignation is, I'd say Didi's voice was as close to it as I'd ever heard.

"Don't you get it?" she asked. "Merilee changed it. My dedication was written to Thomas. I even gave him a copy of the first page with the words written there, so he could see them and know the book was just for him."

A spark of hope glimmered in the darkness that was my investigation. "And this Thomas guy . . . he's still alive? He'll verify that?"

Didi worked over her lower lip with her teeth. "I don't know," she said. "I mean, not about him being alive. I know he's still alive. And I know he would like to tell you all about the book and the dedication and all, but . . . well, he has so much at stake. Don't get the wrong idea about him! He's a wonderful person. But . . ."

Didi's protest and her voice faded. It was just as well; she didn't need to say any more. From what she'd already said, it wasn't hard to fit the pieces together.

"You were in love with him."

It wasn't a question, so I guess I didn't actually expect an answer.

Which was why I was surprised when she raised her chin and looked me in the eye. "Thomas Ross Howell was my boss. And an honorable man."

"And you were in love with him."

"He was married."

"And you were in love with him."

Didi turned her back on me. "Really, Pepper, you don't think a man of his status—"

"Hey, you said it yourself. You said you knew your way around when it came to guys. If he was one of them—"

"He wasn't."

"But you dedicated your book to him."

"He was a good person. I idolized him. I hoped to someday meet and marry a man just like him."

"And I just fell off a turnip truck." Tired of arguing and getting nowhere, I plunked down on the bed. "I'll go see him."

Didi didn't respond, and all it took was one look around the room to see why. She was long gone, and it was just as well. I knew what she would have asked.

Was it smart to go see this Thomas guy?

Heck, I didn't know. In fact, all I did know was that the sooner I talked to him and to Susan Gwitkowski, the better. Because the sooner I talked to them, the sooner I might be able to uncover the truth.

Not Didi's version of it.

Or Merilee's.

Just the whole truth and nothing but.

Because something told me that until I did, there was no way I'd ever really be able to help Didi. And helping Didi . . .

Suddenly and for reasons I couldn't explain, helping Didi had become important to me.

I climbed into bed and pulled the covers up to my nose, but I didn't turn out the lights. Aside from keeping the shadows of Trish's murder away, maybe the lamp helped shed some light on my own motivations, because after a few minutes of lying there thinking, it finally dawned on me.

I knew why I wanted to make sure that Didi got the justice she deserved.

After all, when my relationship with Joel Pan-horst crashed and burned, heartbreak and me, we were on a first-name basis, and being up close and personal with heartache like that . . . well, once you are, it's not hard to recognize it in someone else.

Even when that someone else was a ghost.

It looked like Didi and I were soul sisters of sorts.

There was no way I was going to sleep, not with so much on my mind, so I grabbed my copy of *So Far the Dawn* and settled down to read.

I'd always been a sucker for a good love story.

"Who did you say you were?"

When I waited for his secretary to step out to lunch and ducked into his office, Judge Thomas Ross Howell was busy reading from a fat, dull-looking book. He glanced up at where I stood in the doorway, looked down at the book, and put one finger on the page to mark his place. "Martin? Pepper? Do I know you?"

He didn't ask me to come in or to sit down, but I did both anyway. On foot, I could easily be escorted out of the building. This way, he'd have to lift both his leather guest chair and me to toss me out on my keister, and though he looked like he could do it, something told me Howell wouldn't take the chance of rumpling his thousand-dollar suit.

At eighty, Thomas Ross Howell was still as fit and attractive as he'd been in the ten-year-old photos of him that I'd found at the library that morning. He was tall, athletic, and as tanned as if he'd just stepped out of the Florida sunshine. His iron gray hair was thick and he sported a stylish cut. The Rolex on his left wrist glimmered in the light of the lamp on his desk. So did his gold cuff links.

"You don't. Know me, that is." I smiled like the fact that I'd snuck into his office without an appointment and unannounced was no big deal. "There are some things I'd like to talk to you about."

The judge's brows dipped over his eyes. "I don't discuss cases. Not outside the courtroom and certainly not with a plaintiff. So if that's what you're—"

"It's not about a case."

"I don't give interviews. Not unless I've talked to your editor or your producer first."

"I'm not a reporter."

"Then you should know I don't hand out donations, either. Except through the trust my wife and I have established."

"I know. About the money you give to the orchestra and the Art Museum and all. That's great. Really. But I'm not looking for a handout. I just thought—"

He reached for his phone. "Security will have you out of here in a matter of seconds. So if you think you can get away with trying to rob—"

"No. No. No robbing!" I rushed to disabuse him of the notion, pointing to myself and the conservative brown pantsuit and white blouse I'd hoped would help me blend in at the county courthouse. "Do I look like a robber? I don't want your money. I just want to talk."

"I don't talk to people I don't know."

"But it's important."

"Then you should request an appointment."

"So you could refuse to give it to me?"

He smiled and lifted the phone receiver, and though I had hoped for a diplomatic approach and a little small talk to put the judge at ease, I knew that if I didn't play my trump card, my one and only chance to find out what he knew was going to slip through my fingers.

"It's about Didi Bowman," I said.

The phone at his ear, Howell froze. Slowly, he put the handset back in place. "I don't know who you're talking about."

"I think you do. Didi ... er ... Deborah Bowman. You knew her. Back in the fifties."

I'd caught him off guard, but I should have known the surprise wouldn't last. A man didn't get to be a powerful judge and city leader if he didn't have balls.

Like we were passing the time of day at one of the many fund-raisers he sponsored and talking about nothing more important than the weather, Howell chuckled. "You expect me to remember someone I met nearly fifty years ago?"

"Yeah, I kind of did. You see, I think Didi was more to you than just someone you once met."

Howell's eyes were as blue and as cold as a glacier. From across his desk, his gaze pinned me and turned my blood to ice water. "And that's supposed to mean what?" he asked.

I shrugged. "It's not supposed to mean anything. I don't have time for that kind of crap. I just think you and Didi must have been more than just acquaintances. Otherwise, she wouldn't have been in love with you."

Howell moved pretty fast for an old guy. He was out of his chair and around the desk before I ever even saw him coming. "Now listen here, young lady . . ." He stabbed one finger at me. "If you think you can just waltz in here and start flinging accusations . . ."

"I'm not flingin' a thing." I did my best to act like I wasn't scared shitless. Which I pretty much was. I waved aside his angry protest. "She just said—"

"Don't be ridiculous! Didi didn't just say anything. She's been dead since 1956."

I stood. "I thought you said you didn't know Didi."

He turned away from me and marched around to the other side of the desk. He was buying time and I knew it, but at this point, there wasn't much I could do about it. I was still counting on Howell's information and his help. And nobody knew better than me that right about then, I was toeing the fine line between *All right, let's talk* and *Slap the cuffs on this woman and make sure I never see her again.*

"What do you want?" he asked.

"Just information. Honest. It all has to do with Didi's sister, Merilee, and that book of hers."

"*So Far the Dawn*?" There was no amusement in Howell's laugh. "Is that all anybody in this town can talk about? I'm sick to death of hearing about the damned book. If you're another one of those crazed fans looking for some sort of insight, all I can tell you is that I don't know a thing. Yes, I knew Didi Bowman. There. Are you happy? Since you apparently already know we were acquainted, I see no point in denying it. But you've got your information all wrong, Miss Martin. Didi Bowman was a secretary in my law office. That's *all* she was to me. An employee and nothing more."

Was it true?

The question ate away at my bravado. After all the lies I'd heard from Didi and the way she'd denied any sort of relationship with Howell, maybe I should have known better than to march into the office of one of the city's most prominent leaders and start pointing fingers.

But maybe even the world's best liar couldn't fake the pain I'd heard in Didi's voice when she talked about Thomas Ross Howell.

I held on to the thought because it was the only thing that gave me courage, and right now, I needed all the courage I could get.

I swallowed down my misgivings. "Funny that you remember what year she died. I mean, since Didi was an employee and nothing more to you."

Howell sighed. Not like he was giving in. More like he was exasperated. "Miss Bowman's death created quite a stir in the office. That's one reason I remember it. The other is that it happened the same year my son was born. Also . . ." He looked away and his expression softened. Like he was lost in a memory.

"You're too young to have ever known her," he said. "Maybe if you did, you'd realize that Miss Bowman was . . . how can I put this diplomatically? She was hard to forget."

"A hot little number, huh?"

He tugged at his suit coat and shook himself back to the present. "There were some who thought so."

"But not you."

Howell looked at me hard. "Maybe you missed the part about me saying my son was born that year. My daughter was three years old at the time. So you see, I was happily married." He glanced toward the photo on his desk of an elegant, silver-haired woman. "I still am."

"That's nice." I smiled. "And I'm not trying to contradict you or anything, I'm just trying to make sense of the situation. See, what I don't understand is, if all that is true, why Didi dedicated her book to you."

There was a dimple in Howell's chin. He rubbed one finger over it. "Look, I don't know where you're getting your information, but—"

"If I told you, you wouldn't believe me."

"And you think I can help you, how?"

"Because I think you know what I'm talking about. She dedicated *So Far the Dawn* to you, didn't she? She showed you the first page of it and her writing was on it. It was long before Merilee published the book. And when she did, what did you think? Did you think that Didi had just stolen a page of Merilee's book and pretended to be the author just to impress you?"

Howell studied me with an intensity I imagined he'd used on more than one opposing attorney over the years. I shifted from foot to foot.

"What are you getting at here?" he asked.

It was time to lay my cards on the table. At least some of them. "I think Merilee didn't write that book," I told him. "I think Didi did, and I think you once saw the original copy of her manuscript. If you're willing to talk about the fact that you saw the manuscript and that Didi wrote it, we might be able to prove that she's really the author. See, if she is, then the wrong person has been getting rich on the royalties for a lot of years."

"You're talking about Didi's daughter. You think Judy should get the money."

I shook my head. "Judy's dead. Has been for a few years. But Judy, she had a daughter. Maybe you didn't know that. Judy's daughter. Didi's granddaughter. If we can prove—"

"Hold on! Right there." Howell barked the command. "How old are you?"

The question caught me off guard. "Twenty-five," I told him. "But I don't see how that—"

"Out!" His cheeks flushed with an ugly, dark color, his voice trembling with barely controlled emotion, Howell pointed toward the door. "Get the hell out of my office. Who do you think you're dealing with, little girl? You're crazy if you think you can pull some sort of shakedown scam on me. I know exactly what you're up to, and let me tell you this, you'll never prove a thing. You think you can grab a share of my money and my family's prestige, think again and remember this: If I ever see your face again, you're going to hear the words *restraining order* so fast, your head will spin."

"Excuse me?" Baffled by his sudden mood swing, I stared at him in wonder. "What are you talking about? I only want to know if Didi ever showed you the original manuscript. If she told you that the character of Palmer was based on you. I only wanted to know—"

I guess Howell didn't give a damn what I wanted to know.

Before I could say another word, he grabbed my arm, dragged me out into the hallway, and slammed his office door behind him. Even through the closed door, I heard his voice as he called security and told them there was an intruder outside his office.

Time to beat a hasty retreat.

I made it outside without incident, thank goodness, and while I hurried away from the courthouse as fast as I could, I wondered what the hell had happened up there.

What difference did it make to Howell how old I was?

And why did he think me being there had anything to do with what he called a shakedown and a chance to snaffle up his money?

Unless . . .

I had just started across a street against the light when the truth hit. I stopped in my tracks in the middle of the intersection, and when a couple of car horns blew and a driver leaned out of his window and asked me if I was some kind of crazy, drugged-out freak, I heard the sounds as if they came from a million miles away.

Of course! I should have figured it out the moment I realized that Howell and Didi were connected by more than just the path to the steno pool.

Howell didn't give a damn about *So Far the Dawn* or who wrote it. He was worried that I was trying to cash in on a family connection.

That's why he asked how old I was.

Howell thought I'd shown up out of nowhere to claim him as my long-lost grandfather.

Because Judge Thomas Ross Howell was the father of Didi's baby.

And that meant . . .

Another blast of a car horn got me moving. I scurried over to the sidewalk and followed my train of thought to its logical conclusion.

It wasn't pretty.

Because I was convinced that Howell wasn't just Judy's father.

Thomas Ross Howell was the reason Didi jumped.

Chapter 14

I was all set to run this new theory by Didi—and dare her to prove me wrong—but it looked as if she'd learned a few handy-dandy ghostly tricks from the dearly departed don. As Gus had done so many times when I needed to talk to him most, Didi had vanished.

Pun intended.

I got back to the Bowman house and she was nowhere around.

The rest of the world, though, was.

I had to fight my way through the crowd in the entryway, and when I did, I saw what was happening. One group of workers was moving the last of the display cases into their permanent positions in what used to be the dining room. With a whole lot of pomp and ceremony, a second group was setting the first bits of memorabilia in place in the glass cases in the once-upon-a-time living room.

Members of the press captured the moment for posterity, their cameras trained on the one and only Merilee, who, resplendent in peacock blue, stuck around long enough to primp and smile, then disappeared into her study with the promise (or was it a threat?) of the sequel that was awaiting her attention.

No big surprise that Ella was there to watch it all.

Unknown to anyone but little ol' Gifted me, so were Elizabeth and Kurt.

I waved to the dynamic dueling duo, but we didn't have a chance to chat, and call me cynical, but I knew it was just as well. The two stars were standing near a poster that, according to the plaque next to it, had once hung in the Ziegfeld to advertise the opening of the movie.

"You look embalmed, darling. And stuffed," Elizabeth told Kurt, her top lip curled as she studied him in his blue uniform.

"And you, my dear . . ." Kurt's smile glinted in the light of the cameras that flashed all around. He eyed the cleavage that peeked out from the top of the famous blue velvet dress. "Whoever thought they could pass off New Jersey trash as Ohio blue blood must have been as crazy as a loon *and* nearsighted to boot."

I left them at it.

Good thing, too. As soon as she saw me, Ella latched on to my arm. "Can you believe it?" She tugged me over to a glass case that featured the (fake) diamond and sapphire necklace Opal wore in the scene where she connived a naive banker into loaning her the money to save the family's shipbuilding business. At the same time I wondered what she'd say if she knew Elizabeth was standing right behind her in the same green outfit Opal wore to call on the bank, I made the right clucking noises.

"This is the most exciting day of my life," Ella said, and I didn't contradict her, even though it was what she'd said the day Merilee arrived at Garden View. What was the point in arguing? And what difference would it have made?

Ella was beyond thinking logically.

Her cheeks aglow, and the same shade as the flamingo pink dress she wore with a snappy little matching sweater, Ella drifted from display case to display case, grinning from ear to ear and taking me along for the ride.

"Look! The Opal doll!" She clutched her hands to her heart, and while she beamed at the eighteen-inch doll inside the nearest case, I shook out my arm to get the circulation going again. The doll was dressed as Elizabeth had been the night she'd first popped up in Merilee's study, in the ubiquitous blue gown. She had the same tumble of golden curls, the same sapphire eyes. "I wanted one of these dolls so bad when I was a kid, I got on a bus and went downtown to ask Santa for one." Ella gave me a wink. "Considering that we're Jewish, my mother wasn't exactly thrilled. I did get the doll, though. For Hanukkah that year. You think maybe Santa's interdenominational?"

She didn't wait for me to answer, and that was okay. There wasn't much I could say, and she probably wouldn't have heard me, anyway. Ella looked toward the next case and practically melted in a puddle of aficionado mush. "The *So Far the Dawn* lunch box! Isn't it the most beautiful thing you've ever seen?"

I wasn't so sure. I looked at the twelve-by-twelve metal box with the picture of a smiling Palmer and a pouting Opal on it. Even before I could comment, I heard them behind us.

"Oh, Kurt! A lunch box. The perfect item for a ham like you."

"And for you, Elizabeth. But only if one of the things packed inside is a tart."

"A lunch box like this is as rare as hen's teeth." Ella's comment cut across the sniping. Her sigh fogged the glass case. "It's the one piece of memorabilia I've never been able to get my hands on, and it would be the crowning glory of my collection."

"You're not thinking of a smash and grab, are you?"

I was kidding.

The look of lunch box lust in Ella's eyes told me that maybe I shouldn't have been. Fortunately for her criminal record and for my bank account (because of course I would have bailed her out of jail), her better self took control. Ella pulled her gaze from the lunch box to me. "I'm glad you showed up," she said. "Since I was coming over here anyway, I brought your gown. I hope you don't mind. Bob showed me which room was yours, and I put it up there."

I wasn't sure which comment worried me more. The one about Bob being in my bedroom. Or the one about the gown.

Because the one was too icky to consider, I glommed on to the other.

"What gown?"

Ella patted my arm. "It's gorgeous. I promise. It had to be retailored completely, of course. I mean, you and Trish Kingston . . ." She laughed. "Well, she had such a stick of a figure. And you're so gorgeous and curvy. But not to worry. When I stopped by your apartment to pick up your mail last week, I took the liberty of checking your closet and taking one of your dressier dresses. You know, to the seamstress. She used it for sizing, but of course, you'll still need to try on the gown before—"

"What gown?"

I guess the second time was the charm. Or maybe Ella finally heard me because I spoke so loud. The confusion in her eyes cleared. "The gown? Oh, you forgot, didn't you? Your gown. The one you'll be wearing to the gala."

As it happened, I had not forgotten. I had never been told. I didn't bother to point this out to Ella because just as I was about to (along with the fact that there was no way in hell I was going to wear a hoop skirt or a corset), she spotted something in the next case, and if I'd stopped to talk, I wouldn't have been able to put an arm around her when I thought she was going to collapse on the floor.

"Oh, Pepper!" Tears welled in Ella's eyes. Her shoulders heaved beneath my ministering hands. I don't imagine the folks who designed the museum displays wanted people touching the glass cases, but Ella did anyway. With one finger. Like what was inside was so precious, she didn't dare do any more.

What was inside, according the sign above it, was the original handwritten copy of *So Far the Dawn*.

Merilee's original handwritten copy.

"To be this close to greatness!" Ella was sighing

again, and I had to wipe the condensation off the glass before I could get a good look at the looseleaf pages inside the display. There in front of me was the whole, entire manuscript. It was opened to the scene where Opal heads off to Baltimore.

I scanned the pages, and I'll say this much: There was nothing like seeing Merilee's work to take a girl aback.

I stood there staring. At the pages and the neat, careful writing. At the smudge-free margins and the words that were, by now, familiar. I'd seen them in print only a couple of nights before when I sat in my room and read the book.

Right then and there, every question I'd ever had about Didi and her claims to the authorship of the book washed over me like the cold slap of a Lake Erie wave.

There was *So Far the Dawn.*

Every word of it in Merilee's cramped handwriting.

Could there be any doubt she was the author?

Could I deny the fact that she'd had fifty years to copy the manuscript, word for word, and in her own hand?

The question hurled me firmly back to reality and the mystery I found myself embroiled in.

I actually might have had a chance to think about it further if a camera hadn't flashed from over Ella's left shoulder. Automatically, I glanced that way.

Imagine my surprise (or maybe *irritation* was a better word?) when I caught sight of the photographer just as he finished up and ducked into the hallway.

A photographer who looked a whole bunch like Dan Callahan.

"Excuse me," I told Ella, and honestly, I don't know if she heard me or not. Because I was already on my way to the door when I said it.

When I got there, I had to sidestep through the crowd, and after that, I had to elbow my way through the press of people in the entryway, and when I made my way through that bunch, I was forced to sidle around the gawkers, the reenactors, and the neighborhood busybodies who hadn't been invited to the event and were milling around on the front porch.

Is it any surprise that by the time I clumped down the stairs and into the front yard, the Dan who might not be Dan (but maybe he was) was nowhere to be seen?

There's only so much any woman can take and still hold on to her sanity and her rationality. Believe me when I say this: I had reached that point. Okay, so it took me a while. But hey, I'd been preoccupied.

I was still preoccupied, what with talk of me wearing a ball gown and thoughts of Weird Bob the camera thief in my bedroom, and, oh yes, the mystery I was supposed to be solving.

But all that aside, I was also now officially and completely pissed.

It was a good thing I'd never had a chance to set down my purse when I walked into the house. My car keys were handy, and I didn't hesitate. I jumped into the Mustang, turned the key, and gunned the engine.

I wanted answers and I wanted them now. Bound and determined to find them, I headed to the other side of town and to the hospital where I'd first bumped into Dan the Brain Man.

"Dan, did you say? Dan Callahan?"

Dr. Cecilia Cho had changed little since the day I smacked my head on Gus Scarpetti's mausoleum and woke up in the ER to find her peering down at me, stethoscope in hand. She was still dressed in scrubs decorated with little pastel butterflies. She was still wearing glasses, and her dark hair, of course, was still shot through with gray.

But the day of the accident that had spelled the beginning of the end of my life as I knew it, and the end of the beginning of my Gift, Dr. Cho had struck me as professional, take charge, and competent.

Now as I sat across her desk from her, all she did was look confused.

"I'm not sure who you're talking about," she said.

I blubbered for a moment, and who could blame me? Of all people, I had expected Dr. Cho to provide me with clear and logical answers. Faced with her uncertainty, I found it hard to put together a coherent thought, much less a lucid sentence. "But you've got to . . . You must know Dan," I stammered. "This is where I met him. In the ER. He came into the examining room to check my head X-rays and my CAT scans. Not that first day I was here. Not the day of the accident. It was a few days later. When I came back to see you. You must have a record of the fact that I came back to see you."

Dr. Cho checked the notes in the file folder that was open on the desk in front of her. "You were having trouble sleeping," she said. "And you were exhibiting some strange behaviors. You talked about hallucinations."

It was the day after I'd first met Gus, and at the time, I was desperate to prove to myself that he was nothing more than a brain blip.

These days, I knew better.

"I did," I told the doctor. "Talk about hallucinations, that is. But I didn't. Hallucinate, I mean. And I know I didn't hallucinate Dan. Dan Callahan, PhD. That's what his hospital ID tag said. Cute guy. Really." Thinking about the last time I saw Dan and the way he had appeared out of nowhere, saved my life, and kissed me goodbye, my cheeks shot through with heat. "I wasn't imagining things."

"If you say so." Dr. Cho grabbed a pen and made another note in my file.

From where I was sitting, I couldn't see what she'd written.

"So tell me, Pepper . . ." She tapped her pen against the paper. "When this . . ." She consulted the file again. "When this Dan Callahan stepped into the examining room to talk to you, was I here, too?"

I thought back to that afternoon. "You'd just walked out," I told her. "You must have passed right by him in the hallway. You couldn't have missed him. Shaggy hair. Wire-rimmed glasses." I thought about Dan's fashion sense. Or more accurately, lack of it.

"He always looked like he got dressed with his

eyes closed. You know, navy pants, brown shirt. That sort of thing. And he was smart. Really smart. There are more diplomas hanging on the wall of his office than I've ever seen anywhere and—" In the middle of this logical recounting of the whole mystery that was Dan, my stomach flipped. I took a good, hard look at Dr. Cho.

"Do you think I'm crazy?"

She laughed. It wasn't exactly a silvery sound, but then I wasn't exactly in the mood to be humored. "Of course that's not what I'm saying. We can't possibly know that. Not with any certainty. Not from just what you've told me here today."

"But I didn't imagine him, Dr. Cho." I was whining, and I knew whining made me sound desperate. I told myself to get my shit together and raised my chin, giving Dr. Cho as sane and reasonable a look as a woman who talks to the dead could muster. "I saw Dan. I talked to him. We went out for a drink together, and he walked me home. He called me on the phone and left messages at my office more than once."

He wasn't a ghost, either.

I'll admit it, the possibility of Dan being from "over there" had occurred to me ever since the day he started showing up out of nowhere and vanishing again just as quickly. Then, as now, I dismissed it. Ghosts were incorporeal. They couldn't touch things. They couldn't move things. They couldn't talk to people.

Any people except me.

But to stick to the point . . . I'd seen Dan do all those things. When we went out for drinks together, he'd talked to our waitress. When we met for coffee, he'd gone up to the counter to order my latte. When a hit man had me in his sights and was all set to blow me to smithereens, it was Dan who'd knocked him out with a roundhouse kick and a couple of slick karate moves.

And unlike the time Gus had tried to grab my arm to keep me from walking into the path of an oncoming car, I didn't freeze up like a Sno-Kone when Dan touched me. And certainly not when he kissed me.

Oh no. When Dan kissed me, chilly had nothing to do with my reaction.

"I know Dan is real," I told Dr. Cho, letting her think I was talking about delusions because it was better than explaining about the ghosts. "Like I told you when I walked in here, I keep seeing him around. That proves it, doesn't it?"

"Does it?" Dr. Cho tapped a stack of papers into a neat pile. "I have no doubt you believe what you're telling me, Pepper. Yet if that's so, I've got to wonder why you're here asking about Dan. Could it be that in spite of the fact that you're trying to sound so certain, you're really doubting yourself? That you're looking for confirmation?"

I answered without hesitation. "No. I'm sure I've seen Dan." (I wasn't, not exactly, but this wasn't the time to quibble.) "I'm sure I met him here in the hospital. I even came back a couple of weeks later so that I could participate in that study of his."

"He's conducting research?" Dr. Cho took another note. "Here at the hospital? I don't suppose you can tell me what he's studying?"

"Of course I can. Aberrant behavior and occipital lobes. My high propensity for hallucinatory imaging and—"

I knew I'd stepped in it, but it was too late to call the words back.

Dr. Cho nodded knowingly. "The fact that you've been here twice since your accident is a sign, Pepper," she said.

"It is?"

"Whether you realize it or not, it's a cry for help."

"But I don't need any. Help, that is."

"Are you sure?"

"Look . . ." My frustration was building along with my temper. I scraped a hand through my hair. "I'm not looking to have my head shrunk or anything. So as much as I appreciate your concern, thanks but no thanks. All I need is for you to tell me where to find Dan. This little game of hide-and-seek he's playing is pissing me off and—"

"Have you always had these anger issues?"

"I don't have anger issues!" My protest would have been a little more convincing if I hadn't pounded my fist on the desk to emphasize my point. "The only issues I have are Dan issues."

"And there's only one way I can help you with those." Dr. Cho opened the top drawer of her desk and took out a planning calendar. "We can't possibly know for certain what's going on with you, Pepper, without a battery of tests. They're pretty thorough, not to mention exhausting. Depending on what your health insurer will allow, I'd suggest you stay two nights, and it looks like we can fit you in next week. Let's just schedule it right now, why don't we? This way, we can get everything out of the way, and you won't have to keep coming back."

"For—?"

Dr. Cho reached into another drawer and took out a brochure. She slid the slick paper with its colorful pictures across the desk to me. "It's not nearly as scary as it sounds," she said. "See. Here are some pictures. You'll feel like you're on vacation. Our psychiatric facility is very homey."

"Oh no!" I leaped out of the chair and away from her and the ridiculous (not to mention terrifying) suggestion. "I don't need to be poked and prodded and analyzed. All I need . . ."

All I needed was all I needed all along: to find Dan, and it was clear that Dr. Cho wasn't going to be any help. Without bothering to finish the sentence, I raced to the door and hightailed it out of the ER.

But I didn't leave the hospital.

Just inside the wide revolving door that led to the parking garage, I paused and looked behind me. No little men in white coats. No Dr. Cho. Satisfied that at least for now I wasn't headed for the loony bin, I got my bearings and thought back to the times I'd met Dan at his office. I knew that if I crossed the lobby and went upstairs at the next bank of elevators . . .

Before I knew it, I was standing outside Dan's office.

There was no one around, and when I knocked on Dan's door, no one answered. I turned the knob.

The door opened easily, but not all the way, and I tried again, bumping the door with my hip. When that didn't work, I mumbled a curse, reached around the door, and felt along the office wall for a light switch. With the light on, I could peek inside and see what was holding things up.

What was holding things up was a bucket and a mop. The big, industrial-strength kind.

Weird?

I thought so. After all, the last time I'd been here, Dan's desk was along one wall, and another was filled just about floor to ceiling with diplomas. There was a credenza behind his desk where he kept the file folders for his study. And in front of his desk, the chair where I'd sat the day I came in and he hooked me up to some machine that measured brain waves and proved—at least to Dan—something about that whole high-propensity-for-hallucinatory-imaging thing.

And now . . .

I pushed the bucket and mop out of the way and stepped into the room.

The desk and credenza were gone. Instead of the bookcases that should have taken up most of the wall on my left, there were metal shelves. They were filled with cleaning products, rolls of paper towels, boxes of latex gloves.

"Can I help you, please?"

The voice from behind me brought me spinning around. I found myself nose to nose with a young guy in gray pants and a matching shirt. His name badge said he was Jose and part of the housekeeping staff.

"No, thanks. Really." I stepped across the bare cement floor and back into the hallway. "I was just looking for Dan. You know, Dan Callahan. This was his office. I mean, before they turned it into a utility room."

Jose shook his head. "You're lost maybe? This is the room where we store things. You know, soap and such."

"Yeah, I know. I saw. But . . ." I took another look around just to be sure. "I know I'm in the right place. I've been here before. Why just a couple of weeks ago—"

Jose scratched a finger behind one ear. "I have worked here six months," he said. "And for six months, this is where I come to get my mops and my brooms. This is where I put them away when I am done with them. You are mistaken, I think, senorita."

I was almost afraid to ask the question and it almost didn't make it past my lips, anyway. My mouth was suddenly dry. My voice was tight in my throat. "And Dan?" I asked.

Jose shrugged. "Callahan, you say? Nobody named Dan Callahan ever worked anywhere around here."

Chapter 15

So, was I crazy?

Hell, no.

At least not in the way Dr. Cho thought I was crazy.

Utility room or no utility room, I knew what I knew, and propensity for hallucinatory imaging aside, I knew that Dan Callahan was not a figment of my imagination.

No figment could possibly be as good a kisser as Dan.

My mind made up, I decided I'd deal with him the next time he stuck his cute little nose into my not-so-cute little business, and I put the problem of Dan on the back burner. There seemed no better way to prove my sanity than to get back to work and accomplish something.

But like I said, I wasn't crazy. When I talked about accomplishments, I didn't have Merilee's gala invitations in mind. Or even trying on the gown Ella had brought me to wear to the event. (Though I will admit to being curious about the dress and a little worried, too, since Trish was originally supposed to wear it and Trish was . . .

well, I didn't want to speak unkindly of the dead, but let's face it, Trish was not exactly a role model for the fashion conscious.)

When I said *accomplish*, I was talking about solving Didi's mystery.

With that in mind, I was determined to make the most of the afternoon. Lucky for me, there were plenty of phone books near the pay phones in the hospital lobby. Even luckier, Susan Gwitkowski had never changed her name.

I jotted down her address, but I didn't call and ask if I could stop by. If I'd learned anything from my association with the local mob, it was that there was a certain value in catching people off guard. After all, Susan Gwitkowski must have been just about the same age as Didi, and if Didi were still alive . . .

I did a couple of quick mathematical calculations.

The woman I was going to talk to was by now a little old lady, and believe me, after dealing with two fussy grandmothers and the countless senior citizens groups that came through Garden View on tours, I knew all about little old ladies. I didn't want her to have too much time to think about the past and realign her memories. Better to shake her up a little and see what fell out. About Didi. About swimming upstream in the steno pool. Oh yeah, and about fifty-year-old office gossip, too.

Did I say *little old lady*?

The woman who answered the door of a grand old mansion with turrets, a slate roof, and leaded glass windows that winked at me in the afternoon sunlight was short and slim, and her hair was curly and cut stylishly short. No way was the mahogany color real, but hey, I had to give her credit for trying. She was clad in leopard-skin capris and a skin-tight black shirt, and the whole presentation was accented by her gold lamé sandals and the gold that glittered from the dozens of chains around her neck. They skimmed breasts that weren't anywhere near as lush but were certainly as perky as mine.

I couldn't help myself. I wondered if she was one of my dad's patients.

"I'm sorry to bother you." Even if she didn't look old, I figured Susan would appreciate a show of old-fashioned manners. "I wonder if I might talk to you for a minute."

She looked me up and down. "About . . . ?"

"Well, it's kind of awkward. You see, it's about Deborah Bowman."

"Didi?" The name was the magic open sesame. Susan loosened her grip on the front door and stepped back to let me inside. "Nobody's mentioned Didi's name to me in a long time. Come on in, honey. Have a seat."

She led me into a living room that was twice as big as my apartment, with windows that overlooked a garden where red and white tulips bobbed in the spring breeze. The last of the daffodils brightened up the spaces between lilacs that looked like they were ready to pop.

"It's beautiful," I told her, and I wasn't lying. What I could see of the garden was breathtaking. The house itself . . .

I tried not to stare, but let's face it, I'd never been

known for my self-control. Susan's living room was a cross between a Pier 1 store and a cheap bordello. There was purple gauzy fabric draped across the windows and mosquito netting over the bloodred fainting couch where I sat down. There were sequined pillows on the matching couch across from me, candles everywhere, and incense burning on a nearby table.

It smelled like pine needles.

I sneezed.

"This place is amazing," I told Susan, because I figured *amazing* pretty much covered the gamut. I touched a tissue to my nose. "You must have done really well for yourself in the steno pool."

Until then she had been giving me the kind of hollow smile that said she really didn't understand why I was there. The smile never wavered, but there was suddenly a spark of something more than just curiosity in Susan's dark eyes. "Wise investing," she said, and I could tell from the tone of her voice that it was the last we'd talk about it. She dropped down onto the couch across from mine, and her perfectly plucked and shaped brows dipped into a vee. "You said something about Didi. You're not—"

"Related?" For the second time, I denied any familial connection to the Bowmans. "Not me. But you know, she did have a daughter."

"Judy." Susan reached for a pack of cigarettes and the gold lighter within easy reach. She lit a cigarette, took a drag, and sat back. "I know her, all right. I ought to. I raised the little bitch."

This was news to me, and I could have kicked myself for not thinking about it sooner. Any private investigator worth his (or her) weight in salt would have thought to ask what had happened to Judy after Didi's death. "I just assumed that Merilee had—"

"You're kidding me, right?" Susan blew out a stream of smoke along with the words. "When Didi got knocked up, her family just about disowned her. They didn't want anything to do with Judy. What's she up to these days?"

I wasn't sure if she was talking about Didi or Judy. Then I realized it didn't matter. My answer applied to both. "She's dead," I said.

"Is she?" Susan didn't look particularly upset by the news. "Haven't heard a word from Judy since the day she turned eighteen. Do the math. That was a hell of a long time ago. She up and walked out of here and that was that." She stabbed her cigarette into an ashtray shaped like a camel. "And after all I did for that girl."

"Then you don't know she had a daughter."

Susan lifted one shoulder. "Don't know. Don't care. Hey . . . You didn't show up here because you expect me to be responsible for her or anything, do you? Why don't you ask Merilee for help?" On the coffee table draped with a paisley shawl was a copy of the morning's *Plain Dealer,* and Susan sneered at it and at the story on the front page. I craned my neck to see the headline. SO FAR THE DAWN MUSEUM SET TO OPEN.

"With all her money, you think she could have done something for the kid. But no. Didi dumped Judy with me the night she . . . Well, you must know the story if you know about Didi. That was that. Never talked to any of the Bowmans again. I applied for legal guardianship of Judy and nobody opposed me. Nobody ever sent me a red cent to pay for her care or her education, either. And what did it get me? Nothing but grief. That girl was just like her mother. A liar and a tramp."

"But I thought you were Didi's friend?"

"Did you?" Susan studied me through the haze of cigarette smoke that hung in the air between us. "Who told you that?"

"I talked to Thomas Ross Howell." Not a lie, even if it wasn't exactly an answer to Susan's question. "Was he Judy's father?"

She barked out a laugh. "I worked for Tom Howell for nearly forty years, and if there's one thing I know about the son of a bitch it's that he'd never bare his soul. Not to friends. Not to family. And certainly not to a stranger. Not even a pretty one like you. No way did he admit he was Judy's father."

"But you always thought it was a possibility."

"Why do you care?" She lit another cigarette. "And what difference does any of it make now? Didi's been dead for fifty years. You say that Judy's dead, too. You trying to foist Didi's granddaughter off on Howell?"

"I'm not trying to foist anybody on anybody. I'm trying to find out more about the book."

At the mention of the word *book*, Susan froze. One heartbeat. Two. I shifted uncomfortably against the hard-as-nails couch and wondered what I'd said to offend her. Before I could come up with the right words to apologize, she shook herself free of the reaction and aimed a laser look across the coffee table at me. "You are talking about *So Far the Dawn,* aren't you?"

"As far as I know, there is no other book." Not precisely true. There was the sequel (such as it was) that Merilee was working on. I didn't want to muddy the waters with all that, so I stuck to the subject.

"Yeah," I told her. "I'm talking about *So Far the Dawn*. I think maybe Didi wrote it."

Susan paused as she was about to take a drag on her cigarette, the filter just barely touching her carmine lips. She tipped her head to one side. "Really? You think that? Than you're as stupid as I was. Because there was a time I thought she wrote it, too."

"Then why didn't you say anything?"

"I said *a time*. Believe me, it was a very short time. Didi used to show up at work every morning all excited about what she'd written the night before. We'd sit in the lunchroom together and she'd give me the play-by-play, you know, tell me what was happening in the story and what she planned to do next."

"So when the book came out and Merilee's name was on it . . ."

She took a drag on her cigarette and exhaled a long stream of smoke. "I used to hang out with Didi a lot back then. Even had dinner with her family a time or two. I met Merilee. I knew she was a librarian. I listened to her talk about the Civil War and, hell, I didn't know anything about it, but I could tell she sure knew what she was talking about. So tell me, who would you have believed. A scholar like Merilee? Or a tramp like Didi?"

"And she'd lied to you before."

"All day long and twice on Sundays." Susan laughed. "Not that I held it against her or anything. It was just Didi, you know? She had a heart of gold and an imagination that wouldn't quit."

"Is that why she thought Thomas Howell was in love with her?"

Susan set her cigarette on the lip of the ashtray. Right near the camel's butt. "I'm not sure where you're getting your ideas," she said. "You keep coming back to Judge Howell, and what I don't think you understand is that he was—and is—a good and honorable man. His record is impeccable. His reputation is unassailable."

"I understand all that. But Judy had to come from somewhere."

Susan grinned. "How about from anywhere?"

"Meaning . . ."

The phone rang, and Susan popped up to answer it, grumbling when she couldn't find it anywhere nearby. She headed out of the living room. "Come on now, honey. You're old enough to know what I'm talking about. Didi had plenty of lovers. Any one of them could have been Judy's father. Excuse me, will you."

She must have found the phone somewhere because the ringing stopped, and as I sat there and wondered what to ask her next, I heard the purr of her voice.

"Psst." The sound came from across the room. I looked that way and found Didi standing in the doorway.

"Where the hell have you been?" I asked her. I popped out of my chair and went to stand close to her so I could whisper. "And what are you doing over there? Get in here and help me out. Susan isn't giving me anything to go on."

"Wanna bet?" Didi crooked a finger at me. I could still hear Susan's voice from another room somewhere toward the back of the house. The coast was clear, and I followed Didi.

I found myself in the library. There were windows along one wall and a desk in front of them. Didi looked that way.

"Take a gander at that," she said.

I hesitated. "I can't just go snooping through another person's things."

"Sure you can." She was in her social call gear, and she marched over to the desk and pointed at it with one gloved hand. "If there's something in that person's things that's a thing that doesn't belong to that person."

Rather than try and figure out the sense of the sentence, I went over to see what she was talking about.

An address book sat in the center of Susan's desk next to a stack of unaddressed envelopes. Like she'd just been getting ready to use it.

The book was small, maybe eight inches tall and half as wide. The cover was black, and it was bent and worn. No doubt it was pretty old.

"This is what you wanted me to see?" I could still hear Susan on the phone, so I dared a closer look at the book. "It's junk."

"It's mine."

Maybe the sneer I aimed Didi's way told her I wasn't exactly buying the story.

"Go ahead," she said. "Open it. You'll see.

Check the inside cover. My name and address are written there along with the words *This book belongs to Didi*."

I did.

It did.

"If you need more proof than that," Didi added, "I bet I can recite every name in the book, too. Look for Anderson, James. Antonucci, Tony. Barkwill, David."

Rather than listen to her go through the whole list, I flipped through the pages. There were James and Tony and David, just like she said.

"So why would Susan have your address book?" I asked Didi. "Why did she ever have it? And why would she still have it? What is she doing with—"

"What difference does it make?" With the wave of one hand, Didi urged me to get moving. "Just take it! Quick! Before Susan gets back."

My eyes widened with horror. My stomach clenched. Being a private investigator was one thing. But burglary . . .

"Oh come on, Pepper," Didi hissed. "I'd take it myself if I could, but you know I can't. You're the only one who can do this for me. Somewhere along the line, Susan must have lifted it out of my desk drawer at work because that's where I kept it. It's not like you're stealing anything."

"But she'll know I took it."

"So?" We heard what sounded like Susan getting ready to wind up her conversation, and both Didi and I looked at the door. "It's mine," Didi said. "I want it back."

"But—"

"But think about it. There must be a reason she

has the address book. A reason she *still* has it. It doesn't look like she's kept it as a memento. If she did, it would be on a shelf or packed away in a box or something. It's out on her desk. She's using it. That's not just coincidence. You know that and I know that. There has to be a reason, and the reason has to have something to do with me. I have every right to find out what that reason is, and that means you have every right to take the book so we can look through it later and figure out what Susan's up to."

I may have mentioned that I hate it when ghosts are right. I hate it even more when them being right results in me being a felon.

Was it any wonder I hesitated?

"I dunno," I said, and I probably would have gone right on hemming and hawing if not for the fact that I heard Susan say goodbye to the person on the other end of the phone.

"Sorry!" Her cheery voice echoed through the hallway. "Had to take that call. I'll be right with you."

I'd just run out of shilly-shally time.

When I took the book and tucked it into my purse, my hands shook. When I hurried back to the living room, my legs were rubbery. By the time Susan showed up, I was right back where she'd seen me last, sitting on the couch. The moment she was in the door, I jumped to my feet.

"I've taken up enough of your time," I said, and when I realized I was clutching my purse with both hands and looking as guilty as hell because of it, I slung the purse over my shoulder and headed for the door. "You really have been a great deal of help."

"But I really haven't." Susan followed me, and when we got to the front door, she opened it and stepped aside. "Something tells me you wanted to hear me say that I think Didi wrote *So Far the Dawn*. I'm sorry. I wish I could. Heck, back when Judy was living with me, I used to dream that I'd find something that proved Didi hadn't been lying, that she really was the author. That way, Judy could have gotten all the royalties and she would have had enough money to get the hell out of here."

As sentiments went, hers had all the warmth of a January day on the shores of Lake Erie. I shook off the bad vibes and stepped into the afternoon sunshine. "I understand," I said, even though all I really understood was that Susan was selfish. "But, really, you've helped more than you can imagine."

Before she realized that *more than you can imagine* really meant that I had swiped the address book and that I was deceptive, a fibber, and a burglar to boot, I hightailed it out of there.

I was halfway back to Ohio City before my heartbeat slowed to a rate that was almost normal, and that's when it hit me:

The trip to Susan's wasn't completely wasted. I had something I hadn't had before.

I mean, aside from a guilty conscience.

I had a sample of Didi's handwriting.

What's that saying about all work and no play?

In my case, it was more like all work and all work. I'd spent the day working at solving Didi's case, and as much as I would have liked to hunker down with the purloined address book and figure out what it meant and if it had anything to do with *So Far the Dawn*, I didn't have the luxury.

I walked into the house and straight into Merilee's why-aren't-you-done-doing-what-you're-supposed-to-be-doing wrath.

I spent the rest of the afternoon, all of the evening, and most of the night addressing gala invitations.

By the time midnight rolled around, I was almost done. But as tempting as it was to think of finally finishing, my hand was cramped and my right arm ached. I couldn't write another name or address. I dragged myself to bed, but though I was dog-tired, I couldn't sleep.

Oh, it's not that I didn't try.

It's just that I kept getting woken up by noises that sounded like they came from somewhere above my head.

Like somebody was up in the attic poking around.

I finally dropped off to sleep somewhere around three, and by the next morning when I woke up, I'd convinced myself that I'd imagined the noises.

The dark circles around my eyes told me otherwise.

I was in no shape to look through Didi's address book because if I did that, I'd have to read. And my eyes were too red and too tired for that. If I took on the address book, I'd also have to think. And no way that was going to happen, at least not until I had a couple of gallons of coffee in me and a few hours to get my act together and my head back in the game.

Until then, it was time to satisfy my curiosity. If I had to attend the damned gala, I was entitled to know what I'd be wearing.

Just as Ella promised, the gown was hanging in my closet. I unzipped the bag it came in and peeked inside.

It goes without saying that I am not easily impressed.

Call it inherent good taste. Or maybe it's just the last traces of my upbringing. When you have plenty of money to spare, it's hard not to expect the best and be disappointed by anything but.

Which explains why when I finally saw the dress, I fully expected to turn my nose up.

Big surprise.

At first sight of the dress, my breath caught. When I touched it, my skin tingled and my heart raced.

Eager for a better look, I stripped the bag off and held the gown at arm's length, checking out the golden silk, the wide skirt, the heavy, cream-colored lace at the low-cut neckline and elbow-length sleeves.

Except for my wedding gown (which really didn't count since I ended up not having a wedding and so never wore it), the gala gown was the most beautiful dress I'd ever owned. I couldn't help myself; I knew the hand of Fashion Fate had been at work when Trish died. In the dress, she would have looked like a broomstick that had been all dolled up.

Me? I was going to look like a princess.

I couldn't wait to prove it, so I yanked my T-shirt over my head and stepped out of my lounge pants. It wasn't until I had the gown off the padded hanger that I realized it wasn't the only thing in the bag. There were also a crinoline hoop and a petticoat.

Oh yeah, and a corset.

I eyed the weird undergarments suspiciously, but facts were facts and there was no denying that thanks to the size of my bustline, if I was going to get the gown to fit, I'd have to wear the corset.

I grumbled, but I suppose in the great scheme of things, my brush with old-fashioned undergarments wasn't a total waste of time. After all, Quinn had mentioned that he thought corsets were sexy, and since I was all about appealing to his sense of sexy . . .

I slapped the corset on and fastened the straps and buckles along the front of it.

The laces at the back were another matter.

I reached behind me, grabbing for the laces and tugging them as best I could, and appreciating—not for the first time, I might add—how nice it would be to have a servant. No wonder that back in the day, women had lady's maids. The angle was all wrong. I could have used a little help getting the laces tied.

"Damn," I grumbled, and tried again, grappling with the laces while I cursed a blue streak.

I guess because of all that cursing, I didn't hear my bedroom door creak open.

I suppose because I was so busy concentrating on the laces, I didn't realize that someone had come up behind me.

Not until it was too late, anyway.

A hand went around my neck, and I let out a screech of surprise that was muffled by the wall where I found myself with my nose mashed against the tattered wallpaper. I twisted and turned. Or at least I tried. But the grip around my neck was impossible to shake off. There was no way I could see who had a hold on me.

I kicked and squirmed. I grunted and threw an elbow that connected with nothing but thin air, so busy fighting that it took a moment or two to realize that suddenly it was getting harder to breathe.

The reason hit, and I froze in horror.

Crucial mistake.

While I was busy panicking, my assailant got the upper hand. The laces on the corset tugged and tightened.

And ever so slowly, the air was squeezed out of me.

Chapter 16

"*Pepper!*"

The way I figured it, my assailant must have succeeded. I was a goner.

Me being good and dead, that was the only thing that would explain why I heard Quinn's voice calling me.

At the same time I decided to go with the flow and see where the concept of heaven took me in regards to the city's yummiest Homicide detective, I reminded myself that the dead (or at least the ones I was personally acquainted with) couldn't make use of their bodies.

Which meant that the paradise I thought of when I thought of Quinn wouldn't exactly work.

Call me shallow, but it was enough to make me realize I wasn't ready to die. At least not until I lived long enough to find out if when it came to Quinn, *heavenly* meant a whole lot more than angel wings.

"*Pepper!*"

I heard his voice again, I swear I did. It sounded like it came from far away, and hey, maybe I was limp, trounced, and unable to breathe, but I knew that in my current predicament, far away wasn't going to do me any good.

The sounds of footsteps pounding up the stairs, though, did.

As suddenly as it started, the attack stopped. My assailant let go, turned, and scrambled out of my room.

And me?

I did what any sensible woman would do in the same situation. I collapsed on the floor, sobbing.

That's exactly where Quinn found me when he raced into my room. He dropped down on the floor next to where I lay and gathered me in his arms.

Was I talking heaven?

If I wasn't before, I sure would have been then. It felt heavenly to have him hold me.

And being able to breathe again was a big plus, too.

"What the hell—?" He looked away from me long enough to shoot a look around the room, and I guess he didn't see anything unusual because he looked right back at me again. "What the hell happened here?"

"I don't—" My words staggered along with my jerky respiration. When Quinn propped one arm around my shoulders, I sat up and gulped in breath after precious breath. "Somebody came up behind me." I managed the words between gulps. "I was trying on—"

I guess I didn't need to point out what I was trying on. One look at the way Quinn's eyes widened, and I knew he was taking a gander at the corset and at my breasts where they showed just above the lacy edging. I also knew it wasn't easy for him to pull his gaze away. Big points for him (and tough luck for me), he kept his head and his professional distance.

"Just like Trish."

Talk about insult to injury! My spine stiffened, and I pegged him with a look that told him my pride was hurt along with my ribs.

He rolled his eyes. "I didn't mean the way you look in that thing. I meant the attack. It's exactly what happened to Trish."

"That doesn't make me feel a whole lot better."

"It's not supposed to." He stood and offered me a hand up. I'm not exactly sure how I managed since my legs were mush, but I got to my feet. I turned my back to Quinn, and he knew what I wanted. He loosened the laces on the corset, and I breathed a sigh of relief.

When he was done, Quinn tossed me my T-shirt. "Who was it?" he asked.

I shrugged. Which he didn't see since I was pulling my T-shirt over my head at the time. "I dunno," I said as I poked my head out of the neck hole. "My back was turned. It could have been anybody."

"Anybody with the strength to overpower you."

"Which means what, I'm a candidate for the Women's World Professional Wrestling League?"

"You're not exactly a small woman." He was talking about my height and maybe about my bra size, but let's face it, I had just had a near-death experience. I wasn't exactly thinking straight. Because it seemed a better option than breaking down in tears, I chose to be offended.

"My dress size has nothing to do with—"

"You're right. It doesn't." He tossed me my lounge pants, but I wasn't in the mood to slip them on. I bunched them on my lap and watched while he yanked his cell phone off his belt, hit the walkie-talkie button, and asked for uniformed backup to search the house for my attacker. That taken care of, he dropped down on the bed beside me.

"So what are you up to?" he asked.

"I guess I'm up to being a plus-size woman."

The look he gave me simmered with impatience. "That's not what I meant and you know it."

I crossed my arms over my chest. "It's what you said."

"I'm sorry. All right?"

He didn't sound sorry. I let him know it by looking away.

Quinn rose to his feet. "Let's try this again, okay? From the top. I stopped in to ask Merilee a couple more questions about Trish. Just to double-check my facts. And no sooner am I in the front door than I hear the sounds of a scuffle from up here. And you. Grunting and groaning and swearing like a sailor."

Was I?

Grunting and groaning and swearing, that is?

It was so not attractive; it made me cringe. Unfortunately, I couldn't discount the possibility. Getting nearly crushed to death was all the excuse I needed.

"I came up here and found you . . . well, I'm not exactly sure what happened but I'm going to go out on a limb here and say that the person who killed Trish also attacked you."

"Looks that way." I plucked at the lounge pants.

"You want to tell me why?"

I couldn't. Not exactly.

Number one, because I didn't know.

Number two—and more importantly—because I couldn't get into the whole thing about how I was working for a ghost who might (or might not) have written a famous book and how the fact that I was investigating the possibility that she might (or might not) have written the book might (or might not) have had something to do with someone pushing a wardrobe over on me, a photographer getting mugged at the cemetery where I worked when I wasn't working at the local version of the Bates Motel, and me getting squeezed like a Florida orange headed for the juice carton.

"I don't know why," I told Quinn. It was easier that way.

For a minute, I thought he was going to buy into the whole thing, too. That's how long it took him before his patience gave way.

"You expect me to believe that?" His question echoed through my pitifully small room. "You really expect me to believe—"

"I don't know what you believe. I only know that I don't know what happened. You asked why someone would want to—" It wasn't easy to say the words, but I choked them out anyway. Just so he'd know that I wasn't a weenie. "I don't know why someone would want to kill me the way they killed Trish. It doesn't make any sense. I haven't done anything."

"Just like you didn't do anything the last time someone tried to kill you."

I didn't have to ask what he was talking about. For all Quinn knew, my close encounter with the wardrobe in the attic was an accident. Which meant he had to be talking about Albert, the muscle-bound punk who'd visited my apartment when I was working Gus's case.

"You did save my life that time. And this time. I appreciate it."

A muscle twitched at the base of his jaw. "And you're going to show your appreciation by stonewalling me."

It wasn't a question, so I was not technically obliged to answer. "I'm not stonewalling," I told him anyway. After all, I owed him. Because of the whole saving-my-life thing. "I can't tell you what I don't know."

"And you don't know why anyone would want to jump you."

"I don't know why anyone would want to jump me." I managed to look him in the eye as I delivered this out-and-out lie. "Unless, of course, it was you. But then, if it was you, I don't think that's exactly the kind of jumping on we'd be talking about."

"You're not going to distract me."

"I wasn't trying," I said, because of course I was, and I wasn't going to admit that I wasn't succeeding. "I'm just saying that if you wanted to jump my bones—"

"Which I'm planning on doing one of these days if you'd ever not be in mortal danger long enough for me to have a chance."

"Then maybe—"

"Then maybe, nothing." When I made a move in his direction, Quinn moved to the door. "I'll tell you what, Pepper, I'll give you some time to think about this whole thing. Maybe if you're willing to let me in—"

I looked around my bedroom and lowered my voice. "You're already in, Detective."

"That's not what I mean and you know it."

Outside, I heard a car pull up to the front of the house. I had no doubt it was the black-and-white Quinn had called for backup.

"You want to talk, let me know," he said. "If not, then I guess I've been getting the wrong signals all along."

"But—"

He held up one hand to stop my protest, and it was just as well. I wasn't being honest with him.

Except for the whole bit about wanting him to jump my bones.

The doorbell rang, and Quinn headed out into the hallway. "I'll tell you what," he said. "I'm going to be at that gala of yours. Not that I want to be, but my lieutenant, she figures it's an opportunity for me to ask some questions, talk to some people. Maybe get some answers and finally make sense of what's going on here. You want to talk . . ." The downstairs door opened, and he called to the uniform officers and told one of them to come up and take my statement.

"Save a dance for me," he said.

But before I could tell him that I would—even if I wouldn't be talking—Quinn was gone.

"Just the way he looks at you practically makes me melt like an ice cube in the sunshine."

Not only didn't I know Didi was in my room, I

didn't know how she knew who I was thinking about.

I closed the copy of *So Far the Dawn* I wasn't reading because I was too busy daydreaming (even though it was night) about Quinn.

"You saw him come up here this morning."

Didi was in her pajamas and had a towel wound like a turban around her head. There was green, gooey facial mask spread over her cheeks, nose, chin, and forehead. She nodded, and she didn't even look embarrassed at being caught eavesdropping.

Another thought occurred to me. "If you were here, then you must have seen who attacked me."

"Sorry." She wrinkled her nose, and the goo glistened in the light. "I didn't show up until I heard all the noise, and by then it was too late. I knew something was wrong, and then I saw that cop . . ." She shivered. "He's Tab Hunter handsome."

I didn't know who Tab Hunter was. I didn't care.

"Quinn is gorgeous, all right," I told her. "He's also royally pissed at me."

"Because you won't tell him about your investigation. Or about my book."

"I can't tell him about the book. Not without telling him about you. I can't tell him about how I think someone's been snooping around in the attic. Or about Weird Bob and how he had a camera that belongs to the photographer back at the cemetery. Mostly I can't tell him why someone wants to kill me because I don't know why someone wants to kill me."

"Unless we're close to finding out something someone doesn't want us to know."

I didn't have to ask what she was talking about. As if we'd choreographed the move, we both looked at my purse.

"Your little black book," I said, and even before the words were out of my mouth, I was reaching for it.

Away from Susan's sumptuous library with its paneled walls and plush carpeting, the book looked older and more tattered than ever. Carefully, I opened it.

"You knew the names," I said, reminding Didi of the way she'd recited them back at Susan's. "You said—"

"Anderson, James. Antonucci, Tony. Barkwill, David." Didi went through the beginning of the alphabetical list again.

"Who are those guys?"

"They were my boyfriends."

I flipped through the pages. Except for K, Q, and Z, the other sections all had names, addresses, and phone numbers listed in them. Maybe thirty of them total. My eyes went wide. "All of them?" I asked.

I guess the question must have sounded a little harsh because Didi's shoulders shot back. "You want me to apologize?"

"No. Really. It's just . . ." I thought of Ella and the way she liked to preach about women's rights. Back in Didi's day, the concept of that many men in any woman's life must have been pretty shocking. These days, thanks to Ella and her liberated cronies, we were more enlightened.

"What you do . . ." I corrected myself. "What

you did back when you did it is none of my business," I told Didi, and I meant it. "It's not my place to judge and besides . . ." Quickly I thumbed through the book again. "You must have had one hell of a good time!"

She caught herself just before she grinned and messed up the mask, and I got myself back on track. "So why would Susan want an address book filled with the names of your former boyfriends?" I asked her.

While I talked, I paged through the book again. More slowly this time. That's when I realized there was more there than just a simple listing of names. I whistled low under my breath. "I can understand keeping the names and numbers of former lovers," I told Didi, "but I can't believe you had the nerve to have a rating system. Not in writing, anyway."

"What are you talking about?" She looked over my shoulder to where I pointed. Some of the names were marked with stars.

Didi shook her head. "I didn't put those there," she said. "Which means—"

"That Susan did." I took a closer look. "David Barkwill has one. So does somebody named Jack Edwards. There are four or five others with stars, too." One of them was Thomas Ross Howell but I didn't bother to mention him. There was plenty I wanted to know about him, but I was saving that for later. "Why these guys?"

She squinched her eyes shut, thinking hard. "Read the names again."

I did, leaving out Howell completely. "Barkwill, David. Edwards, Jack. Javits, Michael. Paskovitch, Ken. Simpson, Daniel."

"And the ones who don't?"

This list was longer, but I went through it, too.

Didi chewed her lower lip. "Well, I know Jimmy Anderson ended up in the Ohio Penitentiary. Something about stolen cars. And Tony Antonucci . . ." She shivered and hugged her arms around herself. "He was dreamy. Just like that cop of yours. He drove a milk truck."

"And those names don't have stars. And this Daniel Simpson, he has a star, but it's crossed out."

"Dan Simpson died fifteen years ago," Didi said. "Had a heart attack. He was playing golf at his country club."

Listening, I drummed my fingers against the yellowed pages of the book, and maybe it was the rhythm of the clump, clump, clump that got my brain to work. "The guys who do have stars . . ." I thumbed through the pages, finding the names again. "Do you know what became of them?"

Didi nodded. "Dave Barkwill, he owns a big construction company now. He has scads of money. Kenny, he was a banker. Mike Javits, you've probably heard of him. He played professional football for a while. I think he's in the Hall of Fame. And Jack Edwards . . . well, you must recognize that name."

I didn't and told her as much.

"Reverend Jack?" She looked at me in wonder. "He's the televangelist who has that huge church down in Akron. Writes books and appears on TV talk shows and all. Back when I knew him, he was preaching out of an old gas station. The owner was a member of his congregation who let Jack use the place on Sundays."

Even without Howell, I saw the glimmer of light at the end of a very long, dark tunnel. "What you're telling me is that all the guys who have stars are successful, right? They have money."

Didi thought it over, but I didn't have to wait for her to confirm my suspicions. I knew what Susan was up to. "Didi, she's blackmailing them."

"What?"

"It's Susan. She's shaking them down. She knows that you and these guys were lovers all those years ago. She's holding it over their heads."

"No way!" Didi waved away the possibility. "It's been fifty years. Why would she care? Why would they?"

I pointed to the first name. "You tell me. David Barkwill. Why would he care?"

Didi looked up at the ceiling. "Well, he was married. The money for the construction company? It came from her father, and last I checked, Daddy was still alive and kicking. He was a mean old son of a gun even back then. I bet he's still holding on to the purse strings."

"And Reverend Jack?"

Was that the trace of a blush I saw beneath the green goo? Didi looked away before I had a chance to know for sure. "He preached fire and brimstone," she said.

"And you were the hottest number of them all." I looked at the book. "It's true for every one of these guys, isn't it? Every one of them had something to hide then and they don't want that same something to come back and bite them in the ass. Not even now."

"It's possible."

"It's more than possible," I told her. "I'm sure of it. That's why Susan lifted the address book out of your desk. It's how she's parlayed her salary from the steno pool into a fortune. Wise investing!" I remembered what Susan said back at the house. "She's got something on these guys because you told her all about what you did with every single one of them."

"I may have mentioned them," Didi admitted. "You know, the day after our dates. I may have told Susan what happened."

"And she's been living on it ever since." I told myself it was the last time I'd underestimate a little old lady and watched Didi carefully as I spoke. "She's got Howell's name starred, too," I said, but I kept my voice light. Like it was no big deal. "My guess is that's why she defended him so vehemently. She can't afford to let the cat out of the bag when it comes to Howell and ruin a good thing. She must know some secret about him, huh? I mean, to keep a guy as powerful as Howell under her thumb all these years. What do you suppose that secret is, Didi? Does Susan know that Howell was Judy's father? Do you think she suspects that he was the reason you jumped?"

As if my words were slaps, Didi trembled when they slammed into her. But she didn't run and she didn't hide, and I had to give her credit. Running and hiding were two things ghosts were very good at. The fact that she stayed there to face me and my hunches said a lot for Didi.

"We were supposed to meet," she said. "Thomas and I. That night. On the Lorain/Carnegie Bridge. You know, so we could leave town together."

A nighttime meeting. A married man. A hot-to-trot secretary who'd just had his baby.

It didn't sound like the respectable judge I'd met, but that was then and this was now. Then, Howell was young and his career was just starting. If I stretched my imagination, it almost seemed possible. "He was going to leave his family?"

Didi nodded. "We needed a fresh start and we knew we'd never get it here. He had a busy law practice, a reputation, and big dreams. He couldn't afford to jeopardize any of that. And yes, he had a family, too. Judy was only nine months old." Her voice faded, and I knew if I let her slip too deeply into her painful memories, I might never find the answers I was looking for.

"What about Judy?" I asked. "What did Howell think about having another child?"

Didi snapped out of her thoughts. "He was thrilled. He loved her very much. That night, Judy was with Susan. You're right, Susan knew about Thomas. She knew we were going away together. After Thomas and I were settled, we were going to send for Judy. That was the plan. But then . . ."

"But then he never showed up."

Don't ask me how I knew, I just did. It was the only thing that could explain such a sad ending to a situation that seemed to have held such hope. "You waited, right? And the creep never came to meet you."

"It wasn't his fault." Tears scored Didi's facial mask. "It was all because of his wife, Tammy. You

see, she told him that if she ever found out he'd
been unfaithful to her, she'd kill their children and
then she'd kill herself. I know that's what happened. Thomas tried to leave. He wanted to leave.
More than anything, he wanted to be with me and
Judy. But somehow, Tammy found out. And he
couldn't take the chance that she'd hurt the children. Thomas loved them too much. Just like he
loved me."

"He didn't love you enough to come to that
bridge and explain what was going on." No problem with Didi thinking my comment was insensitive. She never even heard me. Her gaze was a little
out of focus. Like she was seeing through me.
Beyond me. Straight back to that painful night.

"It was one of those damp, gray days in March.
Just past dark. The wind was blowing from the
north, right off the lake." She hugged her arms
around herself, and when Didi turned away from
me, then turned back again, she wasn't in her pajamas any more. The green goo was gone, too. She
was dressed in high-heeled pumps and a black
cloth coat that went down to her knees, and she
had a suitcase clutched in her gloved hands. Her
hair was pulled away from her face and tucked
under a small velvet hat perched atop her head. It
was trimmed with feathers that ruffled in the bone-
chilling breeze that suddenly filled my room.

"Whoa!" I protested, but Gift or no Gift, I apparently had no control over what was happening.
The air was suddenly damp against my skin. A
wisp of fog blew by me, and the lights faded.

When they came up again enough for me to take
a look at the scene around me, I realized that—

somehow—I was outside. With Didi. A spectator to a scene that had happened fifty years earlier.

"The street lamps looked like hazy balls of light." Didi's voice was muffled by the fog that swirled around our feet. We were standing on the sidewalk, and when I looked up and down the street, I saw that she was right. The streetlights glowed a ghostly sort of yellow, their light soft around the edges.

"I remember thinking that I should write down the thing about the streetlights and the fog," Didi said. "So I would remember. Because the whole image . . . well, you have to admit, it's pretty good, and I thought that maybe someday I'd use it in a book. I looked through my pockets . . ." She set down her suitcase and did just that, pulling out a hanky and a piece of gum wrapped in foil before she fished out a folded piece of paper. "But I couldn't find a pen so I repeated it to myself over and over. Hazy balls of light. Hazy balls of light. Just so I wouldn't forget."

She stuffed her hands in her pockets and walked back and forth beside a wall as high as her waist. When she walked past me and down the sidewalk, the fog cleared for a moment, and I saw two giant stone pillars, one on each side of the street. Each was carved with the image of a man holding an automobile, a tribute to the area's industry.

I was a Clevelander, born and bred, and like any Clevelander, I recognized the place. These days it was called the Hope Memorial. Back when Didi was alive, though, it was known as the Lorain/Carnegie Bridge.

Yeah, the same bridge Didi had jumped off.

Realizing where we were, what night it was, and what was about to happen, my stomach knotted. I raced forward to warn her, but it was as if Didi didn't even know I was there. She paced up and down the sidewalk.

"It was quiet," she said. "You know, the way it can be on a foggy night. Like the whole world is wrapped in cotton batting. I heard the sound of a foghorn from a ship out on the lake . . ." The haunting noise echoed through the night. "But I didn't see anyone or hear any cars. After a while, I was so cold and damp . . ."

"That's when you realized you'd been stood up."

She *had* forgotten I was there. Didi whirled around. She shook her head violently. "No. I knew he'd come. I knew he wouldn't leave me. He'd never—" Her voice breaking with tears, she turned toward the stone wall that looked down over the Cuyahoga River, some two hundred feet below. "I waited for hours. I was so cold, I couldn't feel my feet. I walked back and forth, but that didn't help. I told myself he'd come. I knew he would. But then he didn't, and I don't know what got into me. It felt as if there was an animal deep inside me, eating out my heart. I . . . I climbed up on the wall."

She did just that, and though I knew what I was watching was nothing more than leftover traces of the energy that had fueled the tragedy so many years before, my heart raced and my stomach flipped. I stepped forward, one hand out to her. "Didi, don't!"

My words echoed back at me from the fog. At least I think it as my own voice I heard. It was hard to hear when my heart pounded in my chest and my blood rushed inside my ears. I stood there, wondering what I could do to change the course of the events that had happened so many years before, and even as I watched, a figure moved past me and toward Didi.

Man or woman? Honestly, I couldn't tell. The figure was as insubstantial as the fog that swirled around us, no more real than the shadows that hid its face and distorted its shape.

A voice came from behind me somewhere.

"He's not coming," it said.

The voice shook Didi out of the spell that held her. Still perched high above the city, she turned. In the anemic yellow light, her face was radiant. "He will. He has to. He said he'd be here."

"He'll never leave her."

"He said he's coming for me."

"He didn't mean it."

"He wouldn't lie."

"Are you sure?" I heard a chuckle and the sound of something scraping against the concrete. The next thing I knew, the figure had closed in on Didi. It grabbed hold of the sleeve of her coat, holding her in place, keeping her from harm.

Didi took one more look over her shoulder at the panorama of Cleveland skyline and held out her hand to the figure, preparing to step down.

I breathed a sigh of relief.

Maybe things hadn't really happened the way Didi remembered them.

Maybe I wouldn't be forced to watch her die in the fog and the cold.

Maybe—

I saw the figure glance not at me, but at the person who stood somewhere in the shadows behind me.

"Go ahead," the voice said.

The figure nodded, tightened its hold on Didi, and pushed.

Chapter 17

"*Why the hell did you tell me you committed suicide?*"

Okay, so my question wasn't exactly tactful. And I wasn't precisely composed. How was I supposed to act when I had just witnessed a murder? Yeah, yeah. It was a fifty-year-old murder. But still . . .

Safely back in the present and right where I'd started out from, I sat on the edge of my bed, pulling in shaky breath after shaky breath, one hand pressed to my heart and the other swiping at the tears on my cheeks.

"You were murdered, Didi." I said it pretty loud, partly because it didn't seem to be sinking in with my resident victim. Mostly because I was so rattled, I couldn't help myself. "How did you not know you were murdered?"

Across the room, Didi stood with her back to me. Her head was tipped to one side.

"I know it sounds crazy but . . ." She turned to me, and when she did, she looked just like she had before we started our frightening little journey into the past. Pajamas. Turban. Green goo. "I never thought about it before. I didn't remember . . ." As if the fog still sat heavy on her shoulders, she shivered inside her flannel pajamas. "I remember being on the bridge. I remember that first step off into nothingness. It felt like I was flying. But I didn't know . . ." She shook herself. "I was so confused that night. I was out of my head! And, remember, I did leave a suicide note. I heard people talking about it at my funeral. What else was I supposed to think?"

I thought back to the scene on the bridge, and maybe this whole detective thing was finally starting to sink in. Instantly I saw the flaw in Didi's theory. "You left a note, huh? But you didn't have a pen. I know because I saw you looking through your pockets for one. Bet the person who pushed you didn't know that."

Didi's blue eyes widened. "I forgot. I mean about the pen. I didn't—" She shook her head as if she was trying to clear it. "First at my funeral, then over the years . . . I heard *suicide* so often, I really believed it. I thought I killed myself."

The enormity of the news settled in on me. "Shit," I grumbled.

"I'll say." Didi dropped down on the bed next to me. "Now what?"

All right, I admit it wasn't exactly the right thing to do to inspire confidence in a client, but I shook my head, confused. "I guess we've got to wonder if your death had anything to do with the manuscript," I said. "That all depends on who pushed you." When Didi didn't say a thing, I tried a more obvious approach.

"Who pushed you?" I asked. "I couldn't see

clearly. At least I couldn't see any more than shadows. You know, like a TV when the cable is out. Any chance it was Merilee?"

Didi shot off the bed like it was on fire. "Don't be ridiculous. Merilee is my sister. My own sister wouldn't—"

"Steal your manuscript?"

"That's different."

"Is it? If she wanted the manuscript bad enough—"

"She didn't. All she ever did was make fun of my book. I'd tell her about it, and she'd criticize my research or tell me my characters wouldn't do the things they did, that they wouldn't talk the way I had them talking. She didn't want the manuscript at all. Not while I was alive. It wasn't until after I was dead that she realized it would never be published if she didn't—"

"Revisionist history!" I jumped up from the bed and faced off against Didi. "Listen to yourself. Suddenly you're excusing her."

"I'm not. But you said—"

"Hell, Didi, I just saw someone push you off a friggin' bridge. All I'm saying is that we have to figure out who it was."

"No. You're the one who doesn't get it. I'm dead. I've been dead longer than I was ever alive. I missed out on turning thirty. On seeing my daughter grow up. On holding my granddaughter. I never got to marry the man I loved." Her shoulders slumped. "I killed myself, Pepper. That's what everyone said, and they were so sure of it, no one ever even bothered to question it. Everybody just figured I was another unwed mother who couldn't face the humiliation. No one cared enough to even look into my death. Don't you see, after all these years of them not caring, I don't care, either."

I couldn't exactly empathize with a lot of what Didi said. I'd never had a kid—heck, I didn't even know if I ever wanted one—so the whole maternal thing . . . well, that was foreign to me. But I wasn't completely heartless. I did understand what it was to be young and alive. I knew what it felt like to have dreams shattered and hopes dashed, too.

There was also the little matter of justice.

Would Didi understand about that?

I didn't know and I didn't mention it, because frankly, I wasn't sure I understood it completely myself.

What I did know was that royalties or no royalties, name on a book or not, Didi's restless spirit was doomed to roam the earth as long as her murderer remained at large.

Call me a sucker.

I couldn't do that to a woman with green goo on her face.

The good news was that there was no lack of suspects.

The bad news?

See above.

The next day as I sat on my bed and made a list, I realized there were a whole bunch of people who might have wanted Didi dead.

Merilee, for one, and it didn't take much of a stretch of the imagination to figure out why. She knew about Didi's manuscript. If she saw the potential to cash in on what was sure to be a hit, she might have been more than happy to have Didi out of the picture.

Weird Bob because . . .

Well, as far as I could see, he didn't have a motive, but there was no doubt he *was* weird.

Thomas Ross Howell was high on the list, too, though at this stage of the game, there was no way on earth I was going to mention that to Didi. Even after fifty years, she was obviously still in love with him. Sure, she must have known the truth: If her affair with Howell was exposed, it would have ruined his perfect life. There was no use in me pointing out something so obvious. Especially when it would hurt so much.

I continued with my list, writing down Howell's wife, Tammy, next. After all, she had a stake in this too.

Susan Gwitkowski was there, too. No doubt when she worked with Didi, she'd seen the little black book. If she thought it was her key to riches, she might have been willing to kill for it.

Was I missing anybody?

Probably, especially when I thought back to the scene on the bridge and considered the fact that there were two people present. Sure, one of them had pushed Didi. But the other had given the order.

If only I knew where to begin.

I looked toward my dresser, where I'd hidden the little black book beneath the underwear in the middle drawer. "Heck," I told myself, thinking of all the names inside the book, "it could have been any one of them, and between now and the premiere . . ." I sighed. There weren't enough days in the weeks to talk to all the men listed in Didi's little black book. I wouldn't even know how to track them down. Unless . . .

I'd been so busy focusing on the news of Didi's murder and all that it meant in terms of my investigation, I hadn't allowed myself to relax enough to get my brain in gear. It kick-started back to life, and I jumped off the bed.

I yanked open the dresser drawer, scooped up the black book, and went to find what was left of the gala invitations.

There wasn't a lot more I could do until the day of the gala. At least not in terms of my investigation. Of course, that didn't mean I was living a life of leisure. Merilee kept me hopping.

The dry cleaner's, the jeweler's, the florist, the seamstress.

It was no wonder Trish had been worn to a frazzle. Aside from being antisocial, cranky, and a super-duper pain in the ass, Merilee was one tough taskmaster.

But all was not lost.

Thanks to the never-ending demands, I had errands to run each day. And that gave me a lot of freedom.

On the afternoon that I had appointments to pick up Merilee's gala gown and the necklace and bracelet a local jeweler was loaning her to wear with it, I took a detour to Garden View.

Not much had changed since the last time I stopped by. There was still a bevy of reenactors roaming the grounds, and they still gave me the creeps. The good thing, though, was that not one of them looked like Dan the Brain Man.

I put the thought out of my mind and concentrated on my mission. I had a couple of reasons for my visit, one of which was Ella's birthday. It was coming up in just a few weeks, and for all she'd done for me (aside from signing me on as an indentured servant to the Queen of Mean), I wanted to get her something special. I'd gone through the list of usual ideas: bath gel, body lotion, blah, blah, blah. But somewhere between the dry cleaner's and the jeweler's, inspiration had struck like a blast from a Union artillery cannon.

Merilee the Meticulous would never allow anything tacky and modern in her office. If I was going to find the ultimate in birthday gifts, I needed the good, not-so-old-fashioned Internet.

Lucky for me, Ella wasn't around, so I didn't have to explain myself. I said a quick hello to Jennine at the front desk, ducked into my office, turned on my computer, and got to work.

"*So Far the Dawn* memorabilia." I mumbled while I Googled the words, congratulating myself for being a genius and figuring I'd be done with my search in just a matter of moments.

Like I knew there were so many crazy collectors out there?

I glanced at page after page of sites devoted to *SFTD* kitsch and, overwhelmed, decided the best place to start was at the beginning—sofarfrenzy. com, the home of Opal dolls, Palmer pictures, and what was purported to be the original front door of the house used in the scene where Opal first meets Charleton Hanratty.

Not a *So Far the Dawn* lunch box in sight.

"Shit." I hit the back arrow and went on to the next site, and then the one after that.

I could have bought a replica of the nightgown Opal wore on her wedding night, a duplicate of the musket Palmer carried in the war, any number of porcelain figurines, collectible plates, and Christmas ornaments.

"You think there would be one damned lunch—"

My eyes scanned the screen, and my words dissolved into a gurgle of pure, unadulterated disbelief.

For sale. Newly posted, the listing on dawn-dazed.com read. *Original. Valuable. First page from original* So Far the Dawn *manuscript. Age authenticated. Some damage from writing on page. If you're a serious collector, you've got to own it! Truly one-of-a-kind.*

"I'll say," I mumbled, and if I had a fifty, I would have plunked it down and bet it on the spot.

That's how sure I was that I knew the identity of the lister who called himself msman.

I didn't hesitate. Calling myself Number1fan, I composed an e-mail, and in it, I just about begged for a look at the page. I told msman I was the most avid *So Far the Dawn* fan on the planet. I swore I admired Opal and confessed that I'd been in love with Palmer since the moment I'd first read the book. I'd seen the movie dozens of time, I said. I knew every line of dialogue by heart. I wanted that manuscript page, I told him, and I wanted it bad. Price (I made sure I said this in a paragraph of its own so there was no way he could miss it) was no object.

Some of what I told him was actually true. At

least when it came to the part about how much I
wanted to get my hands on the manuscript.

Most of it, of course, was bullshit.

Did I care?

Not even a little. After all, if msman was who I
thought msman was and if the page was real . . .

My heart was beating fast, and when I hit the
send button, my fingers were crossed.

I was so jazzed by the possibility of actually seeing
an original manuscript page that wasn't one of the
"original" manuscript pages in the display case at
the museum, I never did find a lunch box for Ella.
I told myself I'd look again another day, and with
hopes higher than they had been since the day Didi
spooked her way into my life, I continued on with
the second half of my reason for my visit to Garden
View. Back in my car, I cruised over to the new
section.

Lucky for me, when I got to the Bowman mau-
soleum, I saw that nothing had changed there.
There were a few people hanging around, and Rick
Jensen was still waiting for the perfect photo op.

I parked my Mustang. "Hey!" I called to him,
and lifted a cardboard box out of my trunk. "I've
got a present for you."

When I opened the box and showed him what
was inside, Rick's eyes lit. "My camera! Where did
you—? How did you—?"

"It's kind of a long story," I told him, even
though it really wasn't except for the part about
how I never would have been in Weird Bob's workroom if it wasn't for a certain ghost. "Where I
found it doesn't matter except that it might mean

something in terms of who mugged you. I think I know who did it, but I can't go to the cops. Not yet. Not until I get you to confirm a couple of things for me. I want you to think really hard, Rick. I bet if you do, you'll remember seeing the person around here. Big, beefy guy. Kind of old. Long ponytail. He's always dressed in jeans and a grubby denim shirt."

I'll give Rick credit. He tried. He stood quietly for a minute or two, his eyes closed, his forehead puckered as if he was going through a mental list of each and every person who'd visited the mausoleum.

Finally, he shook his head. "Sorry. I don't remember ever seeing anybody like that, but then, there have been a lot of folks ogling this place. Damn, but I wish one of them had been that Merilee Bowman! If I could get just one good picture of her, I could really make a name for myself. But as far as the guy you're talking about . . ." He was deep in thought again.

"Maybe yes," he finally said. "Maybe no. I'm leaning toward the *no*."

This was not something I wanted to hear. Not when I was so sure of myself, my theory, and the undeniable evidence I'd discovered in Weird Bob's workroom. I tried again. "Are you sure? Come on, Rick, this is pretty important. Think! This guy, he always smells like cigarettes."

"Now I know he hasn't been around here." Rick shook his head. "I was a smoker myself. Quit a three-pack-a-day habit not a year ago. Believe me, I'd remember the smell of smoke." He breathed deep, as if he could smell it and was enjoying every cancer-inducing molecule. "What I wouldn't give for a Camel unfiltered." He wiped the smile of nicotine desire off his face.

"Sorry," he said. "I'm pretty sure the guy you're talking about was never here to see the mausoleum."

"But he might have been the one who clunked you on the head."

What was it called on those TV courtroom shows? Leading a witness?

Oh yeah, I was leading Rick, all right. Hopefully to remembering Bob's involvement in the mugging.

Unfortunately, the only place I was leading him was nowhere at all.

He was sure of himself when he said, "I told you, somebody snuck up from behind me. Big guy or no big guy, I didn't see a thing."

I was still holding the box that contained the camera, and I looked from Rick to the long curl of film at the bottom of the box. Maybe there was more than one way to prove Weird Bob's involvement. "You didn't see anything," I said, "but maybe your camera did." I fished out the film. "Will this prove anything?"

He sized up the film. "It's been exposed. It's toast."

"But you could try, couldn't you? I mean, develop it or something?"

Rick wasn't so sure, and I think he would have said so if I didn't play the sympathy card.

And bat my eyelashes at him.

"I found your camera," I said, thinking back to the lessons in the not-so-gentle art of persuasion

I'd learned from Gus. "I brought it back to you. The least you can do—"

"You're right." When I offered it, he took the box out of my hands. "I don't know what you think I'm going to find on this film. I've told you, I've told the folks here at the cemetery who asked, I've told the cops. Nothing unusual happened the day I was mugged. I don't remember taking any pictures that were special that day. That's for sure. In fact, when I think back on it, I don't remember much of anything at all except—"

"Except . . ." I leaned forward, eager to hear more.

Rick looked away. "You're going to think it's crazy," he said.

I didn't bother to point out that as the world's one and only Gifted cemetery tour guide, I was getting used to the fact that pretty much nothing was crazy.

Or maybe everything was.

This wasn't the time to get philosophical.

"Tell me anyway," I said instead. "Maybe between the two of us, we can figure out what it means."

Rick's hands were big. He wrapped them around his camera. "It's just that . . ." He blushed. "I feel so goofy admitting it. I mean, hell, I'm no psychologist, but even I know it's probably got some weird mental health implication or something. You see, my grandmother, she was a drinker. She used to whack me around when I was a kid. You know, when she was drunk. She thought she was fooling us all, that we didn't know when she was hitting the bottle. Yeah, like we were that stupid!" He made a sour face. "She used to try to cover up the smell of the booze on her breath."

Rick looked so uncomfortable about confessing all this, I might have felt sorry for him if I wasn't so busy wondering what it all meant.

"I think that's why every time I think back to the day I was mugged, I have the same weird memory," he said. "You know, like the fact that I was knocked on the head is getting all mixed up with what happened to me when I was a kid and Grandma was hanging with Jack Daniel's. That's got to be why every time I think about the mugging, I have the same sensory experience. I'll bet some psychologist would make a big deal out of that, huh?"

"Depends what sensory experience you're talking about."

"Like I said, it's crazy." Uncomfortable, Rick cleared his throat. "Every time I think about getting whacked on the head, I think about Grandma. You see, that's how she covered up the smell of the liquor. That's what I think about when I think about getting whacked. Menthol cough drops."

Chapter 18

"It's beautiful, isn't it?"

As she looked over the ballroom of the Renaissance Hotel and the crowd of costumed partyers milling around the buffet tables where candles twinkled and champagne flowed, Ella's face was aglow.

Mine . . .

Let's just say that my interest in the scene was a little more scientific.

With that in mind, I took a quick look around. Kurt and Elizabeth were across the room, she in her blue velvet dress, he in his uniform, bickering about which of their pictures (twenty feet tall and hanging at the far end of the ballroom) was better/more attractive/more professional.

With any luck, they'd keep themselves so busy, I wouldn't have to deal.

The rest of the crowd was another matter. From across the massive ballroom, I caught sight of Thomas Ross Howell, resplendent in tuxedo. He had a short, silver-haired woman on his arm (obviously his wife, Tammy) who must have spent the equivalent of one month of my rent on her green gown. Yeah, it was that spectacular. And who was I to criticize? I was a big believer in the if-you've-got-it-flaunt-it theory.

At the same time I proved it by twinkling at President Lincoln, who walked by, looked me over, and gave me a wink, I wondered if Howell knew that David Barkwill, construction mogul, another of Didi's former boyfriends—and fellow murder suspect—was just a few short feet away getting himself a glass of punch.

He might not know, but I sure did. As dazzling as the whole scene was, I hadn't forgotten my primary mission. I had plans to talk to both Howell and Barkwill, as well as to the rest of the men from Didi's little black book who'd responded to my personal invitation in my best handwriting.

As soon as I shook Ella.

Easier said than done.

Her eyes sparkling like the slick sheen of her rose-colored gown, Ella wound one elbow-length-glove-clad arm through mine. "Oh, Pepper. It's as if I stepped into a scene from *So Far the Dawn*. Like a dream come true!"

I tugged at the side of my gown and at the corset beneath it that was pinching my boobs. "Only if you dream about being a masochist," I told her.

She thought I was kidding and laughed. "You look like a princess in a fairy tale," she said.

She was right, and in keeping with the whole got-and-flaunt theory, I wasn't ashamed to admit it. The gold silk gown with its miles of creamy lace edging looked fabulous with my hair and as old-fart, old-fashioned, old-time as the style of the dress was (snug waist, wide skirt, and all), I really did look good in it.

Of course, the off-the-shoulder styling didn't hurt. Neither did the fact that my breasts were pressed, smashed, and mashed against the low-cut neckline. But how I looked and how I felt, those were two different things.

When a man excused himself to get around me, I stepped to one side. My hoop skirt swayed and I slapped a hand on either side of it to keep it from taking off down the dance floor and swinging me along with it. "How the hell did women ever function when they were bundled up in clothes like this?" I hissed. "Between the corset and the pantaloons and this damned hoop—"

"Now, now." Ella scolded me, but she was smiling while she did it. "A proper lady never uses such language."

"I've got news for you, I'm no proper lady."

"That's pretty much what I'm counting on."

The comment came from right behind me, and I didn't have to turn around to know it was Quinn. For one thing, Ella looked that way and blushed from the more-modest-than-mine neckline of her gown all the way to her forehead. For another, Quinn's voice tickled its way up my spine and left a tingly sensation behind. Fire and ice and raw sexual energy.

Not a bad combination.

Not that I was going to let on. At least not this early in the evening.

When I turned to him, I hoped he'd attribute the fact that I was trembling to the crazy wobbling of my hoop.

Nice try.

Because when I turned to him, and saw that he was wearing a tux . . .

Well, let's just say that *eye candy* took on a whole new meaning.

I looked from the tips of Quinn's spit-polished shoes to the top of his head. Top to bottom was A-OK, and everything in between was mighty fine, too.

"Detective." I nodded my hello. "I didn't expect to see you all dressed up."

"Expecting to see me undressed?" His eyes sparkled in a way meant just for me.

A fizz bubbled through my veins.

"I think it's time for me to greet the members of ISFTDS who are here," Ella said. Giggling, she patted me on the arm and disappeared into the costumed crowd.

"Well, that will give her something to talk about at the office tomorrow," I said, even though I knew Ella was too sensible to spread gossip. "You're feeling mighty pleased with yourself tonight."

"And you're looking mighty good." Quinn gave me a careful once-over, his gaze stopping at my low neckline. "No wonder those olden days are considered so romantic."

"Don't get any ideas. Something tells me women back then didn't really show this much skin." I shifted my shoulders, trying not to feel so squashed. "I wouldn't even be this exposed if I tried on my

gown in time to get it to the seamstress for altera-
tions."

The sparkle in Quinn's eyes throttled back to a
slow simmer. "Someone made an attempt to kill
you while you were trying on the dress the first
time, and we never found any evidence as to who it
was. I imagine that was enough to make you reluctant to try on the gown a second time."

"I'll say," I told him, but I didn't mention the
fact that I'd been too busy to try on the gown because of other things, too. Like communicating
back and forth with msman, who, according to his
latest e-mail, still—glory and hallelujah—had not
found a buyer for the original manuscript page.
Unfortunately he also said the price I had offered
(more than I could afford) was a little low.

The question popped out of me before I could
stop it. "I don't suppose you know how I can raise
five thousand dollars in cold, hard cash, do you?"

Quinn's gaze dropped to my chest, and a smile
inched up the corners of his mouth. "I'm not going
to state the obvious."

"You bet you're not."

"So why do you need that kind of money?"

I'd debated about telling him. Not about the
money, of course. Before the words spilled out of
my mouth, I hadn't realized I was going to mention
the money. But there were other things, things I
would need Quinn's help with eventually. Was now
a good time to take him into my confidence? Probably not, but I knew that if I waited for the perfect
moment, it would never come.

"There's something I want to buy," I said. "An
original manuscript page. From *So Far the Dawn*."

He barked out a laugh. "You of all people! Don't tell me you're turning into one of these—"

"Freaks?" I lowered my voice so the freaks around us wouldn't hear. "Not a chance. But listen, I think there's something strange going on. About the book. About the manuscript displayed at the museum." She was all the way across the room chatting with the mayor and the anchor from one of the national news programs, but I glanced over my shoulder at Merilee and lowered my voice anyway. "I don't think she wrote it," I told Quinn.

Something told me Quinn wasn't surprised often, and even when he was, I had a feeling he didn't let it show. Which is why I took it as something of a compliment when he rolled back on his heels, looked from Merilee to me, and whistled low under his breath. "Who—?"

"It was her sister, Didi. At least I think it was. Maybe. I'm pretty sure." I was. I think. "Anyway, I found someone online who claims to have an original page from the original manuscript. If I can buy it and you can get it . . . I don't know . . . tested or dated or whatever it is they do to check the age of things . . . and if you can get the writing on it compared to the sample of Didi's writing that I have . . . then we can prove it. And then everyone will know that Didi really wrote the book."

Even when Quinn was caught off guard, I found out he didn't let it get the best of him. He got right down to business, narrowing his eyes and shooting me a look. "And you know all this, how?"

I shrugged. Was I stalling? Or trying to distract Quinn and get him to look at my chest? Either way, it worked. Both ways, it was better than having to confess how I really knew what I knew. Or at least what I thought I knew I knew.

"It really doesn't matter how I know, does it? What matters is that if Didi really wrote the book, then she should get the credit. And the big, fat royalty checks."

Even Quinn couldn't argue with logic like this. He nodded. "Then let's talk to this Didi and see what she has to say."

"We can't." Technically correct since *we* didn't have the Gift. "She's dead."

"Then how—"

"Can she get the money?" It was better to head him off at the pass than let him ask the obvious question: *Then how do you know?*

"Didi had a daughter," I explained. "She's dead, too, but her daughter had a daughter. Which means Didi has a granddaughter. Which means that if I can prove Didi wrote the book, Harmony—her granddaughter—can cash in on—"

Quinn was a quick study. He didn't need to hear any more. He cut off my explanation with a look designed to intimidate. "Which means you're talking a lot of money. And a lot of money explains why someone tried to kill you. It also tells me that the day you were attacked in your bedroom, you knew exactly what was going on, you just weren't talking. Looks like for the second time since I met you, you've stuck your nose where it doesn't belong."

It was hard to argue. Especially when he was right. So when had that ever stopped me? "My nose is exactly where it belongs," I told him. "Because I know Harmony. Or at least I've met her. The money is rightfully hers, and that means she deserves it. I also know that something isn't right in the world of *So Far the Dawn*. The wrong person is taking credit for a book that millions of people love. Is that enough for you, Officer? If not, consider this. Everyone thinks Didi committed suicide, but she was really murdered, maybe because of the manuscript. And Trish Kingston—you remember her, the woman whose death you're currently investigating?—was involved in the mugging of that photographer over at Garden View. I don't know about you, but I think that means that the mugging might ultimately have had something to do with Trish's murder."

I'd gotten this out as quickly as I could, before Quinn could tell me I was nuts and try to stop me. I ran out of air and sucked in a deep breath.

"So you see," I said, "I've got this moral obligation—"

"To get yourself killed?"

"That's not what I was going to say."

"It's what's going to happen! Damn it, Pepper—" Quinn controlled his temper. It wasn't easy. He scraped a hand through his hair and looked around. We were standing at the edge of the dance floor, and a crowd was gathering around us for the first waltz of the evening. Rather than risk being overheard, he grabbed me by the elbow and escorted me to the perimeter of the room, where floor-to-ceiling windows overlooked the city's Public Square.

"Stay out of it," Quinn said.

I couldn't explain that it was already too late for

that. But then, where was it written that I owed
Quinn an explanation? For anything? "It's too late
for that," I told him. "I'm in it. Up to my neck. But
I can get out of it fast. Or at least I can clear up the
thing about the manuscript. All I need to do is buy
the page. And get it to you. And you'll get it tested
and—"

"I'm not making any promises." The way he
said it told me he wasn't kidding. The way he
looked at me, though . . . well, I was nothing if not
a good judge of people. Quinn's lips said one thing,
his eyes said another. He wasn't making any promises, but he'd do this. For me.

"I'll look around. I'll ask some questions. If your
story holds water, we'll take the next step."

I was relieved, and not just because I'd found
someone to help fund the buy. I had an ally. Quinn.
Somehow, just knowing he was on my side and
watching my back made me feel as if the weight of
the world had lifted from my shoulders. Side, back,
shoulders. Nearly all my body parts were covered.

Nearly.

I stepped closer and smiled up at him. A good
move when it came to flirting. Not such a good
idea considering the hoop skirt. I thwacked it into
submission before it could do Quinn any damage.
"We'll buy the manuscript?"

"We'll buy the manuscript. If—"

There was that knife-edged look again, cutting
to the bone, relentless and waiting for me to cry
uncle.

I caved, and in the great scheme of things, who
could blame me? I almost *had* gotten myself killed.

Over a stupid manuscript. And tens of millions of dollars that in no way, shape, or form belonged to me. The smart thing to do would have been to leave the job to the professionals in the first place.

"I won't do a thing," I told Quinn. "I promise. Not until I hear what you've uncovered."

"Nothing." He looked at me hard. Like he wasn't sure I understood the meaning of the word. "I mean it, Pepper, nothing about this manuscript and nothing about this death that you think is a murder. And why do you think it, anyway, if you say that everyone thinks it was a suicide?"

He didn't wait for me to answer the question. "Never mind," he said. "You can explain about all that later. And about why you think Trish Kingston was involved in mugging a photographer. You realize that's crazy, don't you?"

I did. "I do," I admitted. "But you see, right before he got whacked, Rick, the photographer, he smelled menthol. And Trish, she was always sucking on cough drops and—"

"Enough." Quinn's eyes were glazing over, and he stopped me before things could get worse. He looked toward the dance floor. "Let me talk to some people and see what I can find out."

"And I'll—"

"Do nothing." He said it like he figured I wasn't going to argue, and I wasn't. I had my own personal cop on the case, and for once I could sit back and let him do all the work.

I clutched my hands at my waist. "Don't worry, Officer, I'm going to stay right here and mind my own business. Like a proper young lady should."

"Don't get too proper on me." Quinn's eyes glittered in the light of the crystal chandeliers. "I want you alive, but I don't want you boring."

I was still enjoying the thought when he turned around and walked away.

I'd been so busy talking to Quinn, I hadn't registered the fact that the crowd had quieted down. As soon as I turned toward the dance floor, I saw why. The mayor had moved behind a microphone at the front of the crowd, and he held up both hands, asking for silence.

"Ladies and gentlemen!" His Honor was a tall, thin man with a salt-and-pepper beard, and like Quinn, he hadn't tried to blend in with the *SFTD* crowd by wearing a costume. He was dressed in a tuxedo, a fancy red cummerbund, and a dazzling white shirt. "This evening, I have the honor to introduce you to one of this city's most respected women." He glanced to his left to where Merilee waited in a dress that was an exact replica of Opal's sapphire blue ball gown.

Interesting, since Didi was standing right behind her in the exact same dress.

I looked from her, to Merilee, to Elizabeth, who was watching the proceedings from the sidelines and whose expression made it clear that she wasn't happy that there were three Opals present.

I turned away from her, and across the floor, my gaze met and locked with Didi's. She grinned. *That's me.* She mouthed the words and pointed toward the mayor. *That's me he's talking about.*

It wasn't. At least as far as the mayor knew.

"Tonight's guest of honor is not only a star," he was saying. "She's an institution."

Didi nodded enthusiastically.

"Her blockbuster novel, *So Far the Dawn*, has sparked our imaginations like no other."

At this, there was a smattering of applause, and Didi gave me the thumbs-up.

"It has been translated into dozens of foreign languages, made into one of the all-time classic movies . . ."

More applause, and Didi blushed.

". . . and it has certainly solidified what we here in Cleveland have always known. That we live in a place that is as vital and prosperous now as it was back during the War Between the States. We have one person to thank for all the honor she's brought to our city and all the pleasure she's brought into our lives."

Didi stepped up next to the mayor and beamed a smile at the crowd.

"Ladies and gentlemen . . ." he said, and oblivious to the ghost on his right, he turned and gestured to his left. "Merilee Bowman!"

The place (as they say) went wild. The orchestra played "The Battle Hymn of the Republic," and a group of men dressed as soldiers and standing close to the front led the crowd in a few hearty "huzzahs." (I wasn't sure what it meant, but it sure sounded like a compliment.) It wasn't until the commotion died down that I realized Didi was no longer on the podium. I stood on tiptoe and craned my neck, but there wasn't a sign of hide nor ghostly hair of her.

At least until I turned around.

I saw a whirl of blue velvet over near the windows where I'd so recently spoken to Quinn, and squeezing my hoop to get through the crush, I headed that way.

I found Didi staring out the window, her shoulders heaving. When she turned to me, her face was stained with tears.

"That applause should have been for me," she said. "But instead, look at her!" We both looked to where Merilee—head high and face beaming—was making the last of her bows before she took her place at the center of the dance floor with the mayor. "It's my book, Pepper. Those are my characters. They speak the words I put in their mouths and they do the things I wanted them to do. It's wrong. It's unfair. It's—"

"We're going to get it cleared up." I'm not sure why I thought saying it would help. I'd been trying for weeks to clear up Didi's problem, and yet it was a classic case of so far, no good. "Quinn is going to help us and Quinn—"

"You promised him you wouldn't do a thing." Didi's pout was monumental. She didn't give me a chance to tell her I didn't appreciate the fact that she'd apparently been listening in to my recent conversation with my favorite boy in blue. "He told you not to do anything until he gets back, and believe me, I know the way these things work. What men want, men get. You told me you got all the murder suspects in one place so you could interview them, but you're going to let him take over, aren't you? Not that I blame you or anything. Men are smarter than women. They know more about the ways of the world. They should be in charge. That's how things are supposed to work. It's the way things have always worked. But . . ." She sniffled. "We're just women. I guess there's nothing we can do."

If ever there was a time I wished I could grab a ghost and give her a good, hard shake, that was it.

But I couldn't.

So I didn't.

Instead, I slanted her a look. "Nothing we can do, huh? Says who?"

Her expression cleared. "You mean—"

"I mean we're going to take care of what we need to take care of. And I'll worry about Quinn later." I squared my shoulders and, hoop skirt notwithstanding, glided back into the hubbub of the party. "After all," I reminded her, "tomorrow is another day."

Chapter 19

I was as good as my word.

My word to Didi, that is. Not my word to Quinn.

I talked to David Barkwill, the construction mogul. I chatted with Michael Javits, who, it turned out, owned most of the used car lots in northeast Ohio. I shot the shit with Ken Paskovitch, the banker, and even managed an audience with Reverend Jack, who—for reasons that escaped me since he looked like he'd been stuffed into his powder blue tux by a taxidermist—commanded his own little crowd of admirers.

That was a lot of talking and chatting.

And it got me . . .

Well, as much as I hate to admit it, facts are facts, and the fact is, it got me absolutely nowhere.

After four glasses of punch and four conversations with four old men who did everything from grope me (Reverend Jack, doncha know), to ogle me (the construction mogul), to proposition me (the car lot guru), the only thing I could say for sure was that as far as they could remember—and wasn't it telling that they all remembered even though it was so long ago?—they all had an alibi for the night Didi died.

That, and that I didn't want to talk to another old guy for a very long time.

Of course, a private detective can't be picky. At least not when it comes to a case. I still had Thomas Ross Howell to tackle (figuratively speaking, of course), and just as the dancers were finishing what the orchestra leader called the last quadrille (whatever the hell that was) before intermission, I moved to the edge of the dance floor and looked over the crowd, searching for the judge.

No luck, and I turned to check out the buffet tables. When I did, I happened to glance toward the orchestra—and saw a familiar-looking face behind a bushy mustache and a clarinet.

"Dan Callahan." I grumbled and made a move toward the orchestra, but my timing was off. A lady in a hoop skirt even wider than mine just happened to be dancing by. We met, collided, and ping-ponged off each other. She (no Civil War–era lady, after all) cursed her partner, who was apparently supposed to see me even though he was facing the other way. She cursed me for getting in the way. And as for me, I beat a hasty, head-spinning retreat and ended up over near the tables that had been set up for those who weren't inclined to dance.

My skirt caught on a table leg, and I yanked it free. "Son of a puppy," I grumbled.

"You can dress her up, but you can't take her out."

For the second time that night, I'd been snuck up

on, and I didn't appreciate it. Only this time, the voice I heard wasn't Quinn's, and I wasn't left tingling with anticipation. This was a woman's voice, and where Quinn's had poured through me like warm honey, this one left me cold, cold, cold. I regained my footing and turned to find Susan Gwitkowski staring at me, daggers in her eyes.

"Who the hell do you think you are?" she demanded.

"Pepper." Always the smart ass, I smiled and stuck out one hand to shake hers. "But we've met. Remember? The day I—"

"The day you tricked me into letting you into my house and then stole something that belongs to me."

This was hard to deny. Especially since it was true. I dispensed with the niceties, and since the chair next to where Susan was seated was empty, I dropped into it. "You mean Didi's little black book. The one you're using to blackmail half the male population of northeast Ohio."

Her breath caught, but I had to hand it to her, she didn't cave. Not right away, anyway. "How do you—?"

"Know?" I grinned. "Let's just say a little bird told me. You're not denying it?"

Susan was dressed all in black. Slinky gown studded with beads. Feather boa. Evening bag. Not exactly au courant with the Civil War crowd unless she was playing at being a nineteenth-century hooker. She was sipping champagne (and had four empty flutes on the table in front of her), and she looked at me over the rim of her glass. "You think you're so smart and that I'm going to throw up my hands and confess? That I'm going to feel guilty about what I'm doing? I'll tell you what, there's nothing wrong with taking advantage of a situation. It's justice, that's what it is. It's the least Didi can do for me to make up for leaving me with that brat kid of hers."

Her statement was so calculating, it made me shiver. Not that I didn't understand. In a twisted sort of way, it was payback. "You've made the most of it," I said to Susan.

"You're damned right. I can't tell you how many times I saw Didi with that address book of hers. Writing in a new name. Jotting down another new phone number for another new boyfriend. I can't tell you how many lunch hours I spent listening to her." Susan took a big gulp of champagne. "I'd sit there like a bump on a log, eating my bologna sandwiches and listening to Didi talk about her dates."

Dozens of candles blinked in silver candelabra from the buffet tables. Their light reflected in Susan's eyes, illuminating a truth that was suddenly all too clear.

"It's not about the money, is it?" I asked, but I didn't need an answer. I knew the answer as sure as I knew my own name. "That's not why you do it. The money is just the icing on the cake. And the whole thing about Judy . . . well, that's just you justifying what you've been doing. But it all boils down to jealousy, doesn't it? Didi had the men and you had . . . what?" I knew she wouldn't respond, so I went right on.

"You had nothing but your desk at the office and forty years of working for a guy who never gave you more than a polite nod and a turkey at Christmas. Shit, things were just about boiling in the ol' steno pool, weren't they? You were hot for Howell. Just like Didi was. Only in her case, he noticed, and in yours . . . well . . ." I looked Susan over and had to admit, money or no money, dead or alive, she just didn't measure up to Didi. She wasn't as pretty. She wasn't as sexy. She didn't have half Didi's personality.

"You were jealous," I said, and I knew it was true. "Is that why you pushed Didi off that bridge?"

Until then, Susan had been cool and collected in a venomous sort of way. At the mention of Didi's murder, though, her calm dissolved in a gurgle of outrage. "That bitch killed herself. You know that. Everyone knows that. She killed herself, but not until after she dumped her kid on me. And you think I don't deserve something for that?"

"Oh, I think you deserve something, all right." The music ended, and after the dancers applauded politely, they moved off the floor. Before the hubbub of conversations started again, the room was quiet. I kept my voice low so only Susan could hear. "With any luck, you'll get it eventually."

I didn't excuse myself when I got up and walked away. It would have been a more dramatic exit if my hoop didn't get wedged between a portly guy in a Confederate uniform and a woman in a riding habit. I jerked free and continued on toward where the orchestra was seated.

Was it any big surprise that by the time I got there, the clarinet player's chair was empty?

I grumbled to myself and looked around.

No sign of Dan the Brain Man or anyone who looked like him, mustache or no mustache. But all was not lost. Just as I turned away from the stage, I spotted Thomas Ross Howell standing near a potted palm, chatting with the president of the city council.

I headed that way.

I would have made it, too, if someone didn't grab my elbow.

I stopped. My skirt continued on. I thwacked it into submission and looked over my shoulder. Quinn had his hand on my arm.

"You didn't tell me she died fifty years ago," he said.

I didn't have to ask who he was talking about. Apparently while I'd been hobnobbing with the over-seventy set, Quinn had been doing his homework. Something told me it involved a call to the record room at the Justice Center. I raised a shoulder in the sort of fiddle-dee-dee gesture I'm sure would have played well with this crowd. "You never asked."

"I'm asking now."

Earlier that morning, when I spoke to Ella about the night's festivities, she had insisted I carry the fan that had come packed with my costume. At the time, I told her she was nuts, but now I saw that there was a purpose for everything, even something as silly and old-fashioned as a fan. I snapped it open and waved it in front of my face, stalling at the same time I glanced toward the potted palm to make sure Howell was still there. Reassured, I turned my attention back to Quinn. "You're asking about what?"

"How you know. Why you care. Why you think I should."

"Oh, Officer!" I slapped my fan closed and tapped Quinn on the arm with it, doing my best to be coy and knowing that with any other guy, it would have worked like a charm. "You know and I know, there's no statute of limitations on murder."

"You're not cute, Pepper."

So my isn't-she-adorable routine wasn't working on Quinn. It meant I had to try a little harder.

I stepped as close as the killer gown would allow and looked up into his eyes. "I'm not?"

"No." As if to prove it, he moved back and crossed his arms over his chest. "You can be. But now is not one of those moments."

"But you'll still help me. With buying the manuscript and getting it tested and—"

"And I told you to mind your own business."

"And what makes you think I haven't been?"

"Because you're talking to a whole bunch of people you shouldn't be talking to."

I pretended to take the comment at face value and grinned. "You've been keeping your eye on me!" I stopped just short of whacking him with my fan again. Like I said, with any other guy . . .

Quinn's eyes flared green fire. "Yes, I've been watching you. And I've seen you talking to a lot of people, and I have to ask myself what you'd have to say to a mover and shaker like David Barkwill or a scumbucket like good old Reverend Jack, the biggest scam artist this side of the Canadian border. They sure don't have anything in common with you. Every one of them is close to eighty years old, and pardon me if I'm overstating the obvious here, but you don't exactly strike me as the type who has a soft spot in her heart for senior citizens. There can't be anything in the world you'd want to talk to them about unless—"

As if they'd been cut in half by a cavalry officer's saber, the words died on Quinn's lips. Then again, epiphany moments can have that effect on a person.

He pointed one finger in my direction. "You're nuts," he said.

"You've mentioned that before."

"But I really mean it now."

"You said you really meant it then."

"You think that Barkwill and Reverend Jack and . . ." As if he was sure he wasn't getting it right (though of course he was), he shook his head. "You think one of those men I saw you talking to had something to do with Didi Bowman's murder?"

Now we were getting somewhere. I made a face. "I did, but unfortunately, I've pretty much eliminated the whole bunch," I told Quinn, and I thought back to the conversations I'd had with my erstwhile suspects. "Yeah, they had motive. Every one of them. After all, they were all Didi's lovers at one time or another. Sometimes at the same time. But Barkwill was in Florida at the time of her death. He says he remembers because it was his wife's birthday and they always go to Florida for his wife's birthday. Reverend Jack was preaching on live TV. You get the picture. Every one of them has an airtight alibi. Why, even Susan Gwitkowski over there . . ." I looked toward where Susan was grabbing another glass of champagne from a pass-

ing waiter, and when she glanced my way, I
mouthed the words, *He's a cop* and pointed to
Quinn. Just to make her nervous.

"Susan had her reasons, too, of course, since she
was trying to get her hands on Didi's little black
book so she could blackmail everybody in it. Or at
least everybody in it who had money. But I don't
know . . . I don't think she did it, either. She's
pretty convinced Didi committed suicide."

"So was the coroner."

"Well, he was wrong." I didn't point out that I
knew this for a fact because I had watched the
murder happen. "There's only one other person
. . ." I looked over my shoulder just in time to see
Howell shake hands with the council president.
Their tête-à-tête was finished, and I could see
Howell's wife doing some impatient pacing near
the door.

"Look," I said, "I've got to go. There's somebody I need to talk to."

"Not so fast." Quinn latched on to my arm.
"You need to explain how you know all this,
Pepper."

Howell was starting toward the door.

"I will," I told Quinn. "I promise. But if I don't
get moving . . ."

Though I suspect he could make a scene when
he had a reason, Quinn was too much of a gentleman to do it at the biggest society bash of the year.
He let go, and I took off. I caught up to Howell
right before he caught up to his wife, and managed
to wedge myself (and my hoop skirt) between us
and the door.

"Oh, Judge Howell!" I pretended embarrassment and did my best to make it look like I was trying to get my skirt out of the way. "How nice to run into you. I was hoping we'd have a chance to talk again."

He pulled himself up to his full height. "That's interesting since I was hoping to never see you again."

I tapped his arm with my fan. "You're such a kidder," I said. "And here I thought you'd want to discuss business. It's so much easier to do it face-to-face than it is through e-mail, don't you think?"

It took him a moment to catch on, but hey, you don't get to be one of the most powerful guys in town by being stupid. Howell waved toward his wife in a way that told her he'd be there in a moment and grabbed my arm. He excused us through the crowd and didn't stop until we were through the doors that led out of the ballroom. We ended up next to a fountain that splashed in the lobby.

I pointed at him with my fan. "You're msman," I said.

He was going to deny it. I could practically see the words on his lips. Maybe he decided to come clean because it was the right thing to do. I was more inclined to think it was because he didn't want to pass up the opportunity to make a few bucks.

And I was pretty sure I knew why.

Howell eyed me like a felon he was about to sentence to a term of lock-up-and-throw-away-the-key. "And if I am?" he asked.

"If you are, then you lied to me when I came to

your office. Didi did give you a page of the manuscript. You've had it all this time. The reason you're
trying to sell it now is because you know that with
all the publicity about the premiere, you can get
the optimum price."

"So?"

"So, I'm thinking you need all the money you
can get. After all, Susan Gwitkowski's been blackmailing you for years. What's the matter, has she
upped the ante? Is she asking for so much that
your wife is going to find out? Is that why you're
trying to raise the extra cash?"

Howell's face went pale. His breath caught. Call
me cruel, but I have to admit, I enjoyed watching
him squirm. After all, he was the one who deserted
both his baby daughter and the woman he said he
loved. He was the one who left Didi standing on
that bridge in the fog and cold.

Or had he?

I stepped back and tipped my head, studying
him and wondering if he'd shown up for his ren-
dezvous with Didi after all. Maybe to give her a
little push?

I actually might have mentioned it, just to see if
I could get a rise out of him, but at that very
moment, Didi materialized right beside me.

"He's as handsome as ever." Even though she
smiled, her eyes glistened with unshed tears. "We
would have been so happy together. Instead, he
had to spend his life with her." She shot a look
over her shoulder toward where Mrs. Judge Howell
was passing the time by chatting to a matronly
woman in a navy blue suit. "He's miserable."

I looked over Howell's tux, his gold cuff links,

his tanned and toned skin. "He doesn't look miserable," I said.

"What are you talking about?" Howell shook off his daze. "What do you want?" he asked.

There was no use beating around the bush. "The truth, for one thing," I told him. "The manuscript page, for the other. But let's deal with one issue at a time. Where were you the night Didi was killed?"

Howell wasn't used to being challenged, and needless to say, he wasn't happy about it. He expected me to wither under the force of his glare. Instead, I brushed off his irritation and got down to business.

"I know you were supposed to meet her," I told him, and if he wondered why I tipped my head toward where Didi was standing . . . well . . . he'd just have to keep wondering. "Don't ask me how I know because it's way too complicated to explain. Let's just say that I have it on good authority that you and Didi had talked about running away together. To start a new life."

He shot a look toward the ballroom. "Susan Gwitkowski. It has to be her. As if she isn't doing enough to ruin my life."

"Susan?" I chased away the accusation with a laugh. "Maybe yes and maybe no. Maybe it doesn't matter. What does matter is that I know for a fact that Didi was on that bridge waiting for you. And you never showed."

"He couldn't!" Didi responded before Howell could, a thread of desperation in her voice. "He wanted to, Pepper. I told you that. He couldn't because of Tammy. She found out and—"

"Are you accusing me of something, Miss Martin?" Howell's question cut across Didi's blubbering, and it was just as well. I was tired of listening to her make excuses for this weasel. "Are you saying that you don't think she killed herself?"

"I'm not saying it. I know it. And you should have known it, too. She was a hell of a better parent than you ever were. She never would have left Judy alone. If you were half the man she thought you were, you would have known that the moment you heard Didi was dead. You would have figured out that it couldn't have been suicide. Unless, of course, you knew that because you were there."

"He did know. Of course he knew." Tears splashed down Didi's cheeks. Her voice bubbled. "But not for the reasons you say he knew. He loved Judy and he loved me. He knew I'd never leave him. And he'd never leave me. Not unless she made him. Not unless—"

"You might want to ask Tammy about that night," Howell said, oblivious to the half-hysterical ghost at my side. "She knows I wasn't there."

"Because she found out about you and Didi. She forced you not to go. What did she do, threaten to hurt herself? Threaten to hurt your children?"

However I expected the judge to respond, it wasn't with a laugh. "I have to admit, Miss Martin, I'm amazed by your information. Not that I'm saying it's right or wrong. I'm just saying it's interesting. But even if what you've said so far is true—if—you think Tammy would have done harm to herself? Over one silly little affair? You think she would have hurt our children? You've got quite an imagination! Maybe you're the one who should be writing books."

"That's not why you didn't come?"

Both Didi and I asked the question at the same time.

Of course, Howell directed his answer to me. "You're naive as well as foolish. Yes, Tammy knew about my affair with Deborah Bowman. She knew about all my little peccadilloes. What she didn't know about was Judy. That's what Susan's been hanging over my head all these years, damn her. You see, Tammy understood my tendency to love 'em and leave 'em. But a child?" He cleared his throat as if just doing so could make the reality of the situation go away. "She never would have forgiven me for that."

"Then it wasn't—"

Again, both Didi and I started into the question. Big difference: She didn't have the nerve to finish it.

I didn't have nearly as much at stake.

"Then it wasn't Tammy's idea?" Just speaking the words made my stomach sour. I didn't dare take a look at Didi. I could hear her weeping softly at my side. "You're the one—"

"You're damned right." The judge's nostrils flared. His face darkened. "Didi Bowman was good for a few laughs. Until she got pregnant. Then she turned clingy and needy. She wasn't worth risking my family for, and she certainly wasn't worth risking my reputation for. I was home that night, Miss Martin. All night. My wife will confirm that and if you don't believe it, we were having dinner with some of the neighbors. They're still alive to verify that if you care to ask. And me?" He stepped away from me. "I had no intention of ever meeting Didi that night. And I certainly didn't mean it when I told her I'd run away with her. If she wasn't so stupid, she would have realized it."

"But you loved me!"

Didi's anguished cry echoed through my head.

"But you loved her!" I said.

Howell's smile was as penetrating as a sword. "You think so? Then you should know this: I've never regretted my decision not to meet Didi. Not for one moment. I wasn't responsible for her death, but I never regretted that, either. It certainly made my life easier. Now if you'll excuse me . . ." He turned away.

And I saw not only my investigation into Didi's murder, but my chance of proving she was the author of *So Far the Dawn*, going with him.

"Wait!" When I clamped a hand on his arm, Howell whirled around. "The manuscript," I said, before he could make good on the threat he'd made that day at his office and call security on me. "It's the page Didi gave you, isn't it? It's the one she wrote her dedication on. I've got the five thousand dollars now. I'll deliver it to your office tomorrow. I'll—"

He shrugged out from under my hand. "The manuscript page," he said, "is no longer for sale. Not to you. Not to anyone else."

"But—"

"As a matter of fact . . ." Howell's gaze was as cold as a snake's. "When I get home, I'm going to burn it. I hope you're a smart enough young lady

to know what that means. Don't ever let me see
your face again. There's nothing you can prove.
Not about Didi's death and certainly not about
any wild claims to her writing that ridiculous
book. Good evening."

And before I could even think of something to
say to make him change his mind, Howell was
gone.

When I turned around, I realized Didi was, too.

So much for my plans to break the case wide
open.

I wasn't sure what I was going to accomplish
with my hopes dashed and my mood as black as
the night outside, but I headed back into the party,
anyway. Maybe Quinn would take pity on me, and
we could dance. Or at least talk, if he was through
being pigheaded and insisting I let him in on what
I was doing and why. Or maybe I would just take a
page from Susan Gwitkowski's book. Maybe a
couple of glasses of champagne would dull the
pain and help me forget that on the private investigator scale of one to ten, I was somewhere in the
negative numbers.

I hoped for the Quinn scenario, but I'd settle for
the champagne if I had to. All the buzz without the
grief. Or at least without the same kind of grief.
With that in mind, I headed off after a passing
waiter.

I was just about to snatch a crystal flute from his
tray when an arm went around my waist and a
voice whispered close to my ear.

"You're not drinking and driving, are you?"

Maybe I already was.

Drinking, that is.

At least that would explain why I recognized the voice.

I spun away from the arm and the man it belonged to and turned. Even a bushy mustache wasn't enough to disguise the face looking back at me.

"Dan Callahan, what the hell—"

"Nice to see you, too." Dan sounded pleasant enough, but his expression didn't match his voice. He darted a look around, and even though no one was close enough to overhear us, he bent his head closer to mine. "You want to tell me what you're up to?"

"I'm the one who should be asking that question."

"You mean—"

"I mean, you took my picture at the cemetery. And you followed me to Ohio City. You don't work at the hospital, either, do you? You never did."

For all his cuteness (and believe me, he was plenty cute), Dan could avoid a subject as well as anyone I'd ever known. He could change one pretty well, too. I found that out when he reached into the inside pocket of his jacket and pulled out a photograph.

"We need to talk," he said, and he handed me the picture.

It was a photo of me, taken the night I started unpacking Merilee's traveling library. I was standing in her study and—

"You were spying! Through the window!" I clutched the photo and dared Dan to dispute this.

He didn't even try. "Take a close look," he said.

"I don't need to take a close look. I know exactly what I was doing. What I want to know is what you were doing. What you are doing. Why are you—"

As I talked, I'd clutched the picture to my chest. Dan laid his hand over mine and moved the photo far enough away from my body so I could see it. "I said, take a close look."

Have I mentioned that Dan once saved my life? I'd like to think that I looked at the picture in question to return the favor, but I have to admit, that's not completely true. Though he kept it low, Dan's voice rang with authority. His grip on my hand was like iron. I couldn't have refused if I tried.

I gulped down any feeble protest I might have made and took another gander at the picture. In it, I was standing near the desk. Like I was in the middle of saying something, my mouth was open, but of course, I was the only one in the room.

Or was I?

I squinted and took a closer look.

Barely visible, there were two wisps of white on the other side of the desk. One of them was shaped like a bell. Or a woman wearing a gown with a hoop skirt. The other was tall and imposing, a little more solid-looking. Like a man in a uniform might be.

Kurt and Elizabeth.

My breath caught and my mouth dropped open.

"How—"

Dan didn't give me a chance to finish the question. "Do you have any idea what you're messing with?"

"I'm not messing. With anything. I—"

"Do you know how dangerous this can be?"

"I don't, I—"

He plucked the photo out of my hands, glancing over his shoulder before he looked back at me. "I shouldn't be telling you this. I wouldn't be except that I'm worried. Pepper, you have no idea what you're getting into."

"And you don't know what you're talking about."

Was that my voice? The one that managed to sound pissed and regal and very Opal-like? In an effort to look as sure of myself as I sounded, I lifted my chin.

If I expected Dan to back down, I was disappointed.

He tucked the photo back where it came from and backed away. "It's a friendly warning," he said. "And the only one you'll get."

"A friendly warning?" By this time, my heart was slamming against my ribs. My corset felt as if it was going to pop. I sucked in a breath. "As opposed to . . . ?"

Dan bowed from the waist, the way a proper Civil War gentleman would. "As much as I'd like to, I can't afford to give anyone a second chance. Not even you. Don't forget what I said, Pepper. And don't mess with powers you can't possibly understand."

He backed away another step, and the next second, he was swallowed by the crowd, and I was left to try and figure out what the hell had just happened.

I didn't have much of a chance. The next thing I knew, a voice called to me from the doorway.

"Miss Martin!" It was Rick Jensen, the photographer, and one look at the flush of excitement on his face told me something was up.

"Miss Martin, look!" He hurried toward me, a fat manila file folder in his hand. "My press credentials got me past the front door," he explained, and he pushed the file into my hands. "I'm glad I didn't have to wait until you showed up at the cemetery again. I couldn't wait to show you these."

I flipped open the file, and again I found myself looking at photos. I thumbed through them. I have to say, I couldn't see what Rick was so excited about. At least the picture Dan presented me showed the misty forms of Kurt and Elizabeth. These pictures didn't show much of anything but gray blobs.

I guess my expression said it all because Rick plucked the pictures out my hands and turned them right-side up. "They're hard to see, I know," he said. "Just as you thought, the film was exposed. It took some fancy footwork to get anything out of it. But here. Take a look." He found one picture in particular and moved it to the top of the pile. "Recognize anything?"

I squinted. I tilted my head. I squinted some more.

And slowly, the picture came into focus.

"Holy shit," I mumbled.

Because for the second time in as many minutes, I realized I was looking at a ghost.

The photo showed the Bowman mausoleum. Sure it was blurry. Okay, so it was fuzzy. And yes, the picture (at least from what I could see of it) was taken from pretty far away.

But none of that mattered.

What did matter was what was barely visible in the background: a mousy woman in a nondescript suit and way sensible shoes.

No question who she was.

And no question what she was up to, either.

While Rick had been busy waiting for the perfect photo of perfect Merilee visiting her dear, dear, dearly departed parents, he'd accidentally caught a shot of Trish Kingston.

She was messing with the urn of flowers in front of the mausoleum, and though I couldn't tell what she was doing, I knew one thing. Whatever it was, it had cost Rick his camera and earned him a lump on the back of his head from the marble tip of an angel wing.

Chapter 20

If I discounted the fact that I arrived with Merilee,
who sipped icy pink champagne from the backseat
bar all the way from Ohio City and never once offered me a glass, showing up at the gala in a limo
was not half bad. I could easily get used to having
a uniformed driver open the door of the car for me
and offer me a hand to help me out. I got a buzz
when I stepped onto the sidewalk outside the hotel
and a roar went up from the huge crowd of SFTD
fans who were waiting. Even if they weren't waiting for me.

The flip side, of course, was—photos of Trish
Kingston in hand and a burning need to get over to
Garden View and try to figure out why she poking
around in that urn—I was stuck.

Fortunately, Rick was a good sport.

And he had a car parked right outside.

I offered him an exclusive on whatever it was we
were going to find, and because I couldn't fit into
the front, I squeezed and squashed me and my
hoop skirt into the backseat of his PT Cruiser. We
were off.

We used the employee entrance into the cemetery,

and while the reenactors, the fans, and the cream of Cleveland society were still back at the hotel quadrilling their little feet off, Rick and I stood in front of the Bowman mausoleum.

"You're going to get your pretty gown all dirty," he warned when I made a move for the urn, but I was past caring. I ripped off my elbow-length gloves and went for the flowers.

Of course, they'd been replaced a time or two since that first day when Merilee arrived to visit her dear, dear parents. The current arrangement was composed of white mums and yellow roses. It was long past dark, and the mums glowed like ghostly orbs. The roses made me sneeze.

It didn't take me long to feel along the edges of the arrangement and find the block of wet, foamy stuff the flowers were stuck in. I lifted the entire thing out, handed the whole shebang to Rick, and stuck my hand into the now-empty urn.

Which, as it turned out, wasn't empty after all.

"What is it?" Rick asked when I lifted out a fat, heavy package. It was wrapped with paper, then rewrapped with waterproof plastic and sealed with duct tape.

Like the kind I'd found in Trish's room the day I moved into the Bowman house.

"I think it's papers," I told Rick, because though I'd promised him an exclusive, I wasn't exactly ready to give away the farm. Not until I knew for sure if what I was holding was what I thought I was holding.

"What kind of papers? And what are you going to do with them?"

A good question, and while I considered it,

Rick's curiosity kicked in. He was no dummy. "Does this have something to do with that Kingston woman being murdered?" he asked.

Oh, yeah.

I knew it as sure as I knew that the trek from the car and through the damp grass over to the mausoleum had resulted in a sloppy mess at the hem of my dress and that I'd probably have to pay a fortune for dry cleaning.

Just like I knew there was only one person I could trust with what I'd found.

Like I mentioned before, Rick was a good sport. It didn't take any time at all to convince him to make a quick stop at the Bowman house before we headed to the Justice Center.

"Are you sure we're allowed to be here?"

Rick was standing behind me. He peered over my shoulder into the darkened main room of the *So Far the Dawn* museum. "The museum is closed."

"I work here, remember," I told him, and I guess his nervousness was contagious. When he whispered, I whispered back. "I live here, too. Which means technically I can come in any time I want."

"Yeah, but nobody's around and—"

"That," I told him, "is the whole idea."

Before I could forget it, I zipped into the museum, flicked on the lights, and headed for the glass case where Merilee's "original" manuscript was displayed. Someday, the museum board had promised, security alarms were going to be added for each of what they liked to think of as their "priceless" exhibits. Lucky for me, *someday* had yet to come.

I lifted the latch on the side of the display case and swung open the glass door.

"What in the world are you doing?" When he raced across the room toward me, Rick's face was pale. Like a walleye hooked and pulled from the water, his mouth opened and closed. "You're not going to—"

"Steal the manuscript? Don't be ridiculous! Of course I'm not going to steal the manuscript. If I did, Merilee would notice." I pish-tushed the very suggestion while I reached into the case and slipped a few pages from the middle of the stack. I closed the display case door. "Nobody's ever going to miss a couple of pages."

"But . . ." Rick had that deer-in-the-headlights look. He stood between me and the door, and bless him, he thought he was trying to save me from my baser instincts. "You can't steal them, Pepper. It's wrong. You'll get in big trouble."

The pages clutched in one hand, I tilted my head and propped my fists on my hips. "I thought you were a reporter," I said. "Aren't you supposed to be bold and daring and willing to do anything for the sake of a story?"

"I'm a photographer," he corrected me. "I might be willing to do anything for the sake of a picture."

I shrugged. "So take my picture."

"Stealing the manuscript?" Rick's voice was shrill. "Then the cops would know I was here. I'd be an accomplice or a codefendant or—"

"Don't worry about it," I said and made a motion to shoo him aside. Since he was standing between the display case where Kurt's original uniform was exhibited and a large-as-life (and very creepy because of it) mannequin wearing Opal's garden party gown, there was no other way to get around him. "Trust me, Rick. We're not doing anything wrong. And there is that exclusive to think about."

He might not fit in the bold and daring category, but when it came down to it, Rick was all for the exclusive. He nodded, silently confirming his accomplice status, and turned to leave the room.

In the great scheme of things, it was just as well that he was leading the way.

He was the one who ran into Weird Bob at the door.

Bob planted himself in our path, his arms crossed over his dirty denim shirt. "What are you two doing here?" he asked.

When it came to my walk on the not-so-honest side, Rick might have been ready to speak up. But when it came to facing down Bob, who looked from one of us to the other with his mouth pulled into a thin line and an I'm-gonna-call-the-cops look in his eyes, Rick was a little less articulate.

He turned to me for the answers.

I had taken the momentary opportunity to turn the other way, and feeling both men's eyes on me, I whirled, gave Bob a smile, and pointed toward the Opal mannequin. "I told you so," I said to Rick. "I told you her dress was green. You said—"

"I said blue." Bless Rick, not only was he a good sport, he was a quick study. He slapped his forehead. "Of course. I should have remembered. Green. You were absolutely right."

"And so was the mayor." I looked toward Bob,

letting him in on the story. "The mayor said green, too, and I've got to tell you, after he won that *So Far the Dawn* trivia contest back at the gala, I knew not to mess with him. He insisted green, who was I to argue? I sure am glad we volunteered to come over here and check it out. Everyone back at the party will be glad to have it cleared up."

I sidestepped my way to the door, and when Bob didn't move, I flattened my skirt and inched around him. "I heard the mayor bet five bucks on the side with the police chief. He'll be thrilled to hear the news," I told him.

"But . . ." Bob wasn't the brightest bulb in the box, but I have to give him credit. My story was as flimsy as they came and he knew it. He took a careful look around the room.

But hey, since everything looked just like it had when we walked in, there wasn't much he could say. He looked me up and down, too, and as hard as it was to stand there without barfing when he checked out my body, I clutched my empty hands together at my waist, raised my chin, and gave him an Opal-like glare.

"See you later, Bob," I said, and with Rick scurrying behind me, I made it out the front door without incident.

It wasn't until we were back in the car that he dared to speak. "What the hell did you do with—"

"The manuscript pages?" I grinned and reached under my skirt. "Looks like these big ol' hoops come in handy for something after all."

I paced all night and all of the next morning, my mind bouncing around as my libido had been between Dan and Quinn. Did Dan know about the Gift? About the ghosts? What were his warnings all about?

And where the hell was Quinn when I needed him?

I didn't expect to find an answer to my Dan questions. Not immediately, anyway, and since it was pretty clear I wasn't going to find him until he wanted to be found, I concentrated on the Quinn part of the equation. When my pacing didn't produce a phone call from him, I called the police station.

He wasn't in.

And did he receive the package I'd left for him?

The cop who answered the phone couldn't say. Or maybe he just wouldn't. Either way, between that call and the three more I made that day, the five I put in for Quinn the next day, and the trip I made downtown to the Justice Center so I could talk to him in person the day after that, I learned cops are a closed-mouthed bunch.

Detective Harrison, they told me, was working a case. He'd get in touch when he was able.

In an effort to keep positive thoughts and good karma or blessings or whatever I was going to need to produce the outcome I was looking for, I tried not to hold any of this against Quinn. I went through the motions of my job, fetching and carrying for Merilee, answering phone calls, and scheduling the appointments that were coming at us fast and furiously now that the date of the premiere was approaching.

There were luncheons to attend, book discussion sessions at both the city and the county libraries,

and one overcast day, a signing at a local book-
store, where thousands of fans lined up for hours
in the rain just for the chance to have dear, dear
Merilee sign their copies of *So Far the Dawn*. By
the time that was over and we arrived back in Ohio
City, Merilee (always fragile to hear her tell the
tale) went right to bed, and I was duty-bound to
call the governor, with whom she was supposed to
have dinner that night. Merilee would be there, I
told the secretary to his secretary's assistant (the
only person I could get through to). But she would
be a tad late. After all that autographing, her hand
ached and she needed her beauty rest.

I was in the study and had just hung up the
phone when I saw that there was a piece of paper
resting on top of a stack of books on one corner of
the desk.

For Pepper, the note said, and I recognized the
handwriting. It was the same as that on the sign on
the door of the workroom in the basement. *Someone named Quinn called. He wants you to meet
him. Tonight. He says the bridge. Eight o'clock.*

Tonight?

At the prospect, my heart raced and my imagination soared.

Tonight, I'd—glory and hallelujah—finally know
for sure!

If the tonight in the message was really tonight.

This thought made my heart stop cold, and my
soaring imagination plummet to the ground.

Because the message wasn't dated.

I shot for the door hoping (for the first and only
time since I'd set foot in the Bowman house) to run
into Weird Bob, and fortunately I didn't have to look

far. I found him in the kitchen, and I didn't bother with niceties. "When?" I waved his note to me in the air. The way I figured it, it was the only explanation he deserved. "Why didn't you tell me he called? When? And why did you leave the message there? I might never have found it. I might not—"

"Don't get your knickers in a twist, lady." Bob was making a sandwich. He licked mayonnaise off the knife, then stuck the knife back in the jar, and I made a mental note to myself to avoid the mayo at all costs. "That call came in this morning. I hope it makes sense to you because it sure don't to me. Doesn't that Quinn guy know? There are plenty of bridges in this town."

There were, but I knew exactly which one Quinn was talking about. And if it seemed a little strange that he'd want to meet me outdoors on a night as drippy as this?

Like I said, cops weren't exactly chatty. I was sure Quinn had his reasons, and I for one couldn't wait to find out what they were.

With that in mind, I checked the clock that hung above the stove. It was already after seven. Yeah, I was only a couple of minutes away from the bridge, but I wasn't taking any chances. I raced upstairs for a raincoat and called Quinn to leave a message on his voice mail that I'd be there. In spite of some people's opinion, I wasn't dumb. I also took the time to redo my makeup, run a comb through my hair, and change my clothes, too. If I was going out to meet Quinn, I wasn't going to do it looking as if I'd just spent the day opening books for Merilee so she could scrawl her dear, dear signature on the first page.

Jeans and a lightweight sweater?

I thought not. Not for a meeting this important or a guy this hot.

I opted for black pants instead, a black tank, and a darling cropped jacket I'd gotten online for a song.

A coating of Paris Nights on my lips, and I jumped in my Mustang. With any luck, before another hour was over, I'd find out if the papers I'd left with Quinn for testing were what I hoped they were: Didi's original, handwritten copy of *So Far the Dawn.*

And the sequel.

The Hope Memorial Bridge is a major artery leading from the east side of town to the west (or from the west to the east, depending on which way you're headed). There are four lanes, two in each direction, and a sidewalk along each side of the street. Spectacular views aside—the downtown skyline in one direction and the industrial valley in the other—there is no place to park.

Always sensible (at least when it comes to getting my hair wet and taking the chance of streaking my mascara), I decided not to leave my car at one end of the bridge and walk to look for Quinn. Instead, I cruised between Ontario and Lorain Avenue a couple of times.

I didn't see Quinn or anyone else.

At least I didn't think I did.

It was a little hard to tell. After a day of rain and sky-high humidity, the temperatures had cooled considerably. Fog wafted along the street in front of the car and collected in pockets along the railing that looked down at the river.

"Yeah, the bridge. That was a bright suggestion." I grumbled the words while I made another pass, checking out both sides of the street and wondering what on earth Quinn had been thinking. My window was fogged, and I turned on the defroster. "You couldn't have picked a nice little coffeehouse in some trendy neighborhood like Tremont? Or a cozy little bar in the Warehouse District?"

Maybe he could have, but he didn't.

I was just about in the center of the bridge, heading back east and thinking that I'd do an illegal U-turn at Jacobs Field and make another pass, when the fog parted, and I saw a man waiting on the sidewalk.

I cursed Quinn's flair for the dramatic, wheeled the car as close to the sidewalk as I was able, punched the gearshift into park, and put on my flashers.

"Quinn?" I got out of the car, and thank goodness it wasn't raining. I didn't have to spoil the effect of my outfit with something as fashion-lacking as a windbreaker. As I rounded the car, I wondered if that was good news or bad. A cold wind blew in from the north, over the lake, and I shivered. "You couldn't have found someplace a little dryer? And warmer?" I stepped up onto the sidewalk. "You couldn't have—"

I took one look at the man waiting for me, and words failed. It was just as well. Whatever I was going to say, it would have been blown away on the next blast of chilly air.

See, the man on the sidewalk wasn't Quinn. Or even Dan Callahan.

It was Weird Bob.

Call me a chicken. Or maybe I've just got a whole lot more common sense than most folks give me credit for. I stopped dead in my tracks. Right before I backed away.

"What the hell are you doing here?" I asked him.

Bob didn't answer. He didn't need to.

The answer came from right behind me.

"We can't have you ruining everything, can we?"

Was I surprised when I turned and found Merilee not three feet away?

Honestly? Not a whole bunch. Like the old saying goes, if it walks like a duck and quacks like a duck . . .

This investigation had been quacking at me practically from Day One.

"If I'm supposed to be surprised, I have to tell you, I'm not," I said. What I was, though, was cold. I hugged my arms around myself. "It was all because of the manuscript, wasn't it?"

Merilee was swaddled in an elegant purple cape trimmed with fur. It was a little out there when it came to fashion, especially for early summer, but hey, she'd been born and raised in Cleveland. Like the rest of us, she knew how unpredictable the weather could be.

She tugged at her leather gloves. "I told you," she said, "I don't like surprises."

"I'll bet Trish didn't, either." I heard a noise behind me and glanced over my shoulder to see that Bob had moved a bit closer. Instinct told me to take another step toward the railing. Caution advised otherwise. There was a lot of nothing between that railing and the river far below. I wasn't taking any chances. I held my ground.

"That is what this is all about, isn't it?" I asked Merilee. "Trish found the manuscript in the attic. I don't know how. Maybe she was plain nosy."

"Maybe she was just a pain in the ass." Merilee's words were as cold as the breeze. "Maybe she should have minded her own business."

"Instead, she was minding yours. Trish is the reason the boxes had been moved away from the window. She's the reason the manuscript wasn't there when I looked for it. But she wasn't dumb. As soon as she realized what she'd found, she must have put two and two together. She knew your handwriting plenty well, and she knew that manuscript wasn't written by you. Let me guess, when she told you the news, she didn't show you the whole thing, did she? She didn't need to. She stashed the manuscript over at Garden View—you know, it was in your dear, dear parents' flower urn the whole time— and showed you just a couple of pages, right? Just to prove she had it. And boy, I'll bet when you saw those pages, you just about peed your pants."

"Please!" Like she smelled something bad, Merilee sniffed. "There's no need to be crude."

Bob moved again, and me? I gauged the distance between where I was standing and my car. I might actually have made a run for it if the fog didn't lift for a moment. The light of a street lamp glinted against something in Bob's hand. A gun.

I knew I wouldn't make it to the Mustang, so I pretended a bravado I didn't feel. "That's what Trish was talking about, wasn't it? When she told Ella that things were looking up for her. They were looking up, all right. She was blackmailing you. That explains why she was acting so weird that day at the TV station. And how she was able to afford to get all dolled up." I thought back to the gala and what Thomas Ross Howell had told me about getting rid of the manuscript page in his possession. "It explains why I found ashes in the fireplace in your study, too. After you got rid of Trish, you had to get rid of the pages. The most permanent way was to burn them."

"That's one way to take care of a problem." Merilee nodded, and though I knew it was a signal to Bob, I couldn't move fast enough. Before I knew it, he had one hand clamped on my arm.

The quacking got louder. At least inside my head. If I didn't want Merilee and Bob to see that I was shaking, I would have slapped my forehead. Without a lot of options, I played my trump card, glancing from Merilee to where Bob's fingers were wrinkling my new jacket.

"Just like Didi," I said.

Though she tried to cover it with a toss of her head, I saw Merilee's eyes widen. "Didi? Why are you always yammering about Didi?"

I shrugged. No easy thing when Bob's hand was a vise around my arm. "Maybe because you killed her?"

Merilee's gaze was as emotionless as a snake's. "So Susan was right. You do have this crazy notion about my poor, unfortunate sister."

Susan.

It made sense, of course. I'd talked to Susan at the gala, and Merilee must have seen us. It was only natural she'd wonder why.

"What did you do?" I asked her. "Take advantage of Susan's greed?"

"She's common." Merilee tossed her head. "For a couple hundred dollars—"

"She told you I knew Didi had been pushed. From this bridge. That's how you . . ." I glanced at Bob. And the gun. It was hard to decide which was scarier. "That's how you knew about the bridge. Why you faked the note from Quinn that told me to meet him here."

"Stupid." Bob's laugh was anything but warm and fuzzy. He yanked me closer to the railing.

"Kill me if you want," I said, at the same time I hoped they didn't take the comment seriously. "That doesn't change a thing. I know exactly what happened to Didi. And Quinn knows, too. I told him everything." Okay, so I lied. What did they call it on the TV cop shows? Exigent circumstances?

This was exigent, all right.

"I'll bet Susan's the one who told you Didi and Judge Howell were supposed to meet here that night. That's how you knew where Didi was." I thought back to the scene I'd witnessed. "That explains the scraping noise I heard when she stood here at the railing, too. You figured she had a copy of her manuscript in her suitcase. And that's what you were after."

Because of the lack of light and the wisps of fog that blew around us, I may have been imagining

things, but I could have sworn Merilee's face went
pale.

"You think you're so smart! But you're making
all that up. You have to be. There's no way you can
know for sure. And what makes you think anyone
would believe your crazy story? After all, Didi did
leave a suicide note."

Disgusted, I shook my head. "It's the only convincing thing you ever wrote," I told her. "And the
cops never picked up on the fact that Didi didn't
have a pen with her. You didn't know that, either,
did you? If you were a real fiction writer, you
would have thought through your plot and left one
behind. You know, a sort of clue."

"If I was a real fiction writer?" Merilee's voice
was shrill. "You mean if Didi was a real fiction
writer? You call that trash she wrote fiction?"

"Millions of people do."

"Millions of people are wrong. I'm the scholar in
the family. I'm the real writer. She wasn't educated
enough or smart enough. She wrote about stupid
Opal and stupid Palmer. She made up history."

"But she had the imagination."

Merilee laughed, and shivers shot up my spine.
She nodded, and Bob tucked away his gun long
enough to wrap his arms around me. He lifted me
into the air, but there was no way I was going to
make it easy for him to move me closer to the railing.

I kicked and I squirmed and I screamed, but as I
probably mentioned before, he was a big guy and
pretty beefy. The railing got closer. So did my view
of the Cleveland skyline. Bob lifted me higher.

All the while, Merilee's voice pierced the night. "No, you're wrong. I'm the one with the imagination. After all, I made it look like a suicide and everyone believed me. They'll think the same about you, of course." She plucked a piece of paper from the nether regions of her voluminous cape, and right before Bob swung me over the side of the bridge, she stuck it under my nose. "You see, I've written your suicide note, too."

"And I think I've heard all I need to hear."

Do I need to say how relieved I was to hear Quinn's voice coming out of the fog?

"Drop her," he told Bob.

"Don't tell him that!" I screamed.

Lucky for me, Bob was so surprised, he spun the other way before he did anything. When he dropped me and raised his hands, it was onto the sidewalk. Into a puddle.

I cursed, and on my hands and knees, maneuvered around two uniformed officers who appeared out of nowhere and slapped handcuffs on Bob. What Quinn was doing during all this, I can't say. I'd like to think he was making a move to help me. Something tells me that he was darting in Merilee's direction instead.

Once I realized I wasn't going to die with a splat in the Cuyahoga River, I saw why.

Merilee could move pretty quick for an old lady. She had scrambled up onto the railing.

"I'm not going to jail," she told Quinn and the universe in general. "You're not going to take away my reputation."

"You don't have a reputation." By this time, I

was on my feet. I stood on Merilee's right; Quinn
was on her left. Neither one of us was close enough
to grab her. "You took credit for Didi's work. You
killed her, too."

When she turned to look at me over her shoul-
der, Merilee was smiling. "You bet I did," she said.
"Just like I killed Trish. I lived in a blaze of glory.
And now I'm going to die the same way."

She moved but I moved faster. Right before she
jumped, I grabbed a fistful of her cape. Quinn
moved in the same instant. Between the two of us,
Merilee wasn't going anywhere.

Anywhere except prison.

Needless to say (but I'll mention it anyway), things
got pretty crazy after that.

Merilee was hauled onto solid ground by the
team of firefighters Quinn had brought along just
in case.

Bob was carted away in one black and white
patrol car.

Merilee went kicking and screaming to the Justice Center in another.

Quinn and I were left on the bridge alone.

"Lucky for you I got your message," he said, and
though he sounded hard-nosed, when he saw me
shiver, he slipped off his trench coat and draped it
over my shoulders. "You want to explain how the
hell all that happened?"

"I told you. I got suspicious. Working at the
museum. I knew Merilee didn't write the book."

"And you knew Merilee and that goon of hers
killed her sister, how?"

Just as Quinn asked the question, Didi popped up out of nowhere right behind him. "You can tell him if you want," she said.

"Nah." I shook my head. "Even if I did, he wouldn't believe me."

Quinn turned and looked at the nothing over his shoulder. "Who the hell are you talking to?"

My only answer was a smile.

"All right, I give up." He breathed a sigh of one hundred percent exasperation and reached into his pocket to pull out a small beige card. "Here," he said, pushing the card into my hand.

I knew exactly what it was, and I didn't bother to look at it. "What good does it do me to have your card?" I asked. "I have called. Plenty of times. Are those lab results back yet?"

"No, but something tells me that now we know exactly what they're going to prove." He reached for his raincoat, slung it over his shoulder, and headed for his car. "And the card . . ." He glanced over his shoulder at me. "That's my home number on the back. When you're ready to talk, give me a call."

Didi and I watched him drive away. "You think I did the right thing?" I asked her.

"I don't know. He's not exactly the patient type. And he is awfully cute."

"I wasn't talking about Quinn. I was talking about Merilee. Do you think I should have let her jump?"

Didi looked over the side of the bridge, her expression so thoughtful, I wondered if she was thinking of what it had been like as she watched the world slip past her and knew she was headed for her death.

"I never would have jumped on my own, you know," she said. "I wouldn't have done that to Judy."

"And Merilee?"

"Merilee is going to have her reputation yanked out from under her."

There was no denying that. I'm not a vindictive person, but I knew exactly what it meant. For Merilee it would be a fate worse than death.

Chapter 21

I had no idea how long it took labs to do whatever it was labs did. I only knew that it was too long. The results of the tests on Didi's manuscript and Merilee's copy of *So Far the Dawn* never arrived until the day of the premiere.

After what had happened on the Hope Memorial Bridge that rainy night, I wasn't the least bit surprised by them. The rest of the world, though . . .

Because of its IMAX theater, the new and improved version of *So Far the Dawn* premiered at the city's Great Lakes Science Center, and thanks to the notoriety of the event plus the fact that the author thought to be responsible for the book was being held in the county jail for the fifty-year-old murder of her sister as well as the recent death of Trish Kingston, the place was packed to the rafters and buzzing with excitement.

When Ella walked out on the stage, it took a minute for the crowd to quiet down.

I had to give her credit. Ella was as cool as the color of the minty gown that flowed around her ankles. No easy trick, considering that she was still recovering from the shock of Merilee's arrest and the shock-on-top-of-shock that resulted from the letter detailing the official lab results. We'd each been handed a glass of champagne as we entered the theater, and Ella held hers in trembling hands.

When word first came down about the test results, Ella had herself a good cry, but if I knew nothing else about my boss, it was that she was one tough lady. Her voice was froggy, her eyes were red, but she knew the *So Far the Dawn* show had to go on. She cleared her throat.

"I have an important announcement about a book—and a movie—we all love," Ella said. "It has recently been determined beyond the shadow of a doubt that the handwritten manuscript of *So Far the Dawn* displayed in the museum and attributed to Merilee Bowman is nothing more than a copy. The paper she used was never manufactured until ten years ago. Between that and a scientific handwriting analysis . . . well, the results are conclusive: Merilee did not write the book."

Do I need to point out that, at this, the crowd went bonkers?

They would have gone even crazier if they'd known what I knew: Didi was on stage right next to Ella. In a pink strapless gown with a matching gauzy stole, she looked like a million bucks. Or maybe that was because of the smile that lit her face.

I was sitting near the middle of the pack in an aisle seat right next to Harmony, who'd brought along her foster parents, Doug and Mindy Miller. I leaned closer to the girl and raised my voice so she could hear me over the hubbub.

"Your grandmother is loving every minute of this."

In keeping with her newfound wealth, Harmony sported a rhinestone-studded ring in her eyebrow. She laughed. "Whatever! You mean she *would be* loving this. You know, when I found out they thought she wrote it, I read the book. My grandmother must have been pretty cool."

I turned my attention back to the stage and to the woman who had lived—and died—in her sister's shadow. "Yeah," I said. "She really is."

By this time, Ella was holding up a hand for silence, and though it took a while coming, things finally settled down. A voice called out from the back of the theater. "Then who did write the book?"

Ella cleared her throat again.

"The truth is finally out," she said, and I swear, it must have been sheer coincidence because as she did, she looked to her right, exactly at the spot where Didi was standing. "We have an original copy of the manuscript, and its authenticity has been verified thanks to the age of the paper and a sample of the author's handwriting we were able to obtain." At this, she smiled in my direction. "The real author of *So Far the Dawn* is none other than Merilee's sister, Didi Bowman. It's Didi we have to thank for the story that has captured our hearts and our imaginations. Ladies and gentlemen . . ." Ella raised her champagne glass and, as one, the crowd got to its feet. "Here's to Didi Bowman."

"Didi Bowman!"

The name echoed off the high ceiling, and at the risk of sounding like a softie, I have to admit, the moment sent tingles through me.

I could tell it did the same for Didi. With tears in her eyes, she bowed and waved at the crowd, and as we downed our champagne, she blew kisses at the audience.

Maybe my champagne was too strong?

I looked from my glass to Didi, and even as I watched, she got fuzzy around the edges. Like a TV picture fading, the color of her gown got paler, her face blurred. After a moment, the only color I could see was a soft pink, like the sky immediately before sunrise.

Right before she winked out, Didi looked my way. "Thank you," she said, and when she turned to walk offstage, Kurt Benjamin was waiting in his Union officer's uniform. She wound her arm through his, waved, and the two of them disappeared into a wispy haze of pink light.

"Hey!"

The sound of Harmony's voice caused me to shake myself out of my daze. I saw that the rest of the audience was seated and the lights in the theater had gone down. She tugged at my sleeve. "The movie's going to start."

It did, and did Harmony wonder why I had tears in my eyes as the *So Far the Dawn* title rolled across the screen?

I could always say I had a soft spot for women in gowns and guys in uniform. Oh yeah, and horses.

* * *

By the time it was all over, it was late into the night. No longer secretary to the world's über-est über-author, I no longer had the benefit of limo service. I'd driven to the premiere and parked in a lot near the Rock and Roll Hall of Fame, next door to the Science Center, and even though Harmony offered me a ride in the jazzy silver Jaguar she'd rented for Doug and Mindy (with the promise that they'd have one of their very own soon), I decided to walk to my car. The night was warm, and I was feeling pretty satisfied with myself. I needed a little downtime. I watched the moonlight glint off the lake and the distinctive pyramid-shaped Rock Hall, and took a look at the huge billboard outside the museum.

STILL ROCKIN' AFTER ALL THESE YEARS, it said, and it featured two pictures of the same rock group. One of the photos showed five old guys with pouchy stomachs and wide grins that flashed a message that said they were lucky to have lived through the sex and drugs and rock and roll years. The other photo showed four of the same guys—plus one different one—and it must have been taken decades earlier. In that photo, the rockers were kids with shoulder-length hair and a gleam in their eyes that said the sex and drugs and rock and roll . . . well, that's what it was all about.

I wouldn't have paid any attention.

Except for the guy who was in the old picture but not in the new one. The photo was ancient history, but facts were facts. And fact is, this guy was to die for.

He had long, dark hair, wavy and sleek. His eyes were dark, too, his chest was bare, and he was poured into a pair of leather pants tight enough to ignite every fantasy I'd ever had.

I smiled my approval. Right before I shivered in a sudden chilly breeze that brought with it a sweet and pungent aroma it was hard to place at first. Until I remembered the frat parties I'd attended back in college.

Pot.

I looked around for its source, and that's when I saw a man standing in the halo of a security light over near the door to the hall.

He had long, dark hair. It was wavy and sleek, and he was wearing leather pants that showed off an equally tight butt. His eyes were dark. His chest was bare.

My heart slammed against my ribs, and I looked from the man to the billboard and back again.

It couldn't be! And yet—

"Sure you don't want a ride?"

I hadn't realized a car had pulled up beside me, and I yelped my surprise and whirled to find Doug, Mindy, and Harmony in the Jag.

"Come on!" Harmony hung her head out the back window. "We're going out for burgers to celebrate. We'll bring you back later to pick up your car."

It was a kind and generous offer, but I wasn't exactly thinking straight. Instead of saying yes or no, I pointed at the billboard. "You guys are—"

I looked at Doug and Mindy—nice middle-aged people—and gulped down the *old* that had nearly escaped my lips. "You guys probably know more about rock and roll than I do. Who's that guy? The one in the front of the picture?"

Mindy leaned forward for a better look. "That's Damon Curtis. You know, the rock legend. He was with the group Mind at Large. I hear they're going to be giving some huge concert here at the Rock Hall. Gosh, Damon Curtis . . ." She studied the picture and smiled. "I haven't thought about him and his group forever. He's been dead for forty years."

Dead.

Yeah.

Kind of what I thought.

And exactly why I jumped into the Jag to make a quick exit. As we pulled away from the curb, I glanced back toward the hall.

Yeah, Damon Curtis was still there. And yeah, he was still the hottest thing I'd seen in as long as I could remember.

But in this case, *hot* was just a descriptive term. Because even before Mindy confirmed it, I suspected that this was one cold dude.

And he was watching me.

Oh, shit.

PROWL THE NIGHT WITH
RACHEL MORGAN AND

KIM HARRISON

DEAD WITCH WALKING

0-06-057296-5 • $7.99 US/$10.99 Can

When the creatures of the night gather, whether to hide, to hunt, or to feed, it's Rachel Morgan's job to keep things civilized. A bounty hunter and witch with serious sex appeal and attitude, she'll bring them back alive, dead . . . or undead.

THE GOOD, THE BAD, AND THE UNDEAD

0-06-057297-3 • $7.99 US/$10.99 Can

Rachel Morgan can handle the leather-clad vamps and even tangle with a cunning demon or two. But a serial killer who feeds on the experts in the most dangerous kind of black magic is definitely pressing the limits.

EVERY WHICH WAY BUT DEAD

0-06-057299-X • $7.99 US/$10.99 Can

Rachel must take a stand in the raging war to control Cincinnati's underworld because the demon who helped her put away its former vampire kingpin is coming to collect his due.

A FISTFUL OF CHARMS

0-06-078819-4 • $7.99 US/$10.99 Can

A mortal lover who abandoned Rachel has returned, haunted by his secret past. And there are those willing to destroy the Hollows to get what Nick possesses.

www.kimharrison.net